# NEVER ENOUGH

## BY LINDSAY MCKENNA

**Blue Turtle Publishing**

# Praise for Lindsay McKenna

"A treasure of a book... highly recommended reading that everyone will enjoy and learn from."

—Chief Michael Jaco, US Navy SEAL, retired, on Breaking Point

"Readers will root for this complex heroine, scarred both inside and out, and hope she finds peace with her steadfast and loving hero. Rife with realistic conflict and spiced with danger, this is a worthy page-turner."

—BookPage.com on Taking Fire
March 2015 Top Pick in Romance

"... is fast-paced romantic suspense that renders a beautiful love story, start to finish. McKenna's writing is flawless, and her story line fully absorbing. More, please."

—Annalisa Pesek, Library Journal on Taking Fire

"Ms. McKenna masterfully blends the two different paces to convey a beautiful saga about love, trust, patience and having faith in each other."

—Fresh Fiction on Never Surrender

"Genuine and moving, this romantic story set in the complex world of military ops grabs at the heart."

—RT Book Reviews on Risk Taker

"McKenna does a beautiful job of illustrating difficult topics through the development of well-formed, sympathetic characters."

—Publisher's Weekly (starred review) on Wolf Haven
One of the Best Books of 2014, Publisher's Weekly

"McKenna delivers a story that is raw and heartfelt. The relationship between Kell and Leah is both passionate and tender. Kell is the hero every woman wants, and McKenna employs skill and empathy to craft a physically and emotionally abused character in Leah. Using tension and steady pacing, McKenna is adept at expressing growing, tender love in the midst of high stakes danger."

—RT Book Reviews on Taking Fire

"Her military background lends authenticity to this outstanding tale, and readers will fall in love with the upstanding hero and his fierce determination to save the woman he loves.

—Publishers Weekly (starred review) on Never Surrender
One of the Best Books of 2014, Publisher's Weekly

"Readers will find this addition to the Shadow Warriors series full of intensity and action-packed romance. There is great chemistry between the characters and tremendous realism, making Breaking Point a great read."

—RT Book Reviews

"This sequel to Risk Taker is an action-packed, compelling story, and the sizzling chemistry between Ethan and Sarah makes this a good read."

—RT Book Reviews on Degree of Risk

"McKenna elicits tears, laughter, fist-pumping triumph, and most all, a desire for the next tale in this powerful series."

—Publishers Weekly (starred review) on Running Fire

"McKenna's military experience shines through in this moving tale . . . McKenna (High Country Rebel) skillfully takes readers on an emotional journey into modern warfare and two people's hearts."

—Publisher's Weekly on Down Range

"Lindsay McKenna has proven that she knows what she's doing when it comes to these military action/romance books."

—Terry Lynn, Amazon on Zone of Fire.

"At no time do you want to put your book down and come back to it later! Last Chance is a well written, fast paced, short (remember that) story that will please any military romance reader!"

—LBDDiaries, Amazon on Last Chance.

## Available from
## Lindsay McKenna

### Blue Turtle Publishing

### DELOS
Last Chance, prologue novella to Nowhere to Hide
Nowhere to Hide, Book 1
Tangled Pursuit, Book 2
Forged in Fire, Book 3

*2016*
Broken Dreams, Book 4
Cowboy Justice Bundle/Blind Sided, Bundle 2, novella
Blind Sided, BN2
Secret Dream, B1B novella, epilogue to Nowhere to Hide
Hold On, Book 5
Hold Me, 5B1, sequel to Hold On
Unbound Pursuit, 2B1 novella, epilogue to Tangled Pursuit
Dog Tags for Christmas Bundle/Snowflake's Gift, Bundle 3,
novella
Secrets, 2B2 novella, sequel to Unbound Pursuit, 2B1

*2017*
Snowflake's Gift, Book 6
Never Enough, 3B1, novella, sequel to Forged in Fire
Dream of Me, 4B1, novella, sequel to Broken Dreams
Trapped, Book 7
Taking a Chance, Book 8, sequel to Trapped

# Harlequin/HQN/Harlequin Romantic Suspense

## SHADOW WARRIORS
Danger Close
Down Range
Risk Taker
Degree of Risk
Breaking Point
Never Surrender
Zone of Fire
Taking Fire
On Fire
Running Fire

## THE WYOMING SERIES
Shadows From The Past
Deadly Identity
Deadly Silence
The Last Cowboy
The Wrangler
The Defender
The Loner
High Country Rebel
Wolf Haven
Night Hawk
Out Rider

## WIND RIVER VALLEY SERIES, Kensington

*2016*
Wind River Wrangler
Wind River Rancher

*2017*
Wind River Cowboy
Wind River Wrangler's Challenge

*Never Enough*

Copyright © 2017 by Nauman Living Trust
ISBN: 978-1-929977-37-6
Print Edition

Excerpt from *Sanctuary*
Copyright © 2017 by Nauman Living Trust

This is a work of fiction. Names, characters, places and incidents are either the product of the author's imagination or are used fictitiously, and any resemblance to actual persons, living or dead, business establishments, events or locales is entirely coincidental.

This edition published by arrangement with Blue Turtle Publishing

www.lindsaymckenna.com

Dear Reader,

Welcome to the Delos Series! Readers get to follow Matt Culver and Dara McKinley's continuing story from *Forged in Fire*, after they've met and fell in love.

In Forged in Fire, Dara met Matt Culver, a Delta Force operator. She'd never been so drawn to someone in her life as this golden-brown eyed Army sergeant who was supremely confident, yet so tender with children and with her. While driving out to a "safe" Afghan village to render medical aid with her sister, Callie, they were attacked by the Taliban. After surviving, Dara was slammed back into the real world to finish her pediatric residency in Alexandria, Virginia. Matt comes home a month later, proposes to her and she accepts. After Christmas, Dara goes home to her ranch family in Butte, Montana and introduces them to Matt. While there, she is emotionally drained by the needs of Callie, her sister, who was captured and nearly raped by the enemy during the escape. She loves her younger sister very much. She fights to help her return from that trauma along with Beau Gardener's help, as well as her Grandfather McKinley. Dara is exhausted in every way. Matt takes her to Hawaii to revive, which begins our story of *Never Enough*.

Matt is adamant about getting his beautiful, beleaguered fiancée some vacation time. He knows that Dara loves Hawaii, but has never been to the Islands. Matt wants Dara to have true down time. Only, the peace he had hoped for is interrupted unexpectedly when a Delos charity on Oahu asks for their help.

Let me hear from you about the Culver Family and the Delos series. Please visit my website at www.lindsaymckenna.com, to keep up the latest, exciting happenings with my series.

You will find an excerpt in the back of this novella for *Sanctuary*, Teren and Nolan's story.

Happy reading!
Warmly, Lindsay McKenna

# Dedication

To all my readers who loved the Morgan's Mercenary saga-series! Now there is a new one! Delos series. May you enjoy this vibrant, exciting global family!

# CHAPTER 1

"HAWAII IS SO lush and beautiful even in early January, Matt." Dara smiled over at him. She leaned against him, his arm around her waist. They'd landed in Oahu earlier in the morning and rented a silver Toyota RAV4, and he'd brought her to the biggest shopping district in Honolulu, the Ala Moana Center. He'd grudgingly traded in his normal black T-shirt and jeans for a bright, white and red Tommy Bahama silk shirt with short sleeves. With his new clothes and his military-short black hair, plus his Turkish and Greek blood giving his skin a golden tone, much like that of the Hawaiians Dara had already met, he looked like an islander. Drowning in those golden eyes of his, their large black pupils fixed on her in a hunter's gaze, she smiled warmly, her heart opening fiercely to this man who was going to be her husband in five short months.

"I've always liked coming to the islands," he murmured, watching the sun climb over the sharp-pointed mountain range that ran from north to south down the western coast of Oahu. After their shopping trip, they'd drive around the island to the large town of Waianae. Dara had begged him to stop at the huge shopping center because she wanted to buy some Hawaiian clothes. He'd easily relented, hating shopping but loving the hell out of her. And Matt was glad they'd stopped at the Ala Moana, because she'd bought some knockout clothes that did nothing but enhance that long, sensuous body of hers.

Of course, when she went shopping, Matt took the opportunity to do a little black-ops snooping on his own. He hadn't been a Delta Force operator for nearly ten years for nothing. After moving in with Dara, he noticed she had no personal electronic tablet, so he stopped in at the huge Apple store and bought her a new iPad. He'd wanted to get her an after-Christmas gift, anyway. For his mother, Dilara, he bought a huge, king-size Hawaiian quilt in bright shades of red, yellow, and white at Auana Quilts. Artemis Shipping had red and yellow horizontal stripes painted around each of their container or tanker ships, the company's colors. And Turkey, his mother's home, was filled with bright, clean, beautiful colors. He thought she might like the gift because she adored quilts from around the world. She didn't have one from Hawaii, so Matt knew it would be well received. And then he found a second shop, Hawaiian Quilt Collection, where he bought some quilted placemats for the dinner table with colorful birds-of-paradise flowers sewn into them. He knew she'd love the orange and purple.

He then found Dara in Hilo Hattie, in the women's clothing section. She'd already bought an ankle-length sleeveless dress with a red and yellow hibiscus print. The dark blue background was the same color as Dara's eyes, and he smiled over that. She had also traded in her conservative, dark-brown wool pantsuit and leather shoes for a bright-red, ruched sundress with a heart-shaped bodice, slim shoulder straps, and a hem that fell to mid-thigh. The white hibiscus on it made her look like a *wahine* to him. Plus, it showed off her long, long, gorgeous legs that he was so fond of. She pirouetted around for him, her gold hair laying like a shining cape halfway down her back. Dara knew how much he loved seeing her with her hair down. As a pediatrician due to finish up her residency at an Alexandria, Virginia, hospital in three more months, she typically had to wear her hair up on top of her head or in a ponytail. At home in their condo, however, she always wore it down, much to his pleasure.

Dara had already bought some women's Hawaiian tees, shorts, and white blouses with feminine touches. It was when she excitedly brought out a stunning silk sarong, hand painted in lavender with gold hibiscus, that he about lost it. This sensuous piece of silk could be worn in various ways, all sexy as far as he was concerned. The young Hawaiian clerk, she said, had eagerly shown her the many ways to wrap it and told Dara that she could wear it without a bra or panties. That made Matt take notice, because as Dara pulled out the cloth, allowing it to hang off her arm, he was making all kinds of plans about where she could wear that and how he was going to take it off her. Dara had given him a devilish look that told him she had the very same idea, and he'd given her a feral grin. This vacation was going to be a well-earned reward for both of them.

His fiancée was smiling as he carried all her packages to the parking lot. The morning sun rose warm in a soft-blue sky, and the ocean, which they could see from where they were, was smooth, a marine blue, with sunlight glinting and dappling on its mirror-like surface. "You look damn good in that red and white sundress," he warned her, opening the RAV's door for her.

"Like it, Culver?" she teased, tossing her hair and turning in a circle, giving him some of the hip-roll action that she used in her belly dancing to spark his lust.

"I more than like it," he growled, opening the rear door. "You keep that up and we aren't even going to make it out of our rental house on the other side of the island." Dara's blue eyes sparkled with laughter; she enjoyed teasing him. He liked seeing her girlish side and more of that wild woman he knew lurked deep within her. He placed all the packages on the rear seat.

He had met Dara at Bagram Airfield last November. She and her sister, Callie McKinley, had volunteered to give a belly-dancing performance for the Thanksgiving USO show at one of the larger chow halls. Matt and his team had just come off a long op and were exhausted and sleep deprived. It had been Beau Gardner, another Delta Force sergeant on his team, who had nagged him to come on over, eat, and watch the show. Matt had grudgingly done so. But the first act got his blood pumping and captured his total attention. It was Dara in a bright red belly-dancing outfit with gold coins sewn on to the chiffon fabric here and there, and the sight of her ripped his exhaustion away. As her long, gold hair flowed like sunlight around her lithe, graceful upper body, he felt like someone had stunned him with a Taser. Dara had been beautiful, like a ballerina, as Callie played the music for her slow, sexy dance. Four-thousand men had been in that chow hall, and those two sisters had each brought down the house. Callie looked gorgeous, too, with her red hair shining against a purple belly-dancing outfit with glittering silver coins. Beau was smitten with Callie's hot, fast dance. And now he was in a relationship with her. Delta operators knew how to get the women who entangled their hearts.

Matt saw his Turkish grandmother Damia's diamond engagement ring glittering fiercely in the sunlight as Dara climbed into the RAV. His heart swelled; his grandma Damia, whose rings he had given Dara on Christmas Day, had said on her deathbed that she saw a beautiful woman with sunlit hair who would one day wear the rings she'd worn for sixty-five years. It had totaled Matt emotionally when his mother, Dilara, reminded him of what Damia had said. He needed to feel his way through his clairvoyant Turkish grandma's prediction. It was a good sign, an important one to him. Dara had loved the ring set and was touched to the point of tears. Dara valued family just like Matt did, because she had a very positive, tight-knit family of her own in Butte, Montana.

He climbed into the RAV and glanced over at Dara. She looked delicious in that short, girlish dress with the heart-shaped bodice. She had already traded her winter footgear for a pair of sexy, strappy white leather sandals, showing off the bright-red nail polish she'd painted on her toes the night before. "You look more like a college girl than a doctor," he teased, putting the RAV in gear and slowly leaving the sprawling parking lot.

"I feel like one. This is *such* a nice after-Christmas gift." She gestured out the open window at the velvet-green lava ridge above them. "I love smelling the salt of the ocean, Matt. How many times have you been over here?"

Matt pulled out into the busy traffic in down-town Honolulu, heading north on Ala Moana Boulevard. "I've lost count. When my Delta Force team came over here for jungle-training refresher courses, we were usually out in the mountains opposite the Kaneohe Marine Corps base, which sits northeast of the city. The SEALs also used the same area, and sometimes we'd work in a jungle challenge with one another to sharpen our skills. They're a great group to work with."

Smiling absently, Dara enjoyed sitting back, relaxing, and leaving the driving to him. Matt wasn't a braggart. He had what she termed quiet confidence. She remembered seeing him in action that day the Taliban sent two pickup trucks full of soldiers hurtling toward a market in Kabul, Afghanistan, that they had bombed two days earlier. They were firing off their weapons indiscriminately on either side of the street. Matt had calmly gone outside the orphanage where Callie and Dara were volunteering, gotten down on one knee, and started systematically firing his M4 rifle at the oncoming enemy. Dara couldn't believe how placid he was as bullets flew around him. It was then that she recognized the quiet, steely courage that Matt had. She'd never been around that kind of violence before, and it had shocked her to her soul. Dara had known going over to Kabul would be dangerous, that the six months a year Callie spent working at that orphanage were filled every day with the possibility of dying. But that day, she had seen it.

And now? Had it only been two months since she'd met this incredible man who could shoot to kill one moment, and the next be there to comfort her and the children in the aftermath, calming all of them with his low, soothing voice and his gentle touch? As she languidly rested, watching the heavy foot traffic on one side of the street and looking at the ocean on the other, she felt as if she were in some kind of amazing, ongoing dream. She hadn't intended to fall in love with Matt Culver. She'd had no idea who he was or that he came from one of the richest families on earth. He'd shared a few hints of his family's history with her but never admitted that he was rich beyond imagination, or that he was as generous as he was kind. Dara knew nothing about him except that he drew her to him, and she felt helpless to resist those large, intelligent gold-brown eyes of his that missed nothing.

As the dry breeze passed through the open windows, she closed her eyes, enjoying the balmy mid-seventies temperature, just happy to be with him under less pressured circumstances. The Taliban attack at the orphanage wasn't the only terrifying event they'd had to endure. The Taliban had ambushed them as they'd driven toward a pro-American, Afghan village to render medical aid. Once Matt had gotten her and her younger sister out of that overturned vehicle, he and Beau Gardner, his teammate, had grabbed Dara and Callie and headed off in opposite directions, hoping to throw the attacking Taliban forces into confusion.

Dara had thought they were going to die either of hypothermia in the winter mountains of Afghanistan or at the hands of the Taliban relentlessly tracking them. She thought about the constant, unceasing struggle of the two days they spent running for their lives. Matt was in rugged shape, like a mountain goat, accustomed to climbing up to an elevation of nine-thousand feet in winter weather. She was not. Matt had coaxed her, helped her, and somehow, she'd done it. Without him, she could never have gotten over that horrid mountain and to eventual safety on the other side. Dara would never forget those nightmarish days. Even now, at night, she'd have a nightmare. Matt would awaken instantly, curving his body around hers, his arms holding her close, speaking soothingly to her, calming her, dissolving her fear of being captured by the Taliban.

Dara reached out, sliding her hand across his hard, jean-clad thigh, barely turning her head to catch his glance. "I love you so much, Matt . . . this is such a wonderful vacation to share with you."

He placed his hand across hers, his fingers long and roughened. "We needed this," he rasped. "You went straight from the ambush and running for your life to flying home the next day, going back into your residency. You've not had time to absorb everything that's happened to you, sweetheart."

She heard the concern in his deep voice, felt his care, that wonderful, invisible love that surrounded her as it had so many times before. "Spending Christmas with your family, though, and then two weeks with my mom, my dad, Callie, and Beau at my family's ranch, helped me a lot, Matt. Really, I feel pretty normal." Her lips curved ruefully as she absorbed his classic profile, thinking how ruggedly handsome he was. "But I'm also still floating with unbelievable happiness over finding you . . . you loving me. Me loving you."

She curved her long, slender fingers around his sun-darkened ones. Matt had a golden tone to his flesh, and it wasn't from being in the sun, although he had been in it plenty as a Delta Force operator. He took strongly after his uncle Ihsan, who had the same gold-brown eyes, the same golden tone to his flesh. His Turkish-Greek mother, Dilara, had olive-toned skin and those flawless aquamarine eyes that mesmerized Dara. She'd never seen eyes quite the color of Dilara's. When Dilara was happy, they were more blue. When she worried, they grew more green. She was classically beautiful. Matt had once said that he thought his mother was the goddess Artemis come down into human form. And Dara couldn't disagree. The woman was a world-famous socialite and fashion icon, but she usually kept her fame low-key and didn't seek out attention. Still, Dilara was the face of the Delos Charities, and she would go out into the limelight to raise awareness of what Delos did to help those who had so little.

Dara felt Matt's fingers grow more firm around her own as he drove down the six-lane boulevard between the huge, sprawling Hawaiian city and the endless white-sand beaches with huge hotels built nearby. She loved the gently swaying palms that were eighty to a hundred feet tall. This was the jungle, and she saw many hibiscus, birds-of-paradise, and other colorful bushes here and there.

"You look really relaxed," Matt said, taking the boulevard to the H1 freeway, which would

lead them around to the other side of Oahu and
to the town of Waianae.

"Ohh," she whispered, smiling softly, "am I
ever. I feel as if I'm in a never-ending dream with
you, Matt."

"Well," he joked, "at least this time around
it's a dream and not a nightmare."

Laughing throatily, she said, "No, we had the
nightmare ambush to endure and live through
already. Remember?"

"Helluva way to impress you, wasn't it?"
Matt gave her a warm, amused look. Strands of
her thick blond hair moved restlessly across her
shoulders as they picked up speed on the busy
freeway. The sun glinted through them, showing
the caramel, gold, and wheat tones throughout it.
Dara's hair color was natural, and he'd been
mesmerized by it since he saw her belly dancing
that night at Bagram. Women would die for her
hair, and he knew it. Many tried to create the
look, but Dara was the real deal. She didn't
realize how beautiful she was, how clean her
features, those wide marine-blue eyes of hers,
that lush, full set of lips he would never tire of
kissing and making his own.

"Yes, you impressed me all right," she said,
grinning recklessly. "I was mesmerized by the
color of your eyes, how exotic you looked. After
I found out you were Turkish and Greek, I really
saw it in your face. Your DNA is what made you

so striking."

"As long as you like me the way I am, I don't care what anyone else thinks." Matt lifted her hand, bringing it to his lips and kissing the back of it, inhaling her sweet, womanly scent. Dara was delicious to him. He liked listening to the low, vibrating moans she shared with him when he loved her slowly, building her up, watching her whole body begin to quiver with anticipation of what he was going to give to her. There was no joy greater than foreplay with Dara. She wasn't a neophyte when it came to making love, but in some ways, she was, and Matt delighted in teaching her. She was a fast learner, which made him smile. He was eagerly looking forward to showing her Oahu, the Hawaiian way of life, the blindingly beautiful nature of the island and its warm, welcoming people.

"You really are a shadow warrior, Matt. Callie was right about that."

"Your sister? What did she say about me?" They had spent nearly two weeks up at the Eagle Feather Ranch outside Butte, Montana, the McKinley family's twenty-thousand-acre cattle ranch. Most of the time, they were snowed in, but there were days when the sky was a bright, clean blue and the sunlight was blinding, and they'd ride horses on well-known trails, enjoying the raw beauty of nature together.

"Callie has a lot more experience with you

operator types," Dara said with a careless shrug. "You and Beau were talking with Grandpa one evening, and she said that both of you never really revealed who you were. You gave parts of yourself to the person you were with but were never really fully available to them. Or maybe, putting it a different way, you gave only what you thought the other person needed, but not your full self. Does that make sense?"

Grinning, Matt said, "You know, your grandpa was a Marine sniper during the Gulf War. Did you realize he was black ops, too?"

"No, I didn't. He never talked about his war experiences when he was in the Marine Corps."

"That's because he held a top secret clearance, and he was a sniper. He was blacker than most black ops, Dara."

"But he was able to be vulnerable with Callie and me."

"You were innocent children growing up with him. He could be open with you. You weren't a threat to him; rather, he saw himself as protecting the two of you. As you got older and because of the love and trust you had with him, he could remain open in all ways to you girls."

"That makes sense," Dara said. She slanted him a glance, absorbing the dry warmth and strength of his hand around hers. Matt never hurt her. Never used his brawn or strength against her. "But I feel that way about you. You know that, don't you? I trust you with my life, and I love you. I don't feel any need to parcel myself out in facets to you. What you get is all of me."

He absorbed her serious look; he longed for such deep, searching talks with Dara, because as beautiful as she was, she was equally intelligent and insightful. "Do you feel like I'm parceling myself out to you?" It was a serious concern to him, and Matt knew that after nearly ten years in black ops, there were many things about his behavior that were so ingrained in him that he didn't give them any thought. He saw Dara's broad, unlined brow scrunch, her lips pucker, and he'd studied her body language enough to know that she was in serious thought. His training had finely honed his powers of observation so that he could read a person minutely, and in such a way that they didn't even realize he was analyzing them.

"Sometimes," she said, hesitant. "I mean, I saw it a lot when we were on the run after being ambushed."

"I was working on all cylinders at that time, Dara. I needed to get you the hell out of there, put miles between us and the Taliban. I was spending most of my time reading the landscape, the weather, recalling that area from memory and taking your physical abilities into consideration, too."

"I could feel it, Matt. Don't take what I said

the wrong way, because it made me feel safe. It really did. I could sometimes look into your eyes and I'd see the power of your mind at work. It made me feel secure when I shouldn't have felt that way at all."

"What about after that?" He caught her solemn-looking blue gaze. Dara was a conservative person. Much like his older sister, Tal. She was the oldest of the Culver siblings and had borne the responsibilities of an eldest child. "Do you feel I still parcel myself out to you?" Because he didn't want her to feel like he was giving only a part of his heart to her. She held his whole heart in her slender hands. Dara was a natural healer. Everything she touched was better off for it. Every smile she gave to someone was like blinding sunlight cascading through them, touching their heart, healing their soul. Matt had been privy to that as Dara trustingly gave her vulnerable self to him when they made love with one another.

"When we love one another?" she said tentatively, still putting the right words together. "I feel . . . sometimes, it's just a feeling, Matt. I feel you withholding some part of yourself from me, and I don't know why."

Grimacing, he nodded. "It's Delta training," he muttered. "And it's something I need to work on and fix between us." He kissed her hand again, holding her confused gaze for a moment before returning to driving. Settling her hand on his thigh, he rasped, "It's not easy to be open, Dara. I've spent nearly a decade in situations where lethal threats were damned close to me. It's not an excuse, but that's the reason, okay?" He gave her a concerned look.

"But I'm not a threat to you, Matt. I never will be."

"My heart knows that," he said, his voice suddenly thick with emotion. "My overly-trained brain doesn't. And that's where I have work to do."

She gave him a gentle, understanding smile. "Every time we love one another, it's always better than the last time. It's not about what you sometimes teach me. It's about how I feel your heart is slowly unfurling toward me, embracing me, making me one hundred percent yours. That's what I live for: feeling that magical, beautiful, spellbinding connection with you, Matt. I feel you opening up to me more and more every time, so don't look worried. Okay?"

"But you don't feel it every time I love you?" That tore at his heart, because he hadn't realized it. And he knew Dara wasn't saying this to hurt him. She was not a manipulator. What you saw was what you got. And he loved her fiercely for being her simple, honest self with him. She was that kind of woman, and he wanted to tenderly nurture the beautiful connection between them forever.

He saw her squirm. It wasn't obvious, but he sensed it. Dara didn't like hurting anyone's feelings. Because she was so ultra-sensitive by nature, she was more careful about potentially hurting another person with a wrong look or word. She'd been trained to be diplomatic and optimistic, no matter how bad the news she had to deliver to a parent of a sick child or a mother carrying her baby.

"Hey," he warned her gruffly, "don't hedge on this with me, okay? I've got the skin of a rhino, Dara. I'm not like you—you have no skin." He gave her a teasing grin, hoping to pull her out of her fear of hurting his feelings.

"You do *not* have rhino skin, Matt Culver!" she sputtered, horrified.

"Not with you, I don't," he agreed. "But you can ask Beau Gardner how tough I can be when necessary." Matt loved her tinkling laughter, seeing her head thrown back, her eyes shining with happiness. He lived to make this woman smile, to see her spread her heartfelt sunlight out to others. And like the greedy sponge he was, he lapped up every smile, every loving look, every touch she gave to him. There was something so sacred about Dara that Matt couldn't put it into words. It was a feeling, and it was around her all the time; it made his heart fly open when normally it would have remained closed and guarded. Dara made him want to be utterly vulnerable with her.

"And yet," Dara said, reaching over after pulling her hand from his and sliding her fingertips over a few brown and gold strands of hair above his ear, "you never let that toughness show. I've seen you in a lot of situations and you never shield yourself, Matt."

"I show it only if I need to," he counseled her gently. "You haven't been in that kind of situation with me."

"And I hope I never am. Getting to know you, falling in love with you, is like riding a rocket. I don't know what's going to happen next or where it will go."

Mouth quirking, Matt admitted, "Well, that's true. But I've been like that since I was born, Dara. Things just pop up and happen around me. My mother swears that I carry the energy of a bolt of lightning within me. She loves the old gods of Turkey and Greece. Zeus was the one who carried the lightning bolt, and he was the king of the gods."

"Oh, but wait!" Dara said, giving him a gleeful look. "Zeus allowed his daughter Pallas Athena to hurl his bolts of lightning, too! I'll bet you didn't know that."

Amused, Matt cocked a dark brow. "Yes, I did. I was raised on the myths of Turkey and Greece, Dara. I probably know more about the myths of these gods and goddesses than ninety-nine percent of the world. My uncles would sit us on their knees and ply the three of us with those wondrous tales. Little-known ones. Real gems, because each one was like a teachable moment. We loved when we visited our Turkish aunts and uncles during our summer break in Kuşadasi because they always had a myth to share with us. The three of us are drenched in them, believe me."

"Okay," she laughed, "so who's to say your mom isn't right? Maybe you do carry the lightning of Zeus or Athena within you, and you attract sudden, unexpected, transforming experiences because of it. Do you think it's Zeus or Athena who works with you?"

"Oh, I think it's probably Athena. I'm not like Zeus. I don't want to be a king. I don't need to be seen as all-knowing or all-powerful like he does. There's a statue of Athena where she's holding a coiled snake around each of her upper and lower arms, their heads resting in her opened palms. Uncle Ihsan told us about this statue one morning after breakfast while we were sitting around his rocking chair at his villa. He said he'd heard of it as a boy, that this myth of her with the snakes around her arms had come down from the twelfth century when their family started their shipping company."

"What does it mean?"

"That the snakes are about wisdom, fertility, intuition, and creativity. You know that the head of Medusa is on the shield Athena sometimes carries? Or on her breastplate. Medusa is the woman goddess whose hair is made up of hundreds of living snakes."

"Yeah, but Medusa got a bad rap," Dara said, wrinkling her nose. "The myth we were all told instead, in the later centuries, was that if you looked at her, you turned to stone."

He snorted. "Yeah, that was male patriarchy getting in the way of the real truth about Medusa. My uncles always told us kids that ten-thousand years ago and earlier, the world was matriarchal, ruled by women. Back then, Medusa was the goddess of enlightenment. The snakes on her head represented a connection with the Great Mother Goddess of all. It was as if she were plugged into the loving, creative, and fertile energy and brought it down to this earth, to share with us mere humans to make things better for all of them. She was the light of awakening and being in touch not only with your heart and soul, but with all the world around you. She was known as a great healer, also."

"Well, I sure like that myth better than the one where she petrifies men."

"Well, isn't that interesting?" Matt countered. "The myth was revised by men. Because Medusa was an enlightened woman who was awake, they felt threatened by her. So they reinvented the 'truth' and had her turn men into stone. Men were asleep. They were not in touch with themselves, with their hearts or their feelings. So of course, that was a logical lie to tell about Medusa. They never said that she turned women into stone, did they? Just stupid, foolish men." He chuckled. "As males began to dominate the world, they destroyed the respect they had held for women and their intelligence, creativity, and fertility. And they subjected goddesses to a do-over, too. The patriarchy changed a lot of Greek myths where the goddesses were supreme or at least equal to the male gods. What you see in today's myths is a male remake, distortions, twisted half-truths, or outright lies. And the goddesses have suffered gravely from this injustice. But so do women of our world to this day. That has to change."

"Is that why your Turkish side of the family named their shipping line after the goddess Artemis?"

"Yep, because before the male remake on goddesses in the old world, Artemis was a consummate woman role model who was maternal, helped pregnant women, and was central to a strong, healthy family as well."

"But in the myths we hear today," Dara said, "Artemis, who was called Diana by the Romans, is a huntress. She hates men and runs like a naked wild woman through the forests with her bow and arrows or her spear, killing animals. She refuses to be tamed by a man."

"Well," Matt said drolly, "that's not the Artemis our family knows. And if you look carefully at the beliefs of Anatolia, the ancient name for Turkey, as far back as you can go, she was worshipped by everyone. She was, in essence, the cradle of our country, a strong, wise woman."

"Boy, she sure got the short end of the stick from the patriarchy, didn't she?" Dara said, disgusted.

"If you ask a Turk about Artemis, to this day, she is respected. All the great temples in Turkey, especially the one in Ephesus, were built to her. And as a matter of fact, Turkey is the most progressive Muslim country in the world where women are concerned. Many families still have an altar in their home to her. They pray to her. They bring her flowers, sweet cakes, or other gifts. She's alive and well in our blood. And every ship my family owns, even today, has a small altar to Artemis on board, and prayers are said to her for a safe voyage. That hasn't changed since the twelfth century, Dara."

"I love finding out about your amazing family," she admitted, a little breathless and excited over their discussion. "That's a fascinating tidbit. I'll bet you don't share that with the world."

He shook his head. "No. Remember the sunroom in my parents' home, where I proposed to you and gave you Grandmother Damia's rings?"

"Of course."

"Do you remember seeing a little water cascade on a marble shelf near the window? There was some ivy growing around it, too."

"Yes, I do."

"That's my mom's altar to Artemis. She says morning and nightly prayers to her. She sees the goddess as caretaker of our entire family."

"I've always thought that there's much more to our unseen universe than what is being told or sold to us."

"Sure is, but that's another story for another day." Matt gave her a teasing smile. The openness and joy in Dara's expression blew his heart wide open. She was so childlike in some ways, and he lived for rare moments just like this that he could share with her.

"Let's get back to the core of our talk. You were worried that you weren't opening up entirely to me?"

"Yes."

"You have been opening up to me over time, Matt. I feel that you *want* to. Sometimes, I think you're wrestling within yourself, wanting to be fully vulnerable with me. It's a struggle inside you. I can feel it. Do you?"

He became serious, frowning. "Yeah, there are times when I do, Dara. And I don't want to be that way with you. I want to share myself with you in every possible way. And I'm trying to figure out how to fix this."

She laughed lightly, sliding her fingers through his hair, seeing arousal in his eyes over her tender ministrations. "So typically male. A man thinks if he can fix it, everything will go well. These are emotions, Matt. You don't 'fix' them. You work through them. And since you spent nearly a decade protecting your feelings, your heart, because of the kind of work you had to do, I feel it's just going to take time. I know"—she met his eyes for a moment—"that you will one day be fully open with me. I feel it in my soul, because you love me just as much as I love you . . ."

# CHAPTER 2

D ARA GASPED WITH delight as Matt pulled into the driveway on top of a small hill nestled on the slope of the velvet-cloaked lava mountains. They'd arrived at a small single-story plantation house, full of windows with a teak wraparound porch. There were monkeypod trees lining the concrete driveway up to the white house, which had a slate-colored roof. The teak porch railing gleamed here and there as sunlight cascaded through the trees.

"This is so beautiful!" Dara said, climbing out. Pulling her canvas bag over her left shoulder, she came around the front of the RAV, meeting Matt, who was taking out the keys to the rental. There were small, delicate gray-barked plumeria plants, their flowers pink with yellow centers, their fragrance heady and sweet.

"Like it?" he asked, smiling down at her.

Right now, Dara was like an excited child, and it made him feel giddy with joy as he walked her up the highly polished teak steps to the wraparound porch. Around the bottom of the high porch were glistening, dark-green night-blooming jasmine vines. They had been artfully woven through a low trellis that surrounded the house, so it looked like it was sitting on a shiny green-leafed foundation of vines.

"Love it! Look! Passionflowers!" She pointed at one corner of a huge vertical teak log that supported the roof of the porch. The vines, sporting white flowers with purple and blue in the center of them, wrapped around the log from the ground almost to the roof, nearly hiding it. More passionflower vines wrapped around the other teak support at the other end of the porch. Their scent, combined with that of the plumeria, made Dara smile even more. The house was surrounded on three sides by hundred-foot-tall coconut palms, and behind them was the deep, dark-green jungle covering the slope of the mountain.

She stood on the front porch looking out at the turquoise blue of the ocean and the white beaches. She saw the town of Waianae, a mile away from the curved, pristine beaches. The view was a hundred and eighty degrees from where she stood, and Dara stared at the spiny ridge of the nearby mountains. The sharp peaks marched south toward the end of the island.

"Ready to see the inside of it?" Matt asked, unlocking the door and nudging it open for her. "This is our home for the next seven days. Let's go check it out."

Dara didn't need two invites. She quickly took off her shoes, leaving them just inside the door on a small rug, and walked into the large living room and kitchen area. The floor consisted of long planks of highly polished, golden-hued teak. She looked up at the high cathedral ceiling, painted white, with huge timbers supporting it. The furniture was bamboo with large, comfortable-looking ivory cushions. There were large lanterns of crinkly white rice paper that cast a soft glow when Matt turned on the switch.

In one corner were several jade-colored ceramic pots filled with bright red and green ti plants that were at least ten feet tall, giving the area a dramatic and colorful focal point. Dara walked lightly, appreciating the colors, the calming coolness and quiet of the plantation house. She touched the long white cream drapes, which were pulled open. The most dramatic aspect of the room, and the one she loved the most, was the wraparound windows. They extended from either side of the entrance in the center of the south wall and down the east and west walls. They yielded an incredible view of the slopes running past the town of Waianae and down to the turquoise and marine-blue Pacific Ocean just beyond it.

Matt took her hand, leading her into the large open-concept kitchen. There were white marble counters with streaks of black running through them, a double sink, a Wolf gas stove, and gold teak cabinets, lending warmth to the kitchen. "I like to cook," he confided. "You okay with me doing the duty in the kitchen?"

"Better believe it," Dara said with a smile. She leaned into Matt, sliding her arm around his waist, absorbing the love she could see in his eyes as he placed his arm around her shoulders. "I can cook too, if you need a break."

"That's okay," he murmured, kissing her hair. "This is your vacation. Remember?" At their condo, they split up the cooking duties, but right now Matt wanted her to be free of such things and truly enjoy this vacation with him.

She wandered across the teak floor to a hall that led to a huge master bedroom. "This place is like another world, Matt. It's so gorgeous. I love the teak, the warmth of the wood, all the windows, and seeing all the trees and flowers surrounding this home." There was a white duvet over the king-sized bed and lots of large jade-green silk pillows leaning against the thick, curved bamboo headboard. Below the bamboo foot-board was a bench with cream-colored cushions where one could sit and take off her clothes. The windows were on two sides, their cream drapes drawn back so that the lights of the small towns of Oahu could be seen at night.

"Come see this master bathroom." Matt grinned. "I don't think I'll get you out of it," he said, chuckling.

Dara stepped into the huge L-shaped bathroom. The floor consisted of small, octagonal tiles, some of them clear glass, the rest in white and every color of the rainbow. After Matt switched on the overhead rice-paper lamps, the floor became an amazing burst of fiery colors, and she was mesmerized by it. There was a huge porcelain claw-foot tub. At the other end was a three-person spa. In the center was a huge, frosted-glass enclosed shower for two with expensive rain heads. There was a double sink, and the counter was the same white marble with black striations as in the kitchen. The mirror was at least eight feet wide and five feet high.

"You're right. That tub looks really inviting," she admitted. There were folded fuzzy pink bath towels sitting on the counter, along with washcloths and hand towels. Best of all, Dara saw a huge, red ceramic vase filled with sprays of white and purple of orchids, their sweet fragrance filling the space.

He chuckled. "Bathtubs are a way to your heart, Dara. Let me go bring in our luggage."

"I can help."

"Nope," he said, releasing her, heading for the doorway. "You just get comfortable and think about what you'd like to do with the rest of our day."

She helped Matt to put their clothes away once he brought in the luggage. The windows were open, and there were birds singing outside. A cooling breeze wound through the bedroom, and she could smell the plumeria. After she finished putting her clothes away, she walked over to Matt, placing her arms around his shoulders. A moment ago he'd looked so intensely focused on his unpacking, but as soon as she came and moved her body against his, sliding her arms around his neck, she saw an instant change, and it warmed her heart. She loved affecting him so powerfully. His gold-brown eyes grew amused.

"Uh-oh, I'm being stalked," he murmured, turning around and taking her mouth, sliding against her lips.

The world halted. When Matt devoted a hundred percent of his attention to her, Dara felt like the most desired and cherished woman in the world. She loved kissing him, feeling the passion barely restrained in his kiss as he controlled himself for her sake. Moving her hips suggestively against his pelvis, feeling how thick and hard he already was, sent an instant ache and need of him through her.

"Mmm," she said, easing from his mouth, drowning in the gold intensity of his narrowed eyes. "Now you make me want to stay right here and love you instead of seeing Oahu."

He smiled a little, moving his hand down her supple spine, the red dress beautiful on her. "Up to you, sweetheart. I'm easy either way. We're on vacation, and we can do exactly what inspires you."

She liked being in his arms, leaning against his hard body. "We just had a ten-hour flight, and I'm jet-lagged. Are you?"

Shrugging, Matt said, "Yes and no. In order to adjust to Oahu's time, we should stay up." It was nearly noon according to his watch. "Hungry?"

"Well," she laughed, enjoying the hardness of his cock against her belly, inciting her, making her want to go nowhere, "my body is on East Coast time."

"Then," he said lightly, cupping the cheeks of her butt, moving her sensually against him, "let's do something easy, something that isn't going to drain us further."

"Such as?"

"Let me drive you down to Waianae. It's a pretty seacoast town, nice restaurants, the beach is nearby. You could kick off your sandals and walk in the sand or the ocean itself if you wanted."

"I like that idea. I love the ocean."

Matt slid his fingers through her mussed hair, watching the highlights glint beneath the lamplight above them. "Then let's do that. We'll be lazy today, just kick back, relax, eat when we're hungry, rest when we're tired."

"And make love?" she suggested, giving him a wicked look, cupping his jaw with her hands, leaning up, taking his mouth. Oh, yes, sex! She was ready to pull him down on the bed with her. His mouth was strong, commanding, and he held her firmly against his pelvis. More heat flooded her, and she lost herself in his mouth.

Matt withdrew from Dara's full lips, smiling down into her aroused, half-closed blue eyes, clearly seeing the need in them. "I'm easy, Dara. Just tell me what you want and we'll do it." Because Dara worked twelve to fourteen hours a day as a resident in pedes at the hospital in Alexandria, she always came home exhausted, so he wanted her to be the rudder on this vacation, not him. "What will it be?"

"As much as I want to love you right now? I'm afraid if I do, I'll fall asleep afterward and the jet lag will get worse, not better. I want to be able to adjust and be here, not there. Does that make sense?"

"Absolutely," he murmured, reluctantly releasing her, but not before caressing those fine, plump cheeks of hers hidden beneath that sexy red dress she was wearing. Red always looked good on Dara. The first time he saw her she was wearing that red belly-dancing outfit, those gold coins glimmering and shimmering with every sensual move of her hips.

"Okay," she sighed, unsure. Matt's sensuality and animal magnetism were almost too much for her to walk away from. "The beach and ocean it is." Giving him a playful look, she added, "You're mine tonight, Matt Culver. All of you." He was a sexual alpha male, and they enjoyed making love when she wasn't too exhausted from her medical duties. As Dara eased away, she saw the gleam in his eyes; he was the hunter, and she was his target. It was a delicious feeling to be desired by him, sending even more of an ache into her lower body.

He nodded and growled, "Then let's go, because if we stay here five more minutes, I'm grabbing you and throwing you on that bed of ours, and I'm going to spend the rest of the day loving you."

Moaning, she picked up her purse and exited the room.

Once Matt began living with Dara, he'd found out quickly that she enjoyed sex as much as he did. He had become so in tune with Dara that he could sense her exhaustion when she came home at night after work. Dara was very good at hiding it and had fooled him at first. But after noticing that sometimes after they made love, she would awaken the next morning looking more exhausted than the night before, he decided to tamp down his desire for her. He hoped the vacation would let her catch up on her rest. And he'd made her needs a priority over his. Matt grimaced as he adjusted his cock beneath his jeans, giving him a little more breathing room, and the ache lessened. This was Dara's vacation. And he intended to let her tell him what she needed.

THE AQUAMARINE OCEAN water was warm and felt delicious over Dara's bare feet. Her sandals hung from the fingers of Matt's left hand. The sea breeze infused her with a peaceful feeling, as did the cries of seagulls sailing overhead. Walking on a golden, sandy beach, ankle-deep in the ocean water, made her feel so alive. Matt had taken off his sandals as well. The noontime warmth of the sun fell over her; the temperature was perfect, in the high seventies. The early January weather in Hawaii was very different from the climate she'd left back home in Virginia!

Every once in a while, Dara would spot a small shell in the clear ocean water, and she would stop, lean over, and retrieve her new treasure. Matt knew that locals here would get up at dawn, come down, and scour the beach for shells that had washed up during the night hours. By noon, the beaches were cleaned of any beautiful, whole shells that had been deposited. But Dara delighted in the pieces of colorful shells that she found, holding them like treasures in her hand. His heart swelled with love for her; she was one of those people who delighted in whatever she was doing.

He stopped her and said, "Why don't you put your shells in the pocket of your dress?"

Laughing, she opened her palm, showing him the shards. "They're so beautiful I just want to hold them for a while. Even though they're fractured and in pieces, I want to collect a bunch of them while we're here. I've decided to put them in a small glass goblet with the sand I'm walking on. Next time we come down here, I'll bring some plastic bags. I want to bring some of Hawaii home with us, where I can see it every day."

"So," he said, moving his finger through her many shell pieces, "you're going to put that glass somewhere you can see it to remember this time?" He melted beneath the joy he saw shining in her eyes, those lips so lush, so kissable, and he ached to do just that.

Dara smiled and nodded. "I'm putting this on the desk in my office at the hospital. On tough days, I can sit there and look at it and remember this time with you."

Leaning over, he caressed her smiling mouth with his. Matt could taste the salt air on her lips, the mocha latte she'd had earlier before they walked down to the beach. Easing away, he rasped, "I'm taking a heart photo of you right now . . ." He brought her gently to a stop, easing her against his body, feeling her breasts pressing into his chest, that low, husky sound of pleasure vibrating in her throat as he kissed her long and well. She was such a sensual, sexual creature, although most would never see it. He sure had when she belly-danced at Bagram. And he'd been privileged to go with her to the gym where she worked out and belly-danced to stay in top shape. They always ended up in bed after that, each of them turned on by the other.

Dara closed her eyes, drowning in Matt's cherishing mouth, his arm around her, bringing her into the fold of his tall, lean, hard body. Everything was perfect. Just perfect.

OVER LUNCH AT a small seafood restaurant near the beach, Dara sat at a picnic table beneath a white awning, watching the ceaseless activity of the ocean and the small waves splashing their foamy life against the gold sands of the beach. "This is a dream, Matt." She reached out, gripping his hand, giving his fingers a squeeze.

"My life is a dream come true because you're in it," he told her, meaning it, looking into her eyes, which glimmered with tears because of his admittance. Matt wasn't going to tell her not to cry. As much as tears tore him up, he knew they were a positive release. He still hadn't climbed that mountain of getting comfortable with his own tears. He never cried in public. Instead, while in Afghanistan, after a traumatic mission, he'd cried alone, in a dark corner where no one could hear his sobs. In a way, he admired Dara's ability to cry openly and without apology.

She released his hand, giving him a longing look. "You are perfect for me, Matt Culver."

"Even though when you met me you thought I was just after your body, hmm?" he teased. Well, it was the truth. After watching Dara belly dance? Hell, he was like an alpha wolf in heat, and he'd just found his alpha female. And all he wanted to do was mate repeatedly with her. But there was so much more to Dara than just a sexual being. Never mind her beauty. Or that fabulous blond hair of hers; he would never get tired of running his fingers through those strong, shining strands. No, as he watched her work at the Hope Charity orphanage in Kabul, alongside her sister, Callie, Matt began to realize just how beautiful Dara truly was. Get her around a baby? The woman melted and became so maternal that he wished he were that baby in her arms receiving all the love and attention she lavished on the infant.

That was another facet to Dara: the mother. There was a good reason she was a pediatrician, and Matt had watched her with those babies, those pregnant Afghan women and their small, shy children. His need for her, the reasons for his need, shifted and changed. Yes, sex with Dara would be great. That was a no-brainer in Matt's world. But to watch her blossoming, to see and feel her love and care for others, melted his heart, and at that moment, his feelings for her became about far more than just physical desire.

He had never seen himself falling in love, even though his mother and father were deeply in love with one another. They showed it daily to their children through respect, equality, smiles, touches, and sometimes kisses in front of them. Matt had grown up thinking that his family was like everyone else's. But he quickly found out, after joining the Army at eighteen, that his family really was one in a billion, because so many of his other teammates' lives and families were dysfunctional. Love had been distorted, twisted, made dysfunctional in those families, and he'd seen the emotional and mental damage that had wreaked upon the other Delta Force operators on his team. He began to understand that the family stamping of a child's first eighteen years of life branded them forever. He began to grasp the enormity and responsibility of becoming a parent someday.

When he met Dara, falling helplessly in love with her, Matt had gotten lucky. Or, his mother, Dilara, would archly point out, he'd been blessed by the old goddesses and gods. Dara had come from a family similar to his, he'd discovered over time. They were a Montana cattle ranching family, but her mother and father, and her grandparents, who owned the ranch, were no less in love than Dilara and Robert Culver were. That was a stunning realization that Matt had come to.

He didn't know about her loving family before the ambush, but as he tried to protect her, get her to safety, she showed an emotional courage that he saw in his sisters, Tal and Alexa. And maybe coming from a solid, loving family helped sustain her during that nightmarish humping over a nine-thousand-foot mountain pass in the dead of winter. Matt hadn't been sure they would survive. He'd never told Dara that because she needed to keep her hope alive, keep battling to survive with him, to endure the brutal physical challenges they had to go through. He was a pragmatic realist, and he knew the situation could turn deadly, for both of them. Dara was too slow, not physically fit enough for the mountain challenge, and he was always watching for the Taliban. If not for his tracking skills, and a favorable turn in the weather, Matt didn't think they'd be here, on this sunny, warm beach on Oahu, to appreciate what they had. Still, even now, he was in awe of her emotional strength throughout that ordeal. The fact that she'd come from a family similar to his own explained why she could keep trying, despite her lack of training.

As Dara gazed adoringly up at him, he drowned in her deep blue eyes, which shimmered with love for him alone, and Matt knew how fortunate he really was. All the money in the world couldn't buy a person's love. He knew that, had been raised to understand that money was a tool to do good with, but that it could not buy love or happiness. Love, as his mother had taught her children from a young age, was in the hands of the old goddesses and gods of her country. He, Tal, and Alexa, she told them, would be led to the right man or woman, who would hold their heart peerless and pure within their hands. Dilara was passionate about it, certain, without knowing how or why, that her three children would each attract a mate who would cherish them, love them, and be with them forever—just as she had been drawn to Robert Culver, an Air Force combat pilot, a man from another country, another reality, she gravely told them one night. Their mother would often laugh when they gathered around her feet before bed for a nightly story, and she would tell them of how she and

Robert had met, and how profoundly and swiftly she'd fallen in love with the handsome, young Air Force captain with the broad shoulders and confidence to burn. She said he was a real hero, and he was for her, to this day.

As Matt stood with Dara on the beach, the warmth of the sun surrounding them, the breeze bringing the life-giving scent of salt air to their nostrils, the shrieks of the gulls celebrating his good luck in finding her, he smiled down at her. Matt was no poet; he wasn't good with words like Dara was. His emotions always choked him up when it came to her. He was a man of action. He always would be. All Matt could do was show Dara with his kisses, his loving her, his sensitivity toward her, the way he treated her every day, that she meant everything to him and was his world. As he tunneled his fingers through Dara's loose golden hair, he leaned down, whispering against her lips, "Tonight, I'm going to show you just how much I love you . . ."

# CHAPTER 3

D ARA WANTED TO sneak up behind Matt and place her hands over his eyes. But she knew better. He'd been black ops for far too long; if she silently approached him from behind, she'd be in danger of triggering his muscle-memory response to defend and kill when an enemy tried to catch him off guard. He'd repeatedly warned her never to do that, and she'd taken his advice seriously.

Instead, as he was puttering in the kitchen of their rental home after their evening meal, putting the dirty dishes into the dishwasher, she stood at the entrance to the open-concept living area, her hand resting on the doorframe of their bedroom. They'd gotten home at five p.m.; Matt had bought fresh blue-striped snapper from a local fishmonger and gotten everything else he'd need to fix them their first Hawaiian meal from a local market. By six p.m., Dara was stuffed. They'd sat down on the bamboo couch and caught up with the international news from Al Jazeera America. It was the only station that Matt would watch for what he called "real news," without the sensationalized drama that other news networks trotted out. He also liked BBC World News, broadcast from London, England. Those two, he said, he could sift through and get relevant, true news reporting. They both watched the two news-hour presentations and then discussed the events of the day.

Dara had discovered early on that Matt being a sergeant—an enlisted person in the Army and not an officer—was a fact that had no bearing on his innate intelligence, knowledge, or experience. The truth was, he'd taken courses long-distance and on campus for eight years in order to get his degree in politics. He never used the degree to become an officer in the Army, which he could have done. He liked being in the trenches with his men and his team. That was more important to Matt.

Dara had seen that leadership side of him at Bagram when they'd first met. She'd seen it when he'd rescued her from that ambush and was still seeing it now that he was home for thirty days' leave.

This week in Hawaii was his last on leave. Dara was already mourning the fact that after their vacation he'd have to go back to Bagram to finish out his enlistment, which was up on March 1. Back into the hell of black ops and the possibility that he'd get wounded or killed. She worried a lot about that. She loved him with a desperation she'd never known. Craved his nearness, his thoughts, how he saw the world and how he loved and saw her. She was privy to his gentle side, and how she craved that closeness and tenderness with him! Dara didn't know how she was going to survive without Matt's presence. He was larger-than-life but humble, quiet, and an intense warrior and man. He knew who he was and made no excuses for it. He had a job waiting for him at Artemis Security, heading up the KNR—Kidnapping and Ransom—division. And he was looking forward to becoming a civilian and living with her, counting the months until June, when they would wed. Matt was anxious to leave the Army, anxious to have her in his bed every night and share his life with her.

Would Matt remain safe in Bagram? He had tried to explain to her that, during the winter months, the Taliban left and things quieted down in Afghanistan. It was only when spring arrived in April that there was an influx of Pakistani al-Qaeda and Taliban coming across the border, flooding back into war-torn Afghanistan, and Delta Force had to become more active and vigilant. Dara wasn't completely convinced, because she knew how much Matt hadn't told her during their run from that ambush. Only after the fact did he tell her the real shape they were in and how close they had come to getting captured. And it was all because of her lack of physical stamina, but he'd never said anything of the sort to her. Dara knew she had been too slow, clumsy, out of breath, out of shape, for hard winter mountain climbing. Matt had been like a nimble bighorn sheep, acclimated and enduring physical hardship with ease in comparison to her. But still, she worried about losing him over there when he returned to Afghanistan. She tried to push that worry away and focus on only now, only Matt.

"Hey," she called softly, watching him lift his head from the dishwasher, where he'd placed the last of the dirty dishes. Matt grinned as he straightened.

"That sarong looks damn nice on you," he said, shutting the dishwasher and turning it on.

Her whole body reacted heatedly to his burning inspection. "Like it?" Dara's heart beat a little faster as she saw him wash his hands in the sink, dry them, and drop the towel on the counter, heading in her direction with focused intensity. Her breasts firmed, and her nipples hardened beneath that hooded, hungry look he was giving her as he approached.

"Like it?"

Matt gave her a dark look, absorbing her as

she stood barefoot before him in her sarong. "Sweetheart, you give 'sexy' a whole new level of meaning," he said, reaching out, lightly trailing his fingertips along her naked shoulder. She had fastened the sarong just above her breasts, the two ends of it pulled through a wooden clasp, so that the folds flowed down to her knees. The silk fabric was gossamer, and he saw her nipples clearly pushing outward against it. She had brushed her hair until it gleamed with molten highlights, the strands thick and heavy, curling against the top of the sarong. His erection responded when he saw how that sexy piece of nothing lovingly outlined her tall, graceful body. "I'd like to take a picture of you in that sarong. I want it for my cell phone, so when I'm in Afghanistan, I can open it up when I'm alone, look at it, and remember us . . ." He trailed his fingers up her slender throat, seeing the pulse of her artery fluttering against her thin flesh.

"I'm up for it," she said, her voice wispy, unsteady. His fingers barely grazed her, more like a whisper than actual contact. Dara closed her eyes, absorbing that feathery touch of his, aching in her channel for him, feeling the heat burn bright and strong deep within her. Already, her inner thighs were damp with the promise of what he would share with her shortly.

Matt pulled out his cell phone and then moved back far enough to take the photo. Then he put his phone on the lamp stand next to the bamboo sofa. "You look incredible, like a vision." He approached her, his fingertips trailing from her high cheekbones downward, outlining her lips, which parted beneath his touch. "Or," he rasped, smiling into her upturned gaze, those midnight-blue eyes of hers dappled with gold in their depths, telling him how sexually starved she really was, "you're one of the ancient goddesses. Maybe Artemis herself? Coming to visit a poor, mere mortal like me?"

She sighed beneath the skittering heat his stroke had created, her lips tingling, hungry to taste him, inhale his male scent and open herself up to him in every possible way. "I like Artemis. Can I pretend to be her tonight? And you're that handsome mortal I saw from the marble steps of my temple at Ephesus?"

His smile increased as he studied her passionate expression, inhaling her womanly scent. He knew that Dara had found some plumeria oil, and he could smell its delicate scent on her skin. "I think," he murmured, skating his fingers down her bare arms, making languid, slow patterns across them, "that you put Artemis to shame. You're already my goddess."

His words were so beautiful, so heartfelt, that Dara melted, because she knew Matt always said he wasn't a man of words. But he really was. When it counted, he said the most incredible, heartwarming things to her. She stood quietly, allowing him to do whatever he wanted with her. She trusted him with herself. And always, he approached loving her as if she were indeed some beautiful goddess from the ancient past, worshipping her, respecting her, pulling her into himself, allowing her the freedom of her innate feminine expression, sharing it with him. Dara had never felt so valued, so important, to any man as she did with Matt. He adored her. And she'd never been cherished by a man until she met him. Before she could say anything, he scooped her up into his arms. She gave a little cry of surprise but quickly relaxed against him, feeling his strength, his hardness, and relishing that dark, hungry look he gave her.

"Well, goddess of mine," he told her while walking her into their bedroom, "I am going to love you so well tonight that you will agree, upon waking tomorrow morning in my arms, to remain with me all week. Are you in agreement with my desire?"

She kissed his sandpapery cheek, inhaling him, tasting the salt on his skin, the scent of Hawaii upon him. "*If* you love me well enough, my mortal, I will deign to remain in your presence."

"I believe," he said smugly, depositing her on the bed, "I can please you, my lady. Stay there. I need to get a quick shower. I'll see you in a few minutes."

Dara sat there, her legs tucked beneath her, the folds of the sarong partly open between her thighs. She was sure Matt would find that exquisitely sexy. The man loved it when she wore seductive nighties, because he so enjoyed the slow torture that he put her through as he removed each scrap of cloth. It would be no different tonight because Matt, she had discovered, was a very tactile person. Taste was vital to him—licking her skin, driving her to distraction with that skilled tongue of his. He would inhale her scent and she would hear him growl with satisfaction, because he loved the fragrance of everything about her body. She was amazed that he could discern the subtle differences in the skin between her thighs, her breasts, her neck, and behind the lobe of her ear. He had an unerring sense of where the thinnest areas of her flesh were and would wring pleasure out of those super-sensitive areas until there were times when Dara thought she would faint from the intense sensations he gave her.

She was so deep in thought about him, she didn't even realize he was coming out of the master bathroom until he was halfway to their bed. He'd washed his short hair, and a few strands dipped across his broad brow. As he drew near, she could smell the subtle odor of lime around him, and her channel tightened from that scent alone. Matt was teaching her how such subtleties all combined to make a session of lovemaking so very, very special and one of a kind.

"I'd take a cell photo of you just like that," he said wryly, dropping the thick pink towel he carried over a nearby chair, "but if someone ever got on my phone and found it, they'd accuse me of downloading pornography." He closed the bedroom door, shutting off the light. She had lit two tall yellow candles that sat on the dresser opposite their bed, and they lent just enough light.

She laughed with him as he knelt on the mattress, which dipped with his weight as he moved behind her, trapping her between his opened thighs. "Well, we wouldn't want that, would we?" She could feel the heat of his body, inches from her own, her breasts tightening with anticipation. His thighs were long, incredibly honed, hard-feeling against her outer hips as he bracketed her. Matt was teaching her to use her sense of smell, and she inhaled the dampness of his skin as it tantalized her flaring nostrils, that teasing hint of lime combined with the sensation of tense, controlled masculinity. Dara wasn't sure where imagination began or ended with him. Matt had admitted once that Delta Force put them through a lot of training to enhance their six senses, and yes, he was sharing what they'd taught him with her. Only he was opening up those remarkable, intriguing senses in a sexual way, which only made her burn hotter, need him more and much sooner. Dara was impatient to release her orgasms, which he could easily trigger. But he was what she termed a slow lover, someone who appreciated sensual nuances, gloried in them, drowned in them, before moving on to the next level, which was orgasms for her and a climax for him.

She groaned as he sat behind her and rested his hands on his long thighs. "You aren't going to tease me to death tonight, are you, Matt?"

She heard him chuckle, that rumble across the expanse of his broad, dark-haired chest. "Why?" he asked, lifting her gold hair, moving his tongue languidly across her nape, feeling her react, hearing her breath catch, the sound feathering through him, telling him how much pleasure that one small touch gave her.

"Because," she said poutily, turning, looking into his shadowed face, his eyes almost a gold color, "I'm hungry for you."

"I thought you were tired from the jet lag."

She gripped his thighs. "I'm not *that* tired, and you know it! It's just thinking about you all day today, wanting more of you, more closeness with you . . ." She saw his eyes grow thoughtful, and she felt his male energy surrounding her almost like magic. He hadn't touched her, but she felt him wrapping warmly around her, as if to say that he loved her, that he would always be this close to her whenever she needed him. "I mean"—her voice faltered as she held his gaze—"you're going to be gone in seven days . . ."

"That's it," he rasped, leaning forward, licking her nape once more, holding that thick, silky hair to one side in his palm. "I'm always with you, sweet woman. You know that."

The grittiness of his low, hungry voice thrummed through her, and her fingers dug into his thighs. "Matt, I need you. I want you to take me fast tonight, not slow. Can we do that?" She searched his hooded eyes, his mouth curving faintly as he lightly skimmed her shoulders with his fingers.

"You can have anything you want. You know that. You just have to tell me."

Usually, that was true, but Dara had encountered times when fast still meant slow to Matt. "Then," she said archly, "I'm taking over," and she unwound from her position, slid off the bed, and turned around. She pulled on the clasp of the sarong and its folds fell to the floor, revealing her nakedness. She stood in the shadows, appreciating the primal expression that instantly came to his face. There was amusement in his eyes, and she knew he was pleased with her feminine assertiveness. Dara wondered, as she pushed him back on the bed, allowing him to straighten out his legs before she straddled his hips with her thighs, if sometimes he was teaching her how to go after what she wanted.

"I like my alpha goddess," Matt teased, sliding his hands around her flared hips, bringing her wet core down across his erection. The moment her juices encased his length, he groaned, closing his eyes, feeling the zings of pleasure coursing through him like ragged bolts of heat and lightning.

"Well," she warned him throatily, her hair cascading across her shoulders as she leaned down, her hands flat against his chest, her core sizzling and needy as he slowly moved his hips, sliding her back and forth, "you're right. I'm feeling very alpha tonight."

A pleased expression came to Matt's face, and she felt him tightening his hands around her hips.

"Then come and get what you want, sweetheart. I'm all yours . . ."

A dream come true! Dara gave a pleased sound deep in the back of her throat. "About time," she said, and returned his curving smile, loving him for allowing her to be who she needed to be, not what he wanted her to be. Normally, Dara wasn't this assertive, but tonight, for whatever reason, she was starving for some orgasms. Maybe it was the right time of month for her, the hormones pushing her. Right now, she wanted this man inside her, swelling, thickening, so hard and stroking her insides until she erupted and one of those long, throbbing, delicious orgasms rippled down through her.

"Ready?" she asked, challenging him.

"More than you'll ever know."

She gave him a wary look but became convinced when Matt easily lifted her off him just enough for her entrance to settle over him. That made her quiver, and she shut her eyes, lost in the sensations of their centers suddenly and unexpectedly meeting, the juices thickening and quickening within her. World burning up, fire cascading through her as she eased down upon him, impaling herself on the warm, hard steel of him sliding deeper and deeper within her, she luxuriated in the delicious fusion. She didn't need a lot of foreplay to get her ready for Matt. Just his slowly moving her up and down upon his willing shaft, feeling him grow and swell within her, made her moan with anticipation.

There was giddy power in taking him, doing exactly as she needed to do to gain that wonderful, building orgasm. He'd hardly even touched her nipples, tasted her, or licked her at all. She was so ready, and when he brought more weight down on her hips, her orgasm triggered. A scream caught in her throat, she threw her head back, her long torso arching as he prolonged the milking of that explosion swiftly undulating through her. The world stopped existing and there was only her, riding that orgasm, being hurled into light, tumbling, free, the pleasurable sensations moving up and down her spine like burning lightning. Floating, unaware of anything in those moments, Dara heard a hoarse cry tear from her throat. Her fingers dug spasmodically into Matt's taut chest, her entire body flexing around the melting orgasm that was flooding every sense she had.

The sensations were like small tidal waves of heat combined with tinier explosions, racing outward, making her surrender and collapse against Matt's long, damp body. He caught her, easing her down against him, her hair swirling around his face and shoulder where she nestled her brow next to his jaw. Dara's breath was ragged and she couldn't move, lost in the satisfaction glazing her heart and soul as he continued to gently thrust into her, initiating more sensations, prolonging the initial orgasm for her. Her heart exploded with such fierce love for Matt. He cared for her, he cared that she be gratified fully and completely. Never had a man been so focused on her needs. How lucky she was to be loved by him.

Later, Matt lay quietly, feeling Dara's ragged breathing begin to calm. He loved her long, sinuous form paralleling his, the dampness of her flesh, the plumeria scent combining with the lime of the soap he'd used earlier. The tickling warmth of her blond hair against his neck and jaw made him smile. There was no part of his woman that he didn't love, want to touch, lick, kiss, and nip as the occasion arose. She was an ongoing dessert to him, to his wide-open senses, and he smiled, eyes closed, luxuriating in her fully and completely.

As Dara slowly emerged from being dazed, and he kissed her hair and rasped, "Better now?" He felt her laugh. No sound escaped her, but he felt it and smiled, his hand resting lightly against her back, skimming her damp skin, hoping to give her more pleasure through his touch. Very soon after that, she fell asleep. He tugged the nearby sheet upward, drawing it over them. Matt was more than content to have Dara sleep on top of him. Her weight was half of his, and she was like a warm, fragrant blanket poured over his body. Dara was tired, and he knew the past few months were catching up with her. Matt didn't have the heart to move or disturb her now. It was going to be a deep, healing sleep.

He lay there, his one arm resting against her waist, the other across her opposite shoulder, the thick strands of her hair beneath his fingers. Never had he loved anyone so deeply, so completely, as he did Dara. She slept like an innocent baby in his arms, trusting and vulnerable in every possible way. Closing his eyes, he felt filled with happiness. Matt was sure he was going to burst wide open from the intense emotions he felt for her. He'd never had a woman pry him open, steal his lonely heart, and then hold it with such sweet, innocent love as she had for him.

Matt felt her breath against his body, absorbing the moisture of it against his neck and upper chest, his mind moved languidly to the weeks they'd spent on her family's ranch in Montana. Callie, her younger sister, was improving after the trauma she'd suffered, with the help of Beau Gardner, who was there to fortify and support her. Callie had nearly been raped by several Taliban soldiers while they were running for their lives after that ambush. Beau had taken her in the opposite direction from Dara and Matt, hoping to split up the Taliban faction. It had been a brilliant strategy, but all told? Matt had taken Dara into the mountains. Beau had elected to take Callie toward the river in the valley and then thirty-five miles south through a lot of hilly country, to reach Bagram on foot. And they were within miles of Bagram when Callie disobeyed his order to hide and not move as he went to engage a group of Taliban coming their way. She was a civilian and didn't realize how crucial it was to follow Beau's instructions. As the Taliban had drawn closer to where Callie was hidden, she'd panicked and bolted. She'd brought six enemy down upon her, and they were in the midst of tearing her clothes off to rape her when Beau heard her screams and came running back to save her. It had been close. *Too close.* Callie had been emotionally broken by that attack. They never got to rape her, but it was close enough to shatter her. Beau had saved her life and ended up getting a leg wound out of the deal as he placed himself between her and their enemy.

Taking a slow, deep breath, Matt moved his hand across Dara's sleeping form. Thank God, she'd listened to him at every turn. She had never panicked as Callie had. She'd done exactly as he'd requested. His admiration for her courage under lethal circumstances rose. Because Dara had done what he asked her to, they'd survived.

At the McKinley ranch, Beau was falling in love with Callie. But the guilt she felt because she'd disobeyed him at a critical juncture in their escape, drawing down an attack that had left her damaged and Beau wounded, had driven deep into Callie. In that week when he and Dara had visited after Christmas, there had been a lot of tension in the McKinley family. And it was Dara, the big sister, who had slowly pulled Callie out of her shame and guilt over her actions. Matt had seen how hard it had been on Dara. Every night, when they went to bed, he'd hold her and she'd cry quietly in his arms. And then he would slowly love her, getting her to release the pain her sister was going through, to focus on her pleasure, on them, instead. And he'd purposely moved slowly as he made love to her, because her attention was centered on Callie, not on herself or him.

By the end of that week, he'd watched Dara begin to drag. Dark smudges appeared beneath her eyes because of her long, emotional, intense late-night discussions with Callie. Unlike her sister, Dara was not likely to fall into the emotional trap of allowing her feelings to run her. As a doctor, she couldn't do that and still be of help to her suffering patients. But Callie wasn't built like that, so it took extra energy, emotion, and sheer physical endurance to reach Callie and get her to look at the necessary changes she had to put into place for herself.

It had been a long week for Dara, so Matt wanted to make these last seven days before he had to leave hers. Dara needed to heal from that intense family drama with her sister. The McKinley family was flummoxed by how to help Callie. Beau had become her anchor, and Dara was the chain attached to that anchor. Both of them had helped Callie out of the hellish guilt that she'd carry forever if she were allowed to do so. Dara and Beau had talked privately to one another on how best to pull her sister out of the notion that everything that happened to them was her fault. After all, it had been Callie who had persuaded a reluctant Dara to go out to that Afghan village with her. When things went sideways, Callie took all the guilt onto her shoulders.

Matt spent many hours talking with her sister as well. Beau helped a lot, too. Their grandfather Graham McKinley had been a Marine Corps sniper during the Gulf War. He had earned medals, including a Silver Star, for his black-ops heroism, which the world would never know about. He was instrumental in helping Callie reorient and see that her actions were forgivable. After all, she was not a trained military person, but rather a civilian with no training. And anyone in her place would have done the same thing. Between the three parties, Callie had finally emerged from that dark hell that had entrapped her. And Beau was there to welcome her back into his arms, love her, and support her.

The toll on Dara was something Matt saw daily, but he couldn't say anything. He knew how devoted Dara was to her little sister. He was the same with Tal and Alexa. They were family, and when shit happened, families came together to support one another, no matter what it took out of them. This was one of those times for the McKinley family, but Dara had paid the steepest price, other than Callie herself. There were days when Matt could swear that Dara had given part of her life energy to Callie to help her survive. He'd seen other situations where a person's soul or their emotions had been fractured, fragment-ed, or parts of it had been torn away from them forever. It was the worst kind of wounding in

Matt's opinion. He was lucky. He'd only experienced physical injuries, and the body healed up a helluva lot faster than emotions and minds.

But Matt knew now, more than ever, that love could heal the most egregious wounds in another person. And as Dara slept innocently across his body, the sweet smell of her skin an aphrodisiac to him, he knew that tonight, this was what she needed. He didn't try to figure out why; he just tried to love her as completely as he could. And if that meant he didn't climax, that was all right. Some things were more important than personal sexual gratification.

That was the last thought Matt had as he slid into a deep, healing sleep himself, the woman he loved more than life in his arms. He would never get enough of Dara, those warm feelings flowing through him like light chasing away darkness. She flooded him with her joy, taking him into a place where only promises of bliss existed and held him in their embrace.

# CHAPTER 4

D ARA AWOKE SLOWLY, wrapped in a warm, loving dream of Matt holding her. As she slowly opened her eyes, she realized it was dark in the bedroom. Matt was curled around her backside, his arm beneath her pillow, his other arm draped protectively across her waist, hand against her belly. The sense of security, of being loved and shielded, flowed like a warming river through her. She had never feared being alone or being in a strange place until she started going over to Kabul at Callie's pleading. Because she was a pediatric physician, and the Hope Charity orphanage desperately needed a doctor to examine the fifty children who lived there, Callie had talked her into it.

Those yearly jaunts always filled her with a sense that she was doing the right thing for the right reasons. By nature, Dara was a worrywart, and she knew it. She tried to tamp down her concern about the dangers of being an American woman in a country that hated women like herself, women who were different, who didn't follow Muslim traditions. She worried about being attacked or shot or, worse, killed. She worried for Callie, who was over there six months out of every year, but Callie seemed to thrive on the edgy danger that always existed in that country. Dara did not.

She pressed her cheek into Matt's biceps, her nostrils flaring, drinking in his scent, stirring her awake, stirring her sexual appetite, which he always triggered effortlessly within her, once more. Memories of loving Matt earlier came with the drowsy realization that she'd dropped off into exhausted sleep without giving him a chance to have his own climax. That popped her eyes wide open as she lay there curved with him, his large, lean, muscled body cradling her. She had never allowed that to happen before. They'd always loved one another fully and totally. What was the matter with her?

Groaning internally, Dara knew the answer to that one: her week of blistering emotional ups and downs with Callie and trying to pull her sister out of that shock and trauma she'd experienced in Afghanistan had exhausted her. Literally, Dara felt drained of lifeblood from that marathon emotional wringer with Callie. It had all been worth it, though, because she, Beau, and her grandfather Graham had united and supported Callie. Dara didn't regret it, but now, she hazily realized she was paying for it. Matt had said that she was tired to her soul. At the time, she had laughed it off and shaken her head. Now she was feeling it, how badly that week of drama and emotions had pulverized her.

Lying safe and warm in his arms, Dara closed her eyes, her mind and feelings now awake. Matt had been right. She was fatigued on every level. She felt guilty that she hadn't loved him in return before dropping off to sleep. She was a fair-minded person. She knew how to give as well as receive. It didn't feel right or good that she'd taken from Matt and given him nothing back. Dara had a sensitive conscience, and it was the rudder that steered her ship in life. Matt didn't deserve this. Not at all. He'd pleased her so well, and her body still vibrated in memory of that long, ongoing orgasm that had swamped the shores of her exhaustion, feeding her, helping to heal her.

"I can hear you thinking."

Matt's voice was gruff with sleep, vibrating softly through her. She felt his arm tighten around her waist, drawing her closer to him. She could feel his erection pressed against her cheeks, and she hummed with need once more. "I just woke up," she admitted, her voice thick and raspy. She skimmed his forearm with her fingers, then tangled them among his.

"I love you," he growled, nuzzling between her strands of hair, finding her nape, kissing it, then licking the sensitive flesh and nipping it just enough to send skitters of sensation straight to her breasts and her hardening nipples.

Relaxing into him, Dara smiled and closed her eyes, pressing her head against his jaw above her. "I love you, too."

"So? What were you chewing on? I could feel it."

"I swear, Matt, you're scary psychic."

He pried one eye open, noticed it was three a.m. according to the clock on the dresser. "Remember, Grandmother Damia was clairvoyant. There's a long line of seers in our family. People who can see in the dark, so to speak."

She heard the amusement and teasing in his low, sleep-ridden voice. It felt so good to be held so closely by Matt. All her fears and her concerns melted away when she was with him. He fed her confidence with that undeniable courage and strength he possessed. "Did I really wake you up?"

"Doesn't matter," he rasped, nipping her nape again, feeling her quiver, feeling her satisfaction over the small pleasure he was giving to her. "When you love someone, you're aware of them twenty-four-seven, Dara. That's not a bad thing in my book; it's a good one." Matt stirred, releasing her, bringing her onto her back while he remained propped up on one elbow, watching her shadowed expression. He moved some strands of hair away from her face, caressing her cheek, leaning over, seeking, finding her lips. They were soft, warm, and she opened eagerly to him. Groaning, he hardened, reminded him once again that he needed a release. Her mouth was hot, wet, and as he slid his tongue in invitation against hers, she rolled toward him, her fingers moving slowly up and down his erection, sending him into an immediate heated spiral.

Matt lost his thoughts completely as her skilled, slender fingers massaged him. Growling her name as he left her lips, he gripped her hand, stilling it around him. He saw her pout and give him a disapproving look. Okay, she was serious. Normally, they made love before going to sleep because she was utterly exhausted and would sleep the night through. Seeing the arousal in her darkened eyes, how wide and black her pupils were as she silently beseeched him, he nodded, releasing her hand. "I thought you needed your sleep," he groaned as she pushed him down and onto his back.

"I got it," she told him archly, pushing the sheet aside and getting to her hands and knees, facing him. "Now it's your turn."

He reached out, burning this moment into

his memory and his heart. She was long in the torso, lean like a greyhound, that thick golden hair of hers a cascade and frame around her classic features, those large eyes trained on him. She looked delicious naked, her small breasts firm, those nipples begging to be tasted, and he slid his hand around her neck, drawing her forward to him. "Come here," he urged her gruffly.

His mouth settled on one of those tight peaks and he suckled her strongly, causing her to cry out with pleasure, her hands gripping his broad shoulders, pulled toward him, a willing captive as she surrendered. As she lay on Matt, her hips against the hard slab of his belly, he began a serious campaign to tease each of her needy nipples, sending sheets of sparks jaggedly down through her, making her channel contract with hunger. Her own ideas of how to pleasure Matt were scattered to the four directions, as it was obvious he was in alpha lion mode with her, hungry and not slow at all. She loved these times when he acted starved to have her in every possible way, relaxing against him.

Matt eased her onto her back. In moments, he'd positioned her, easing her thighs wider, his cock pressing against her wet opening, demanding entrance. Her hair was a dull gold halo about her face, her eyes half-closed, sultry, as she pleaded with him to move into her, and he wasn't going to disappoint her at all. Matt placed his hands around her hips. He rested on his heels, pulling her toward him until she was at a low angle on his thighs, open and vulnerable.

There were times as he was about to make love with Dara that Matt felt a deep, dark shift within himself. It wasn't anything bad, it was just . . . different. That feeling had always been inside him. As an operator, he lived off that dark, unknown inner world, and it had kept him alive when he should have died so many times in the past. It was the primal alpha animal within him. His mother had given him the middle name Aslan, which meant "lion" in Turkish. All the stories his uncles and his mother had told him made Matt wonder often if she'd had a premonition that there was a lion spirit around him, keeping him safe, giving him the courage, the strength, and the very necessary survival instincts that he needed as an operator.

Dara was the only woman in his life who had ever awakened the sleeping lion, as he referred to it, within him. And now, as that shift was made, his human, thinking mind dissolving, he felt himself morphing into the consummate hunter finding his mate, taking her and making her no one's but his. His feelings were visceral, and they drove him as nothing else ever had. With Dara, he wanted to place his seed in her, wanted her pregnant with his child, wanted to protect her, love her, and keep her forever at his side. To his surprise, as he felt that shift into his more primal self, Dara responded willingly, not afraid of his strength, his growls, his impassioned need to mate with her so intensely. She loved it. She loved him. And as he moved slowly into her, allowing her small body to shift and adjust to his girth and length, Matt could feel her juices spilling scaldingly around him, pulling him deeper, lavishing him with her woman's way of welcoming him into the cradle of her body.

Gritting his teeth, he controlled that wild, restless animal pacing within him, wanting to stamp her with his seed, make Dara his. It was like shifting to another world with this invisible being who had always been a part of him. He'd never talked to anyone about it. Not ever. But Dara had sensed that change in him. She had one night innocently asked him if he had a lion as a spirit guide. Matt had laughed and teased her about it, saying only Native American and indigenous people had those spirit beings with them. He didn't. She seemed perplexed, looked deep into his eyes, and said nothing more, but he could feel her thinking, feel her digesting his answer. Her eyes told him she thought he had such a spirit being with him. Matt hadn't pursued it with her.

She must have felt that dark shift within him now, because she responded effortlessly to it, lifting her hips, pulling him deeply into her. Tonight, though, she was hungry, and he swore he could feel her own primal animal not only awaken but go on the prowl, starving and wanting him sexually as much as he wanted her.

They came together in a sudden clash, her cry one of passion, not pain. She'd arched into him, dragging him forward across her so he was fully seated as deep as he could go into her, her fingers around his forearms, strong and not taking no for an answer. As he pumped into her, their bodies slapping against one another, he saw a shadow of a satiated smile coming to her parted lips. He took her hard and fast and without mercy, and she coaxed him fiercely to do just that.

She was lush, tight, and wet. Matt could feel her body beginning to contract, heard her cries climb in urgency, felt her hands dance and grip his upper arms as she arched fiercely against him in that hungry rhythm they'd established with one another. Her lower body violently contracted around him. A deep rumble rolled out of him as the bolt of heat slammed down his spine, exploding through his tightened balls, the scalding fluids bursting through him and into her. All he could do was inhale their combined sex scents, listen to her little cries of heightening pleasure, feel her fingers dig deep into his biceps as he continued to plunge in and out of her, riding her, mating with her, and taking her for his own in every possible way. The animal feelings were dark, hungry, and possessive, and as he continued to prolong her powerful orgasm, he could barely hold on to his reality.

All of his six senses flew open and he was aware of her skin, how thin or how soft it felt, her breathing shallow and her voice hoarse with cries as he continued to gratify her. He lost track of time, of where he was, only knowing he was with his partner, the one being he fiercely mated with tonight with the single intent of impregnating her, making her with his child.

The utter satisfaction of being the lord, the primal male, with her as his mate and equal, soared through him as they finally collapsed together, both breathing harshly. Matt found what little strength he had left and encircled Dara with his arms, his hands resting against the top of her head; she was completely covered and protected by his larger, muscular body. It was a fierce, undying need in him to shield her, keep her safe, and he held her tenderly now as he licked her slender neck, tasting the salt, feeling the pulse of her artery beneath the paper-thin skin. He felt her breasts sliding against his chest, felt those nipples still ripe and pebble-hard even now. She smelled so good to him, her scent an aphrodisiac, and he inhaled it deeply into his lungs, his heart. He never wanted to forget this exquisite moment with Dara.

He kissed her, feeling her smile weakly beneath his mouth, opening to him as he caressed her tongue and then kissed the closed lids of her eyes, tasting the salt of tears as they leaked from beneath her lashes. The joy filling them and knotted between them was palpable. Matt had never felt as euphoric as he did right now, holding her beneath his body, fused within her, his arms cradling her shoulders and head. It was such a profound moment that it opened his soul in a way that surprised him and flooded his senses. His love for Dara was so real, so deep, there was no end to it, and now he was within her body, his seed alive and strong, and he knew . . . he damn well knew, without knowing how, that just now he had gotten her pregnant. And nothing in this world meant more to him than her carrying his baby. Their baby. And he would love that child as much as he loved the woman he'd just mated with and who now carried this new being deep within her loving body.

DARA FELT DAZED and elated; her body throbbed and glowed from within. She had no words to express how she was feeling right now, cradled within Matt's body and arms. There were no words for the powerful sense of love he was giving her right now. Wonderment flooded her, the feeling of him still so thick and hard within her, feeding her, a part of her, an intimate sharing like no other. There was a heightened awareness within her, without words or understanding. But it was beautiful. It was forever, and she smiled because the beauty of their lovemaking had grown to a new magnitude. An incredible, magical level.

"Ohh," she whispered as Matt slowly eased up on his elbows, studying her in the shadows. "What just happened?" Her voice was wispy, sounding otherworldly even to her. She saw the amber intensity in his narrowed eyes as he studied her, his fingers moving lingeringly across her scalp, once more giving her such pleasure.

Shaking his head, he rasped, "I don't know . . ."

She licked her lips, turning her head, seeing the time on the clock. Gazing up at him, she said, "I felt . . .I don't have words for what happened, Matt . . . I feel . . . different . . . wonderful." When he nudged his hips forward, she smiled. "This was more than just sex . . . more than just an orgasm or climax . . ."

"Yeah . . . something . . . you look over-whelmed, but in a good way."

Dara drew in a deep, ragged breath, framing his face. "It's all good. Wonderful. I've never felt so whole as with you in me . . . loving me . . . I just can't honestly describe what happened, Matt. I loved it. I love you." She smiled softly into his golden eyes, which shone with his love for her. It was so real, almost visible, and she could reach out and touch that feeling that hung silently around them, embracing them even now.

He leaned down, cherishing her lips, tasting her, wanting to continue mating with her. Until he could figure out what had happened, he wasn't going to try to talk to Dara about it. In his line of work, even though he lived off his intuition and senses, he still had to create reports and missions based on what he knew or sensed. This experience was so lofty that he didn't know where to begin giving it shape or words. Resting his mouth against her lush lips, he whispered, "I've never had better sex than I did just now, with you."

"Mmm, me, too," she sighed, searching his calm expression. There was a primal intensity within him. It was almost palpable. "I liked your animal side." He looked surprised for a moment and then frowned, digesting her words. "When we make love, Matt"—she threaded her fingers through his short brown-and-gold-streaked hair—"sometimes, for whatever reason, I feel a shift in you. I know I tease you about becoming an animal, but I feel a change deep within you, and when you love me, it's fierce, passionate, and so much more intense."

"Like tonight." He frowned. "Did I hurt you,

Dara?"

"No." Her cheeks turned a dull pink color as she avoided his sharpened look.

"Sometimes sex is just wild, unchained, or unfettered between two people. They both have to want it that way. Otherwise, it's very uncomfortable for the person who doesn't want it."

"Oh," she said, "I wanted it. I wanted you. I loved the freedom I felt, as if I were a wild horse running free across a plain."

"It was really intense for me, too. I wasn't sure I could control it, and I didn't want to scare or hurt you."

She smiled faintly. "You've been teaching me a lot about sex, Matt. This is just another new facet for me. And I liked it. A lot."

"Well, it's something we need to communicate about before we do it. *Both* people have to want it, or it's a no go."

"I still feel your spirit animal around you. I know you laugh at me when I tell you this, but it's true . . ."

He gave her a disarming look. "It's your acute sensitivity picking up on something about me. When you love a person, don't you think you're in tune with them on all levels? Whatever those levels are?" He saw her expression turn thoughtful. Dara was like Tal, his big sister. Both were deep thinkers, and neither of them rattled off an answer to a question like many others would. Instead, they seriously thought about it before answering. He moved a silky curl of her hair through his fingers, far more sensitized to how it felt, the scent of it, the glistening beauty of the moonlight filtering around the drawn drapes at the other end of the room, highlighting some of the strands. Matt could feel her moving through layers of possible answers to him.

"I have always been sensitive, that's true." Dara's brows moved down a little as she studied him. "But with you? Ever since I met you, Matt, we've shared something much deeper. Unknowable to me, but I can feel and sense it around you. I like being sensitive toward you." She caressed his cheek, looking into his narrowed eyes, feeling his love for her. It was so real. So wonderful. "Remember how I told you that you weren't vulnerable to me sometimes? That I felt as if you were giving me a piece of yourself, but not all of you?"

Nodding, he took her hand, placing a slow, wet kiss in her open palm, hearing a soft intake of her breath, watching her eyes widen as he gave her pleasure from that small but oh so meaningful act. "I do."

"Tonight . . . just now . . ." Dara began haltingly, her voice suddenly quavering with barely restrained tears. "I-I felt *all* of you, Matt. For the first time. That's the only way I can describe it. At first, I knew something was happening, but I didn't understand what it was, because I was so drugged by you, your fierceness, your passion, your need for me. It was so intense that I felt overwhelmed, utterly consumed—but in a good way—by it."

"It was the same for me, sweetheart."

"Did it feel good for you?"

"Yes, I was like you: floating and euphoric. In fact"—Matt smiled at her, kissing her soft mouth, never able to get enough of her—"turn over onto your hands and knees. I'm still feeling it right now. I want to take you from the rear . . ." He saw radiance in Dara's eyes at the suggestion, and she did as he asked. Matt knew this was her favorite position, and it was his, too.

Coming up behind her, Matt settled his hands over her rounded cheeks, holding them firmly as he thrust his hips slowly forward into her wet, ready entrance. It was as if his recovery time almost didn't exist any longer. "And I want that same incredible sensation and feeling I shared with you before." Whatever was happening, it was driving him so profoundly he could barely control himself or his urge, which nearly overwhelmed him. Matt needed her in every possible way.

Dara moaned his name, pressing her hips back against him, establishing a slow, delicious rhythm between them, her juices flowing heavily as he made her forget everything but him. Matt

Matt turned her over, positioning Dara on her back. She opened her arms to him as he spread her thighs, coming to rest between her knees. He leaned down, taking her mouth roughly, kissing her, breathing his breath into her, infusing himself into her on every level. Dara felt as if she were in another universe, enjoying a hedonism that few would ever experience. And she was living it with Matt. The pleasure intensified to the point where Dara felt herself floating off into the darkness, fainting from the overwhelming feelings that deluged all her ripened, opened senses.

# CHAPTER 5

MATT WATCHED DARA slowly awaken, her blond hair mussed, an angel's halo about her head as the dawn rays leaked in around the drapes in their bedroom. Her face was utterly free of tension, a slight tinge of pink staining her cheeks, those thick blond lashes quivering, telling him she was drifting up through the layers of sleep toward wakefulness. He was propped up on one elbow at her side, the sheet scrunched around her waist, the rest of their bedcovers on the teak floor from the wild, hungry sex he'd shared with her last night. He ached for her again, tenderness toward her winding like a quiet breeze through his chest as he absorbed Dara's slow awakening.

Usually, Dara was up and gone by the time he'd rise in the morning, the condo cold and lifeless without the sunshine of her energy within it. Matt hated awakening with the sheet beside him cool to his touch, indicating she'd risen long ago, taken a quick shower, and hurriedly driven over to the hospital. And she could arrive home as late as midnight on a bad day where there were a lot of emergencies involving babies.

Smoothing her hair away from her brow, his touch feather-light, Matt hoped he had not disturbed her. He knew her work could be draining, though she seemed to have been energized by his arrival at her condo in mid-December. In the ensuing days they spent with one another, Matt had watched Dara bloom beneath his care and love, just as she was helping him. He'd loved having this time for them to get to know one another outside the stressful circumstances of Afghanistan.

Her soft mouth compressed, and then she licked her lower lip. There were other ways to share and show his love with her. As he moved a few more strands of her hair, the silk sleek between his fingers, he knew these days in Hawaii were a dreaded countdown for both of them. Already, he could see shadows in her eyes sometimes, her worry about his returning to the war zone. About losing him. And Dara was the biggest worrywart he'd ever met. To give her credit, she was very good at cloaking it, but with his senses blown wide open, he could damn near read her feelings.

It was more sensing than actual telepathic words or thoughts, but it kept him in touch with Dara when she tried to hide her anxiety from him. Matt would never tell her just how much he could read her. He could smell her fear, her concern, and her happiness. Just as he could sense her sexual need of him. He'd discovered early on that there was a subtle shift hormonally, and, like the animal who'd lived within him since he could remember, he smelled that change in a woman's body. He knew which woman was attracted to him and which wasn't. Which one wanted sex with him. With Dara, her scent was far more complicated and layered. He wasn't that good that he could mentally understand it all. But with her? Everything shifted dramatically, changed and became beautiful, haunting, and Matt craved only her presence, her intelligence, how she saw life, what touched her, what brought her to tears, or made her smile. And that smile of hers went straight to his heart and directly to his soul. Matt wanted to put all those revelations into words and share them with her.

He wrestled daily in Dara's presence to articulate his feelings. It wasn't his forte. Frustrated by his inability to share all this with her, he tried to communicate his heart, his appreciation of how she lightened his soul with her quiet, steady presence, through his touch, his kisses, and by giving her a sense of protection. Her lashes barely lifted, and Matt smiled down into her drowsy, dark-blue eyes, her black pupils large. He leaned down, cupping her chin, guiding her mouth to his, kissing her slowly, deeply, wanting to convey the powerful love he held only for her. She made that sweet humming sound in the back of her throat, her body moving sinuously against his.

Slowly, Matt eased from her wet, warm lips, holding her drowsy gaze. "How about I make us breakfast? And I'll get a tub of hot water ready for you." He wanted to do small things, give gifts from him to her, find nonverbal ways of letting Dara know that he loved her and couldn't conceive of life without her. He saw her lift her left hand, the sparkle of Grandmother Damia's engagement ring caught in the dawn light as she caressed his jaw.

"That would be wonderful . . . thank you," she said, her voice low and slumberous.

"You got it."

DARA FELT GROGGY even after a nice, hot bath. She had put on a pair of white linen slacks with a pink, cap-sleeve tee. Knowing how much Matt loved her hair down, she had brushed it until it shone like old gold. She inhaled the scent of bacon in the air as she left the bedroom. The morning sun had not yet risen enough to come over the spine of the sharp-toothed volcanic mountains. She'd seen a map in a picture frame in the bedroom and studied it. Oahu, like all the other Hawaiian Islands, had been created by a series of eruptions over millions of years. She was struck by how the volcanoes had created this particular island, the mountains rising sharply above it, down the eastern side of it, reminding her markedly of a human backbone. She was always amazed at the way life mirrored nature and vice versa.

"Mmm," she called, letting Matt know she was approaching him from behind as he worked at the stove. "That bacon smells really good."

He barely turned his head, catching her smile as she approached him. "Hungry?" Dara looked good enough to eat as dessert, the pink color of her form-fitting tee bringing out the soft blush across her cheeks. Never had he seen Dara look so relaxed. No longer were there smudges beneath those large, intelligent eyes of hers. There was no more tension in her face, either. She walked languidly, like the lioness he always thought of her as. That sway of her hips made his cock swell with need beneath the zipper of his jeans. With Dara, his senses were always on, always in tune with her, and right now, that faint smile tugging at the corners of her mouth made him go hot with longing for her. She was an aphrodisiac, he decided. It didn't matter what

Dara did or didn't wear. He was simply addicted to her in every possible way.

She came up behind him and laid her head against his back, her arms going around his waist, resting lightly against him. "I'm hungry, and you look sorta good yourself. Never mind the bacon."

He chuckled. "Funny. I was thinking I could have you for dessert after we eat breakfast." Her breasts were pressed against his back, his skin prickling with fire and hunger beneath them. He felt her laugh, her arms tightening momentarily around him and then releasing him, and she moved to the counter beside him.

"Men," she muttered, shaking her head. She picked up a woven basket and placed some paper towels in it, handing it to him as he scooped the bacon out of the iron skillet. "You know, as a doctor, I understand hormones. And I know males have a much higher testosterone level than we women." She smiled wickedly, seeing the gleam in his gold-brown eyes, feeling that dangerous sensuality he always exuded. "And that testosterone makes you male, but it also stains your brain with sex, too."

"Oh," he deadpanned, handing her the basket, now filled with bacon. "I know about the studies where men think about sex every five minutes during every waking hour. Is that what you're referring to?" He saw the merriment dance in her eyes as she pushed away from the counter and took the basket over to the bamboo and glass table in the dining area.

"Most definitely," she shot back, giving his crotch a significant look. "I'd say the study was right, hmm?"

His mouth curved. "Looks like I can't hide the evidence, can I? Guilty as charged." Matt took an egg and milk mixture and poured it into another awaiting skillet. Earlier, he'd chopped up some sweet Maui onion and sharp cheddar cheese and added some Middle Eastern spices into the mixture. He listened to her husky laugh, meeting her smiling gaze. "You inspire me. What can I say, sweet woman?" He gave her a sizzling look that made it clear he wanted to make love with her. Matt enjoyed this kind of repartee with Dara. She wasn't at all challenged by what he needed sexually from her. She was enough of her own woman, confident enough within herself, to tell him yes or no.

Good thing Dara didn't know he already knew what her answer would be, based upon his sensing abilities. That would be his secret. Matt found her easy to tease because she possessed a wonderful sense of humor, and he would never hurt her by being rude or harsh with her. He wanted her trust, her vulnerability. And right now, he felt equally vulnerable with her. It was a new feeling within him. Somehow, last night, things had remarkably changed between them as they mated like two animals starved for one another. It was an evolution in their lovemaking. And it had surprised both of them last night, judging from the expression on Dara's face as they came together like fire and oil tossed upon one another.

"Well," she said, trailing her fingers down his left arm, "I *really* liked what happened to us last night. That was new, Matt. It was"—she sighed, leaning her hips against the counter, watching him make the omelet for them—"incredible, heady, euphoric, and I can't even find the words to really describe how wonderful it made me feel." She lost some of her smile. "Did it do the same for you?"

"Oh, yeah," he assured her, casting her a quick glance as he folded the omelet with the spatula. "Whatever happened last night, it happened to both of us. And I'm not sorry for any moment of it. Are you?" Matt gave her a questioning look. And last night, they'd gone at it pretty hard. That kind of rousing sex wasn't for every woman, and Matt knew that. It seemed to suit both of them at that moment, however, but he didn't want to take any chances. In the cold light of day, when they weren't ruled by their hormones, they needed to discuss what had occurred.

Dara brought down two, bright-blue ceramic plates that had colorful pink and white hibiscus flowers painted on one half of the rim. "Some-thing happened," she murmured. "I can't explain it. I could sure feel it, though." Moving to another drawer, she pulled out the flatware. "I loved it." And then she grinned, giving him a teasing look. "I wondered if it was the water we drank last night or something. Is there something magical in Oahu's water, you think?"

A rumble of a chuckle rolled through his chest as he divided the finished omelet, placing half on each awaiting plate. The toaster popped up four pieces of toast, and he handed the plates to Dara. "I don't think it was the water. But if it was, Oahu has one helluva aphrodisiac on its hands. They'll sell bottles by the billions if everyone who drinks it experiences what we did last night."

Laughing outright, Dara placed the plates on two colorful, quilted placemats that had bright red and yellow Hawaiian designs on them. "You're right about that!"

Matt brought over the buttered toast on an-other plate and pulled out her bamboo chair, which had a thick, jade-colored cushion on the seat. Dara gave him a look of thanks and sat down. "I feel it was us. And maybe," he mur-mured, setting the plate of toast between them and going to the fridge, "it was the magic of Hawaii. Of getting into a stress-free climate." He found guava jelly in the fridge, brought it over to the table, and sat down at her elbow.

"I'm not sure, Matt. I'm still feeling odd and different inside, but it's not a bad thing. It's a good thing."

"Could you describe it?" He sliced into his fragrant omelet after capturing four pieces of bacon and placing them on his plate.

Dara frowned, opening the jar of pink jelly and taking a piece of toast into her hand. "The closest I can come to describing it is, it's like when you drink champagne. You know that bubbly, happy sensation your tongue gets when it hits it?"

Raising his brows, Matt gave her a look of pride. "You're pretty good at this. I'd say the same thing now that you've drawn me a word picture of it."

"Are you still feeling bubbly and happy, then?" She crunched into the guava jelly–slathered toast, a satisfied look coming to her face.

"Yep. It's very nice." He held her amused blue gaze, seeing how much she relished that island jelly on the toast. Dara was artless when it came to hiding how she felt. She simply couldn't do it, and Matt was grateful. The only time she hid her feelings, or tried to, was when she became worried or anxious. Which was a lot of the time. He wondered if something in her childhood had triggered that reaction in her and silently promised himself to ask her that while they were on vacation. He'd find the right time and place to delve more deeply into her family past.

She set the toast on her plate, picked up bacon from the basket, and took a bite of it. "Were you hiding that aspect of yourself from me, I wonder?" She held his hooded gaze.

"It's always been a part of me, Dara. But I try to monitor and find out what my woman wants, not what I necessarily want. Making love is a two-way street. It has to be mutual."

"But it was mutual last night, Matt."

"Sure was," he said, meeting her winsome smile. Her blue eyes were shining, and he could feel her love enveloping him like an invisible embrace. They had never had this kind of downtime to sit and talk deeply, to explore one another in so many areas that needed to be plumbed in depth.

"I loved it. Nothing had ever felt so right with you. I felt . . ." She rolled her eyes upward in thought. "I felt like we were two wild animals circling one another, both powerful, confident, and so sure of themselves. It was so freeing. I've never felt so untamed or primal before."

He almost choked on a piece of the omelet, quickly picking up a glass of the pink guava juice he'd poured earlier for them. Taking a slug, Matt swallowed hard, seeing the sincerity, the searching and questioning in her expression. Dara was expecting an answer from him. "Well . . . yes," he managed to say, his voice a rasp as he cleared his throat. "I suppose you could put it that way."

"Your mom named you Aslan, which is Turkish for 'lion,'" she pointed out, cutting into her omelet with zest. Her knife and fork hesitated above it as she studied him intently. "Now, I know you have mystics in your family, Matt. And even your parents and your uncles have all said that you three kids are psychic. That it's a gene that has come down from the Turkish side of your family line."

Dara was like a lioness on the trail of a scent. He supposed that to be a doctor, one had to be like that. She would find a piece of evidence, a symptom, then run it down like a hunting animal. She'd put those symptoms together and come up with a diagnosis. She had a very scientific and logical mind, which he respected, and he found it interesting that she was homing in on his family's seer-like ability. Matt tried to downplay it. "Well, that's true, but it's more sensing than anything else, Dara. I don't see the future, for example."

"But your grandmother Damia did." She triumphantly flourished her left hand, where she wore that diamond engagement ring he'd given her. "She definitely saw the future. She said her rings would go to a fair-haired woman. That was me."

"Well," Matt hedged, seeing her get excited,

that look of the hunter who'd found her prey, "but none of the three of us have that exact ability. And it's differently expressed in Alexa, Tal, and me."

"So, you've known about this all your life?"

"Sort of," he muttered, keeping his head down, paying a lot of attention to his food, hoping she would let this go and stop hunting. "Tal and I have powerful sensing abilities at times. It comes and goes in me, like it does in her. And maybe that's why in a dangerous situation, which we were always in over in Afghanistan, it served to help keep us alive and out of ambushes."

"But you didn't sense that ambush we got caught in going to that Afghan village."

"That's right. Like I said, sweetheart, my sensing ability comes and goes. When it comes, I'm always grateful to have it, but when it goes, I can't control it or ask it to come back to serve me. It's not something I can will into happening. It's sort of like an ocean tide; it just does what it wants, when it wants."

"That's fascinating," she said, consuming everything on her plate and going back for more bacon. "It's really what people call intuition. It's our sixth sense, which scientists have pooh-poohed but have never really studied. Shame on them."

*If only she knew.* But Matt said nothing because

he had a top secret clearance, and he wasn't about to tell Dara that he was part of an ongoing, remote-viewing program within the CIA, where people were found and used for their psychic abilities. And even that ability came and went. There were times he'd get a flash, a picture. Other times, he'd get nothing. Everyone thought that the sixth sense of human beings had been shut down, but it hadn't. If Dara found out about it, God, she would hound him about his skills. Maybe one day he would tell her the full scope of his psychic aptitude, but not right now. This was vacation. A time to relax, to enjoy one another, not delve into the depths of something he still didn't fully grasp himself.

Matt could see the ongoing curiosity about his skills in her eyes and knew that Dara wasn't grounded in the psychic realm at all. And for now, that was okay with him. He reached out, squeezing her lower arm for a moment. "I just think that we hit a new level within our growing relationship last night. It was great sex combined with the love we hold for one another, Dara. And it worked for us." He saw her expression lighten; she was satisfied with his explanation sans the psychic element attached to it.

"Life is so interesting to me," she said, giving him a grateful look. "People are all so different. You, especially. You're like a Rubik's Cube. Continually fascinating to me."

"What? We're all just petri dishes to be studied by you, doc?" He slid her an amused look.

Bursting out with laughter, Dara wiped her lips on her white linen napkin. "That's unfair, Matt! I've never seen *you* as a petri dish! God forbid!"

He had her going, and he couldn't stop a grin from emerging. "No? Am I not one of your favorite scientific experiments? You just admitted I fascinated you. I can always see the curiosity in your eyes about me."

"Well," she said, stumbling over her words. "Not like *that*! You aren't some scientific experiment to me, Matthew Culver."

Uh-oh, now he'd gone and done it. Dara didn't take that tone of voice with him often and rarely called him Matthew. But when she did, it meant he'd wounded her, and he hadn't intended to do that. Sometimes, his teasing didn't come out playfully and she took him seriously instead. Matt knew this was one of those times, and it left him scrambling. "I didn't mean it quite that way," he parried, cleaning off his plate and setting it aside.

"I sure didn't," she blustered, scowling at him. "You've *never* been any kind of experiment to me. Now, I agree, I love science, and I dearly love being in a lab, and I find petri dishes swiped with viruses or bacteria absolutely fascinating. But I've never seen anyone, much less you, as one."

"Just consider me instead as a canvas that you can paint on to your heart's content," he coaxed, giving her a warm and apologetic look, hoping she would forgive his poor communication skills, which obviously needed work. Instantly, he saw that she liked that visual much better than the petri dish.

"Oh, I love that idea!"

"We are sort of empty canvases to one another," he said, now serious, holding her interested gaze. "I'm sure we'll paint facets of ourselves on one another over time, Dara. Right now, we really are blank slates, because we've only known each other for less than two months."

"That's true," she murmured, finishing off her omelet. "But I fell in love with you anyway, Matt."

"And I certainly fell in love with you from the first moment I laid eyes on you at that Bagram chow hall where you and Callie belly-danced." Her cheeks became a deeper pink and Matt could feel how excruciatingly vulnerable she was right now with him. He could feel the continued openness between them since their lovemaking last night, and he could feel her emotions so much more intensely and brightly. Far more than normal. Was Dara feeling or sensing him as much as he was her?

"Well, you sure made an impression on me that night at Bagram," she whispered, reaching out, caressing his recently shaved jaw. "I fell so hard for you, so fast."

"It was mutual," he agreed, his voice thick with feelings, catching her hand, kissing the back of it before releasing it. She colored prettily and once more, that shining love for him returned to her eyes. "What would you like to do today, Dr. McKinley? The day is yours to do with as your heart desires." That would get them off this line of inquisition as far as Matt was concerned. Dara perked up, suddenly smiling, and he was warmly drenched with her reaction of utter enthusiasm and childlike excitement. Nothing made him happier than to see the beautiful glow that came to Dara's expression when her heart was in-volved.

"Well, don't be upset with me, but Dilara was telling me there's a Delos charity located in Waianae, a branch of the Safe House Foundation. I would *love* to drive over there, meet the director, and spend the day, if they need me, examining the little ones."

Matt smiled, loving Dara even more than ever before. She was a healer, pure and simple. He'd seen her with the children of the Hope Charity in Kabul, working tirelessly, caring for infants, children, and pregnant mothers. He'd seen her in action for five days straight at that charity, and the Afghan mothers carrying their sick infants or holding their toddler's hand, hope in their eyes, as Dara utilized her medical expertise to help them. When their infants improved or their small children became healthy, it meant everything to them. And he saw the fierce dedication Dara had to each of them as well. Her being a doctor wasn't a career choice. It was a heart choice. It was who she was and always would be. So how could he blame her or be upset that she wanted to be with babies, moms, and children here in Hawaii?

"Sure, that would be fine," he said. "You've got your doc's bag with you. We could make a phone call to the director and find out if she wants your medical services."

"That's a good idea," Dara agreed, suddenly eager to be off. "I have everything I need. I'd just like to help out medically if they need me."

He chuckled and rose, stacking the plates and picking up the used flatware. "Yeah, asking you not to help out that charity would be like asking a hunting dog to sit on the porch when she spots a bear ambling by her door." He chuckled, loving her.

"Well," Dara offered with a wry smile, "I just thought since Delos has a charity on Oahu, it might be nice to drop by for an hour or so. I am marrying you, and I've never stepped foot into one of your mom's charities, so I think it's a great win-win. I'd like to see what one looks like and how it operates."

He swallowed another chuckle as he put the dirty dishes into the dishwasher. "I'm fine with you doing it," Matt assured her as she came over with the jar of guava jelly and the emptied toast plate in her hands. "In fact, I'm surprised you didn't ask me earlier," he teased, adding a smile so Dara knew he really was okay with her choice of what to do with their day. Matt had other plans in place, but this wasn't about him. It was about them.

Dara didn't see being a doctor as work. For her, getting her hands on those squirming babies was play and fun. Never work. Matt wanted whatever would make her happy and stress-free. And tykes always made her glow with passion and eagerness to be helpful to those who needed medical care. How could he say no?

# CHAPTER 6

MATT CURBED HIS smile as director Alani Phillips, a Hawaiian woman of fifty, led Dara down the highly polished, white-tile hall toward the medical examination room located near the rear of the Safe House building. The call an hour earlier had made Alani shriek with pleasure. A pediatrician coming? Oh! They had fifty mothers with children and all could use her services! He didn't know who was smiling more: Dara, dressed in her white lab coat over her white linen pants and pink tee, the stethoscope looped around her slender neck, or Alani, whose black hair was up in a tight knot on top of her head. She was dressed in a colorful Hawaiian muumuu that came to her knees. She was about five feet seven inches tall, around a hundred and eighty pounds, apple-cheeked, just bursting with compassion and energy. Saying she was a human dynamo would be understating Alani's enthusiasm and the caring that radiated around her like sunlight.

Matt loitered out near her office, which was located a few steps from the main reception area. Safe House was a place for abused women who had left their live-in mates or their husbands. The children came with them. There was a three-story barracks-like building out in back of the office complex that had apartments within it where the families lived. There was a large nursery near the medical examination room and beyond that, an airy dining room where the mothers and children had three square meals a day, plus snacks. He was impressed with this Safe House, having seen many of them around the world. His mother, Dilara, made a point of traveling to at least fifty of the eighteen-hundred Delos charities every year. And from age twelve onward, her children had often accompanied her on her travels. She wanted to show them the suffering in the world and that something positive could be done to help alleviate it. His mother always brought an entourage of people who could be resources and provide help for each director.

Looking around the bright, white-painted walls of the glass-enclosed office where Alani worked tirelessly, Matt was pleased to see everything was spotless and organized. His mother insisted upon a high level of cleanliness,

wanting everything to be sanitary within the
buildings as well as outside them. He had met the
receptionist, Halia Parker, who had just graduated
from college with a degree in social work. She
was twenty-five, her smile shy, a true introvert,
but her heart was open and she was very kind.
Halia was the perfect person to greet a harried,
threatened, beaten woman who came through
that teak door carved with the Delos rising sun.
The logo was a symbol of hope: light for a new
day.

The place was busy, all the employees wom-
en. This was a safe haven for beaten and abused
women who needed to be protected from the
men who were abusing them, whether it was
someone they lived with, someone they were
married to, or a male family member, such as an
uncle, grandfather, or cousin. Not only did the
Safe House Foundation keep women and
children here until they could get back on their
feet, they also trained the mothers and gave them
skills with which to make a living. Many abused
women had no marketable skills in today's highly
computerized society, and Safe House gave them
experience and education to close that divide.

Matt moved down the hall, and on the left
was an L-shaped room that held twenty-five
computer stations. There were large windows on
one side, with black, wrought-iron bars across
them, telling Matt that this place might not be as

"safe" as it appeared. He wondered obliquely if Safe House was in a poor neighborhood or near one. Usually, Delos charities were placed in economically depressed neighborhoods to help the poor and needy. And often, that meant they could become a target of theft—or worse, which is why Artemis Security had been created, to deal with the threats that existed in today's brutal world.

The educational center was impressive. It was neat and organized as well, and all manuals and anything else that would be needed by students were available to the women being trained to operate a computer and use business software.

"Ah, there you are!" Alani said, pushing the door open. "I thought I might find you in here, Matt."

He smiled, turning toward the energetic woman. "This is a really nice setup, Alani. You're doing a great job here."

She walked up to him and gestured toward the bank of windows. "Only problem is, we have gangs around here." Her lips thinned. "There's a local gang, and the leader's name is Mano—that's 'shark' in Hawaiian. Two-and-a-half years ago, he and his boys, young men in their teens and twenties, broke the windows one night and took all twenty-five of our Apple computers from this room. I was devastated."

"You didn't have bars across the windows at that time?"

Shaking her head, she sighed. "No. Our Safe House is on the edge of an impoverished area, but these local gangs usually hit tourist cars on the beaches. But because of a police crackdown, the gangs started moving inland, across the city. They began looking for opportunities to commit theft other than just breaking windows on cars. They hit us." She pushed her bangs off her forehead, frowning. "We have twenty-four-hour-a-day video cameras in every room, for many good reasons. The video captured all the thieves, and I recognized Mano. The police were able to round up the whole gang. As director of this Safe House, I testified in court against them. They put Mano away for two years in the nearby federal prison. That was two years without constant break-ins happening in the surrounding area."

Grimly, Matt said, "He's out now?"

"Yes, unfortunately. There was a turf war when he was released." She gestured around the room. "He and the Shark gang own about ten city blocks of what they consider their turf, and they defend it against three other rival gangs who are in the town as well."

"Then how are you doing for security?" He looked around, his Delta Force operator's experience telling him that this place needed a serious upgrade. He was glad Artemis was being created. They could provide the directors of Delos facilities just like this one with another layer of protection.

Shrugging, she said, "The police said I needed more. They gave me information. To be honest, I can't handle it with the present budget I'm given. I'll feed my people first before putting up a ten-foot-high cyclone fence around our property here."

Matt nodded. "Do you mind if I take a walk with you around the premises sometime? Look at it through security eyes?" Alani had never met any of his family. His mother had not visited this charity yet. And he was sure the director did not know he was presently in military black ops and knew a lot more about security than most people. She didn't have to know, either; since he was the son of the owner, he was sure Alani would give him anything he asked for.

"I can use all the help I can get. Any security suggestions you have, I'm open to. It's just a question of whether or not I can afford to install them. Now, just to warn you, our housing barracks are for our women and children. That's off-limits to any men. That includes you. These women and children have been abused or threatened by men. I can't have a stranger, unescorted, going into the barracks alone. And I like to give the families there at least twenty-four hours' advance notice that a man they don't know will be in their building, so they don't think you're a lone wolf in a herd of sheep working to hunt down one of the women who is living there."

He smiled faintly and nodded. "Yeah, no problem, Alani. Why don't you go ahead and put out that info to them? Maybe you can assist me tomorrow or the next day, when your schedule permits? Then I can go through the barracks and see what kind of security upgrade they need, too."

"Sure, that would work. By any chance, could your fiancée, Dr. McKinley, come back tomorrow, too? Word has flown like wildfire through the barracks, and I've already got thirty-five women and children begging to see her."

Matt curbed a smile. "Let me talk to Dara. It's her decision."

"Well, if she says yes," Alani said, a hopeful look on her face, "while Dara is here with us tomorrow, you and I could go through not only the barracks but all the other buildings, compile a list of security needs, and maybe you could pass them on to your mother?"

"I'll do exactly that," Matt promised. "But let me go talk with Dara to see if she wants to come back tomorrow."

★

MATT AMBLED DOWN the busy hall. There was nothing but women here, and he liked the low-key, warm, nurturing energy that pervaded the place. All of the people he saw were women working under Alani's direction. Running this place took a lot of paperwork, a lot of people who knew the law enforcement and other governmental systems that were in place to help women who were trying to escape abuse. He located the examination room and saw ten women with squirming babies or toddlers in hand, waiting patiently in line.

They gave him a wary look, and Matt felt bad for them. He was male and a stranger to them. Therefore, a potential menace and threat. He saw the door to the examination room open as a mother with a six-month-old baby in her arms left, smiling, relief in her expression. Matt smiled and nodded hello in her direction as he came and stood in the doorway. It looked like Dara had a girl of twelve whom she was teaching how to be her assistant. The young, curly-haired redhead was pulling the paper over the examination table, preparing it for the next patient.

"Hey," Matt called softly, seeing Dara lift her head from the form she had been filling out on her last patient. "Got two minutes?"

She smiled. "Sure." She turned to the carrot-topped preteen girl.

"Stacy? Can you tell our next patient I'll be

ready in just two minutes for her? See if she needs anything while she waits."

Stacy gave Matt a very distrustful look and edged warily toward the door near where he stood. "Sure, Dr. McKinley."

"Thanks," Dara called, giving her a smile. She pointed toward Matt. "This is my fiancé, Matt Culver. His family owns Delos. He's a friend, he won't bite . . ."

That information erased the fear in Stacy's large green eyes.

Matt could literally see the girl's slender shoulders drop, and she instantly relaxed. He held out his hand toward her. "Hi, Stacy. I'm Matt. Nice to meet you." She appeared to be around twelve, with bright copper freckles across her nose and cheeks. He felt her trepidation over shaking his hand. He was going to withdraw it, but suddenly, she gave a little cry and threw her arms around his waist, hugging him with all her child's strength.

"Thank you! Oh, thank you!" she sobbed into his belly. "You saved my mama, my brother, and me!" She broke into a gale of tears, clinging to him.

Matt swallowed his surprise and he curved his arms around her, patting her gently. "We're here to help you all," he murmured, running his hand over her tousled red hair. It needed to be cut. She looked like little more than a ragamuffin, her feet bare, the muumuu she wore thin, in some places torn and in need of mending. Her little body shook as she cried in relief. Matt was glad the door was shut. This little girl had gone through and probably seen too much. Casting a glance over at Dara, who sat there, tears in her eyes, he fought back his own. A child's crying always ripped him up the most. He'd seen too much of it in broken Afghan villages that had been raided by Taliban. Smoothing her hair with his hand, he eased her arms from around him. Crouching down, he offered her a tissue from a nearby box. "It's going to be okay, Stacy," he murmured, looking into her tear-filled eyes, watching her wipe them and then blow her nose.

"W-we were so scared," she whispered brokenly, clutching the damp, destroyed tissue. "My daddy hurt my mommy. He hurt me. He was going to hurt my baby brother. We were so scared. We had nowhere to go. But Mama came here and Mrs. Alani took us in." She wiped her reddened eyes, whispering, "We thought Daddy was going to kill us. We're afraid he will if he ever finds us."

"You're safe here, Stacy. You, your brother, and your mom. How long have you been here?" He eased a few strands of hair sticking to her damp cheek behind her ear, trying to give her some comfort.

"T-two weeks. I-I never slept at night. Here,

I sleep. It's wonderful." She shyly reached out, touching his shoulder. "Thank you for saving us . . . thank you . . ."

"You're more than welcome," he said gruffly, trying to stuff his own emotions back down deep within himself. "Listen, I need to talk to the woman I love and am going to marry this coming June. Could you let us have a few minutes? And then I'll leave and you can come back in here and help Dr. McKinley?"

"S-sure," she snuffled. "Just . . . thank you . . ." She turned, quickly exiting the room and closing the door quietly behind her.

Slowly rising, Matt saw Dara watching him. "Is it like this with every patient?" he asked her quietly, moving to the desk and sitting on one corner of it, searching her glistening blue gaze. He could feel how deeply Dara had been touched by Stacy's admittances. Matt hoped he was a better male role model than Stacy had ever dealt with, to let her know there were men out there who would not harm her or her mother.

Dara reached out, sliding her hand down his cheek. "Yes. You don't hear the worst cases." She motioned to the six boxes of tissues stacked up on her desk. "By the end of this day, they'll all be used up."

"How do you take it?" he asked gruffly, searching her softened expression, loving her so fiercely it felt like his heart would burst wide open. He saw her lips move into a compassionate pucker.

"Crying is healing. Sometimes a mother comes in with her baby or toddler, and she just needs to talk it out. Talking is strong, healing medicine, Matt. And so are tears." She looked fondly at those six boxes of tissues. "One of the best investments for a place like this? Getting tons of boxes of tissues in house." She smiled tenderly, giving him a look of pure love.

Leaning over, he caressed her lips lightly, wishing they were alone so he could kiss her until they shared one another's breath, not coming up for air at all. Easing away, he rasped thickly, "You're the best guardian angel these women, children, and babies could have. What would you think of coming over here all day tomorrow, too? Alani and I are going to do some serious security checking around the property and get this place protected so there are no more break-ins."

"I'd love to do that," she said, her voice quavering. "But are you sure, Matt? I mean . . . this is your vacation, too."

He slid his fingers through her hair, moving heavy, glinting strands of it across one of her shoulders. "I'm positive. How late do you want to go tonight?"

"Six? There's so many women and babies who need to be examined, Matt. Some have some serious issues that need addressing by a specialist."

"Yeah, no problem. I'll meet you at the reception desk at six, then?"

"I'll be there," she promised, her voice low with emotion.

Matt felt her joy, felt her gratefulness for his understanding. If this wasn't love, what was? He gave her a quick kiss, rose, and said, "See you later, angel of mercy . . ."

AS THEY ATE Chinese takeout that Matt had picked up on the way to their rental house, he was amazed by the energy around Dara. He thought she'd be worn out from seeing twenty patients in one day, but she wasn't. Coming home, she'd taken a quick shower and changed into a pair of sexy white shorts and a bright-red tube top that outlined her breasts to perfection. Her hair gathered up behind her head with two huge red plastic clips, Dara looked like a young college-aged woman, not the pediatrician who wore her heart on her sleeve.

"Mmm," Dara said. "This is so good, Matt. Brilliant idea to grab takeout on the way home."

"I know you love Chinese."

"I love you more. Does that count, big guy?"

He grinned over at her, absorbing that wicked glint in her eyes. "You're feeling pretty frisky tonight, Dr. McKinley."

"It was all those babies," she sighed, sitting back in the chair, taking a moment for her gobbled food to digest. "They are *all* so cute! Every last one of them. I just love picking them up, smelling that sweet baby smell they all have, hearing them gurgle, seeing them smile."

"That's why you're high."

Nodding, she scooped more of the brown rice from the cardboard box and onto her plate. "I can't explain it, Matt. When I get around a baby or child, my heart just turns into a puddle of love for them. They are all innocent. Little blank slates to be written upon. And they trust without being wary." She shared a warm smile with him. "I got my baby love today. That's why I'm feeling so frisky."

"Yes, and you get another ten hours of it tomorrow," he reminded her drily, watching her lips draw into a happy smile, eyes glinting with excitement. *Nothing made Dara more happy*, he thought, *than being with her babies and children*. She was bred to the bone for motherhood, for caring for and loving these little tykes. He didn't feel jealous. Instead, he felt so damned proud of Dara for having the raw courage to live her life through her heart's passion. He was sure, after seeing how tight-knit and loving the McKinley family was, that Dara had been given full support by her parents and grandparents to simply be who she had become. There weren't too many parents who did that with their children. In his own family, his mother and father had followed that same philosophy. They allowed their three children to grow, bud, and then blossom into whatever they were destined to become. Dara was lucky enough to come from just such a family herself.

"Well," she murmured, giving him a quick look to see how he felt about her hours, "Alani said their budget allowed for a physician to come for only so many hours a month, and they always need more than that time. That means that the survivors and their children have no medical attention for usually two weeks out of every month."

"What would they do if there was a baby or mother who was seriously ill?"

"They'd call an ambulance and take her or the toddler to the hospital. Then"—Dara shrugged—"it becomes a medical paper chase for Alani."

"What if they had a doctor on call more often?"

"Some of the cases I saw today? They're totally preventable. For example, a child with a sore throat? If care isn't taken to find out if it's strep throat or not with just one swab, that child might have strep, and it's missed. And then that cascades into some life-threatening condition later on down the line. I always carry strep swabs in my physician's case. And I'm sure two little ones, a tiny girl of four and a young boy of seven, both have strep. I'll find out tomorrow when the hospital lab calls over the results."

"So, that's why you want to go back?" Matt smiled to himself. It wasn't that Dara was trying to hide her real reasons for wanting to spend a second day of her vacation doctoring those who needed it. It was really about getting lab results and going from there. Being responsible and following through, taking care of her patients.

He saw her eyes sparkle as she glanced up at him, mouth full of rice.

"That's okay, I get it." He laughed, shaking his head. "I'll bet you give your attending doctors special hell with all your tricks."

Swallowing, she took a sip of her white wine, wrinkling her nose. "Oh, come on, Matt! There are just different work-arounds with some of the attendings, is all. I got in trouble with some of them because I showed my emotions. I figured out ways to hide them but still share them with my patients later, just out of earshot. Heck, you're black ops. You more than anyone else in this world are an ace at that kind of thing." Giving him an evil look, she muttered defiantly, "I'll bet you'd make my choices look like kinder-garten compared to what you Delta Force boys pull off routinely."

"Guilty," he admitted, holding up his hands, looking into her laughter-filled eyes. "What I love about you—one of the many things—is that you never apologize for what you have to do to help a sick person. I saw you doing it at the Hope Charity in Kabul. I'm seeing it here."

"Well," she murmured, her lips tugging into an unwilling smile, "just don't *ever* let on to my attending physicians about what I'm doing. When they see me coming, they turn on their heel and find the nearest door and run into the office, locking it behind them so they don't have to talk to me. They don't even want to deal with me."

"Your fame precedes you."

"Or something like that, yeah." And then Dara frowned, scooping more rice onto her plate. "I'll tell you, I will *never* let anyone—not an agency, not law enforcement or anyone else—put one of my patients in medical jeopardy. I just won't listen. I'll figure out a way to get what I want for that child."

"Do they call you Superwoman in the hospital?"

Nearly choking, she admitted, "Well, I wouldn't go that far. The attendings have pet names for me I can't reveal or repeat. They're not exactly glowing adjectives I'd want anyone to hear."

"But your patients," he said, sliding his hand down her arm, "love you. They worship the ground you walk on."

"I want nothing more in life, Matt, than to be able to ease someone's suffering. That's my endgame. And I can guarantee you that I'll move heaven and hell to get whatever I need for that little baby or suffering child, in order to ease his or her pain."

"I believe you." He almost wanted to say that she was truly a copy of Artemis. The ancient goddess who was the fierce mother bear, caring for children, babies, and families and protecting them. Matt's heart warmed at that parallel. He'd met a modern-day Artemis. And she was his. And she was going to be his wife. There was nothing else he wanted in his life but her. And the children she would carry would be formed out of their love for one another. Matt had never felt more blessed or more grateful for his life, for having met Dara.

# CHAPTER 7

**"I** WANT MORE of what we did last night," Dara whispered against Matt's damp hair. They'd just shared a shower, messed around a lot, and her lower body was burning with hunger and need of him. She lay on her stomach in the center of the bed, the sheet cool against her warm, moist flesh. Dara tucked a pillow beneath her head. She had put her hair up into a topknot; the ends were still damp, but she didn't care.

"Good," Matt growled near her ear, nibbling on the lobe and then moving behind it, where her skin was so sensitive. "So do I." He licked that area.

A low sound of pleasure whispered from her. "You sure? Aren't you tired?" Fire began sparking down behind her ear as he licked her flesh, as if he were appreciating a special dessert he was going to eat. Dara swore she could feel him turning into that lion, even his tongue feeling furred and rougher against her delicate skin, but oh, so pleasurable! She knew it was her imagination, but it added to the wonderful sensations he was beginning to build within her body.

"Not me. I'm not the one who saw twenty patients today," Matt said, amused as he smoothed damp strands of hair away from her exposed nape, one of the choicest of morsels on her supple body. Licking her nape, he heard her gasp once more, seeing through the semidarkness her arms gripping the pillow a little tighter in response to his exploration of that special erotic region. He could feel her enjoying his stalking her. And that's exactly what he liked to do: hunt her, capture her, and then make her his. It was a very predatory need, and his mind was dissolving as he felt that spirit awakening with hungry intensity within him, sending his everyday mind into unknown ether, no longer functional. All that was left was primal emotions, feelings of powerful potency within himself. There was an inner knowing that Dara was his mate for life, an eruption of fierce love tunneling through his heart, making his chest expand so much he thought he might burst open with that sharp, intensifying feeling he held for her alone. And along with it was wanting to always protect this beautiful, vulnerable woman who fearlessly followed her heart without apology.

Dara laughed huskily, feeling him straddle her thighs and then lean forward, kissing her back here and there. Just having her thighs pressed together told how badly she wanted Matt inside her once more. "That," she whispered in a sigh, "feels so good, too . . . don't stop what you're doing . . ."

He scraped his teeth lightly across her nape, drawing her soft, velvet skin between them, holding her in position as he smoothed his long, roughened fingers along the curves of her breasts, feeling her quiver in response. Then he gently released her nape, licking the area tenderly several times, to soothe any possible discomfort he might have caused her by claiming her in such a primal way.

"Why do you do that, Matt?" Dara lifted her head, turning, barely meeting his eyes, which shone like shadowed gold in the dim light given off by the two candles on the dresser.

"What?"

"Nip my neck. You've done that from the first time you loved me at Bagram. No one else has ever done that to me."

He shrugged, kissing her, then drawing wet patterns back and forth across the area with his tongue. "I don't know. I've always done it. Does it bother you?"

She smiled and shook her head. "No . . . just the opposite, I love it. When you hold me like that, something wild and wonderful bursts open in my lower body. I can't explain it . . . it's so . . . primal, I guess is the word I want."

"I'm primal," Matt assured her darkly, sliding his hands around the curves of her breasts once again, watching her lashes lower, hearing that soft gasp of pleasure slip past her lips.

"What does it mean?"

He leaned forward, placing his teeth gently where her neck connected with her shoulders, holding her flesh and muscle firmly but not hurting her. And then he released her, laving the area with his tongue and lips, soothing it. "Why," he rasped thickly as he licked behind her delicate ear, "do I want to bite you right there when I mount you from the rear? I don't know. It just feels right to me. It's ancient. In the end, all humans are."

"I love when you bite hold of me there," she admitted huskily, relaxing beneath those tiny nips that caused momentary pain followed by intense sensations of fire flowing even more hotly from that region, through her firm, swollen breasts and straight down to her clenching channel. Her nipples ached for his skilled touch, his tongue, his teeth rasping and then worshipping them until she screamed with pleasure. Oh, her man definitely knew every little nook and cranny on her body and took foreplay to the level of art with her. Dara knew she was lucky to be on the receiving end of his slow, hot buildup that brought her to such an intense peak and so many orgasms that she lost her mind—but in a good way. Matt made her forget about everything except the scalding gratification he was giving her.

"I like it, too. Biting you very gently makes me feel . . . well . . . powerful. Like I'm mating with you."

"Mmm, I like it when you take me from the rear and then, when we're crazed and mindless, you bite and hold my neck or shoulder. I can't tell you the incredible sensations it causes in my lower body. I have the best orgasms when you do that."

"Hmm," he murmured, kissing the thin, soft flesh along her neck. "Is that what you'd like me to share with you tonight? It's your favorite position and mine, too. I like mounting you, taking you . . ."

His voice had dropped to that low, vibrating growl that feathered through her, made her clit swell and ache, her juices drenching her channel in a flood of anticipation. "I love everything . . . anything . . . that you share with me."

"Well," Matt murmured, lifting his head, slowly licking her spine, nipping her skin and then laving it with his tongue, "there's one place I haven't really shown you that is a stunning erogenous zone."

"Really?"

He chuckled as her head came up and she twisted a look over her shoulder at him. He could feel his animal spirit on the loose within him once more as it paced, wanting her. "You're like a kid," he laughed quietly, continuing to worship each vertebra of her spine, feeling her getting hotter, needy, and that sex scent of hers surrounding him, teasing him until he could barely constrain himself.

"What? I thought you'd shown me all of them."

Matt hungered for that incredibly strong, nurturing side of Dara as her emotions swept through him, linking with his male hunger to love her. The sharpened emotions lifted him, spurring on his soul hunger to claim her, make her his own. Only his own. As he thrust into her, holding her hips, holding her in place, the animal within him was loose and joyous. Sex had never felt this good, this fulfilling, this satisfying as he stroked into Dara's receptive body, which urged him to take her, as if some long-lost song were coming back to them from a time when humans were animals. It was to be sung between them once more. Time, places, ages unfurled beneath his tightly shut eyes, his teeth clenched as she pushed back upon him, wanting all of him, challenging him to take her fully without thought, the overwhelming instincts gripping both of them as he felt them melting together as one. The sensations were starkly vivid, raw, overwhelming his blown senses, allowing all of himself into her. Because he couldn't stop his thrusting as he slid effortlessly in and out of her tight confines, those gripping sensations building swiftly in her, knowing she was riding the wave of a gratifying orgasm to come, so wild and free, that she was fused with him.

It was impossible to remain coherent. The animal was loose within him, roaring, the reverberation rolling through him as he plunged deeply. That knowledge, that mating sense, so hungry and vibrant within him, made him lean over her, as he felt the first slamming heat rip out of him and into her. Dara called his name as her body contracted around him, bathing Matt in wave after wave of scalding fluids that slid and enfolded the entire length of him, a rumble tearing out of him, pure satisfaction. He gripped her nape with his teeth, holding her firmly, forcing her head and neck backward toward him, exposing her throat as he repeatedly thrust and took her in the most elemental of ways. The mating hormones, that scent of them combined, blossomed in his flaring nostrils, his breath tearing out of him, sweat running in rivulets down his taut, shaking body as he felt his life seed bathing her chamber, where all life began. The moment was seminal, paralyzing, exultant, the climax seemingly never-ending. Finally, he buckled upon her. Dara moaned, utterly weakened by her own powerful, ongoing orgasm, which stole all her physical strength. Matt released her nape, gently licking the area. Dara collapsed with a moan upon the bed, his body fully covering and cradling hers.

Enfolding her tenderly afterward, Matt was fused deeply inside of her, feeling Dara quiver with the strength of that imploding orgasm still rocking through her. He kissed her hair, whispered words of love, of need of her. All Dara could do was whimper and tremble violently in the wake of their loving one another. She weakly gripped the pillow, her body damp-smelling, but it was an alluring perfume to him. Licking her shoulder, her nape, kissing her repeatedly, crooning thickly to her as he held her close, Matt supported Dara with his larger body. He wanted to hold her forever, the need driving and soul-deep. His fierce, undying love for her overwhelmed him. He felt it being absorbed by Dara as she continued to pant and breathe raggedly, her long, slender rib cage expanding and contracting quickly against his arms as he held her firmly, with all his love and need.

Matt could never have envisioned a perfect lover as suited to him in every possible way as Dara was to him. Each time they made love with one another, it was better than the last. This time, his mind was barely functioning. He was lofting like a cloud, floating out of control within some alien galaxy filled with the love he held for her, his senses overwhelmed but absorbing every smell, every taste of her flesh, hearing her little moans and whimpers of satisfaction. She was so open to him that he belatedly realized he was opening fully to her as a result.

Was this what was really happening? He'd never experienced that rich, bold trust of fully connecting with someone before. It felt as if it were binding them on levels Matt had never known existed until just this moment, when he was so deeply posited within her tight, small, flexing channel, which was still contracting from her last orgasm. There was such a sense of oneness with Dara. Matt could feel each of her jerky breaths, feel her heat, feel the pleasure thrumming exquisitely through her glowing lower body, which radiated heat with such a blistering fever, infusing him, burning him up in the best of ways.

To say that they had climbed to another level with one another couldn't begin to explain how Matt felt right now. As he embraced his woman, his arms folded around her shoulders and head, the rest of his long, lean body covering hers, the driving desire to protect her was flooding him in a new, sharpened way. Warmth drizzled around them like a blanket of sunlight designed to bring their breathing into oneness, slowing it, flooding their dazed senses and keeping their everyday minds caged, not allowing them to reconnect with them right now. They were drowning in sensations, ancient, encoded emotions, exhausted but pleasantly so, craving one another's nearness, wanting to remain coupled.

Matt felt Dara's breathing steady over time, become less harsh, the panting dissolving, her skin not as damp as before. He moved his hips, thrusting slowly into and out of her, feeling her weakened response—she wanted to participate but was incapable of doing so at the moment. He felt her trying to match the unhurried rhythm he was establishing with her, but she was just too weak, too exhausted from their hard, physical marathon with one another to do so. Matt understood that, slowly rocking in and out of her, prolonging her pleasure, hearing those sweet little whimpers that made his heart swell with male pride, knowing he was continuing to pleasure the woman he loved, fully and completely.

After a few more minutes, he rasped, "I love you," kissing her temple and easing out of her, turning her over and bringing Dara alongside him, cushioning her against the length of his body. She sighed and laid her head on his shoulder, fingers moving languidly across his dampened chest.

"Wow, there's something in that island water

for sure, Culver. If I didn't believe it last night, I sure do tonight."

His mouth curved. "Could be the greatest marketing boon Oahu's ever known." His heart expanded as she laughed softly against his neck, placing several kisses along it.

"I can see it all now," Dara went on breathily, continuing to touch him, fingertips lingering here and there, appreciating his incredibly strong, masculine body. "The headlines could be something like: 'Water Turns Humans into Rutting Animals in Heat.' Or something like that."

It was his turn to laugh, the rumble moving through his chest. "'Oahu's Water Induces Mating Heat.'"

"Really," she intoned drily. "That's what it truly feels like to me. I lose my mind. I literally stop thinking. I never used to do that, but since meeting you? My brain goes to sleep and I feel myself shifting to a more basic part of myself. It's all strong emotions, my limbic grain riveting me, driving my feelings."

He moved his fingers through her hair, gently grazing the strands. "Maybe it's us. It feels like we've shifted to another level with one another. In a good way. Just . . . different."

"Mmm, better," Dara whispered, leaning back on his shoulder and gazing into his glittering, dark eyes, which were thoughtful-looking, though she still saw smoldering heat in their depths as well. "I feel like we're truly joining one another on a much more important level. I love that," Dara said. She eased up into a sitting position next to him, crossing her legs, her hand resting over his heart as she held his dark, sensual gaze. Matt was handsome in what she termed a classical Greek way. His nose was straight, cheekbones high, and he had a broad brow and wide-spaced eyes that never missed a thing.

"I've seen you in combat," she began in a low voice, moving her hand gently across his chest, luxuriating in the dark hair across its expanse. "I've seen you with children. I've seen you in many different situations, and you were always gentle, except in combat. I saw how you held Stacy this afternoon. She was so starved for a positive, loving male presence, Matt. I don't know if you knew that or not, but she's so fractured by the fact that her only male role model is her abusive, dangerous father, and you were the exact opposite of him in every way. She sensed that about you, too. And that's why she suddenly threw her arms around you and clung to you." Her lower lip quivered momentarily, her hand stilling on his chest. "You invite everyone to you. It's just a natural part of who you are. I've seen you with your Delta Force team, how they automatically gravitate to you. Even when we were running for our lives, you were always gentle and sensitive toward me, toward the fact I couldn't run fast enough or keep up with you as we were trying to escape. You never glare at anyone, never fall into harsh words with a person, and never treat others severely."

The glimmer of tears, of love, shining in her eyes made him swallow hard. Matt always appreciated post-lovemaking time with Dara. Some of their most serious discussions, where they delved into one another's hearts and souls, happened in those moments. She was utterly present with him. The last two nights, had reached a new and heady level for both of them. His emotions were even stronger tonight. He slid his hand over her small, slender one. "Blame that on my parents," he said, giving her a warm look. "They are great role models, as I suspect your parents and grandparents were for you and Callie. You're like me in that respect, Dara. You never look cross; even without coffee, you're nice in the morning when you wake up."

A smile edged her lips, her eyes dancing with amusement. "You're right, but I do need my IV of coffee."

He grinned and nodded. "That's true." Becoming serious, he murmured, "Stacy was starved for a man to be kind to her. I could feel how desperate she was to be loved by her father . . . by any man . . . to help her heal from what he did to her and her mother. She's totally traumatized."

"I know," Dara said, anguish in her tone. "I don't know why people don't realize how sensitive children are, that they feel, too. That they get scared and need to be held." She turned her hand over, entangling her fingers among his. Hers were smooth, long, and soft. His were long, roughened, and yet Dara could feel Matt's gentleness as he squeezed her fingers as if to reassure her.

"My mom has often said this earth of ours is like a cosmic high school for souls. They come here to learn how to be better human beings through lifetimes." He shrugged. "I don't know about that. All I see down here is suffering, and I told her that when I was twelve." He smiled a little, the memory fond. "Mom said that people who lived lifetimes down here on this planet were coming to the high school of pain. That pain was the great teacher here."

"Ugh," Dara said, sniffing. "Why not a planet where a person can learn right from wrong with love instead? With good feelings? Not having to learn through a process of pain? That's pretty damning. It sure wouldn't make me want to live lives down here. Who wants to learn through pain?"

"Well," he said, turning philosophical, watching how the moonlight leaking around the drapes silhouetted the gold hair lying around her shoulders, "everything I've learned in life has been through a painful experience of some kind. How about you?"

Thinking about it, Dara said, "No . . . you're right. I can't think of one thing in my life that I've learned without pain. How depressing." She saw him flash her a grin, but it wasn't a "gotcha" kind of smile. It was one of commiseration. "In fact," she said, allowing her hand to rest upon his chest, "even childbirth is done through a process of pain. And it's one of the happiest moments I can think of."

"Do you want me to give you another orgasm? That's happiness multiplied and there's no pain." Matt saw her eyes glint, teasing in them.

"No . . . I'm very, very satisfied, Mr. Culver. It's just that you are too hard to resist."

"Was that a pun, Ms. McKinley?"

Her laughter was rich and full.

Matt loved her so much. Dara had tipped her head back, all that wealth of blond hair sliding across her shoulders and halfway down her long, graceful back. He liked a woman who could laugh like that, not cover her hand with her mouth and titter away. She got up on all fours, looking down at him. The smile faded and she leaned down, her breasts, those hardening nipples, grazing the flesh of his chest, tightening his growing erection. Groaning, he lifted his hand, sifting his fingers through her hair, absorbing the happiness deep in her shadowed blue gaze. Dara pressed her lips against his mouth, that large, generous heart of hers contained in that torrid kiss. She had the most delicious mouth, a sinner's mouth, really. He opened to her, taking her lips tenderly. This was their special time together, a place and space where they could share their love for one another in so many different and satisfying ways. Sometimes it came in the form of their talking about something. Other times, small caresses here and there over their bodies. Or a kiss like this one. Deep, searching, lush with promise and with so much love that Matt almost wanted to weep with joy over finding Dara. And she was his. He still woke up sometimes at night, amazed that he'd found her. That she loved him just as fiercely as he loved her. They were friends, lovers, and so much more. And every moment spent with Dara was an exquisite gift to Matt. One that brought only joy. Never any pain.

# CHAPTER 8

THE MORNING WAS coolish as Matt walked Dara into the Safe House reception area. It was eight a.m., and by eight thirty, Dara wanted to be ready to start receiving her patients down the hall. Alani met them at her office. Matt dropped off some papers for her to look over before he sent them on to the Delos HQ in Alexandria, Virginia, then grabbed coffee in a smaller office down the hall. He held a lei of white plumeria in his hand. There was a vendor on the street corner selling them, and he'd bought two. One for Dara, who was delighted and quickly placed it over her head, and one for little Stacy, who was her helper for today. Matt wasn't sure she'd accept the lei from him, but he was driven to try. They'd find out soon enough.

Matt spotted Stacy standing patiently at the closed door to the exam room, looking so serious and far more mature than she should have at her age. Her small hands were clasped in front of her. Her curly red hair, which had been in a wild frizz about her head when he'd met her yesterday, was now combed and neatly tamed into a ponytail. Not only that, but he saw some of the smudges on her face were gone, too. And he'd swear that thin, ragged muumuu she wore had been pressed; there were no wrinkles in it anymore. She had made an effort to clean up, no doubt. Matt wondered if it was because she had an important status now that she was helping Dara. Unsure, he felt concerned that the lei might not be the right gift for her, but Dara was positive she'd love it. His instincts told him differently, and he hoped he was wrong.

As they approached, Dara called out a hello to Stacy, lifting her hand, talking warmly with her. Matt saw the girl respond positively to Dara, but she refused to meet his eyes. He'd seen too many abused Afghan girls who knew only fists from the males in their families, and they would never meet a man's eyes, either. To meet their gaze was to invite retribution and more abuse. They learned very early in their imprisoned lives to keep their gazes anchored to their dusty feet. Matt knew the value of always crouching down to eye level with a child. That way, they weren't as fearful or threatened by the tall, big man standing over them.

"Matt found something he thought you might like." Dara gestured toward the lei in his left hand.

Stacy's eyes widened enormously as Matt crouched down and he held out the fragile, fragrant white plumeria lei toward her.

"I bought one for Dr. McKinley," he told her. "And since you've been such a great helper to her, I thought you might like to wear one, too." Matt held his breath, not sure she was going to take the proffered lei. He saw so many emotions, good and bad, pass through Stacy's huge green eyes as she stared down at it. And then he saw her cheeks turn a bright red, making those freckles even darker than usual.

"Really?" she asked Matt, staring at him almost uncomprehendingly.

"Sure," he murmured. "Dr. McKinley and I are engaged, and it's always nice if the man who loves her, which is me, can get her something to match her beauty. When I bought this for her, I thought you might enjoy wearing a lei, too. If you don't want it, maybe your mom might like it? Or you know a friend who would enjoy it?" Matt wasn't going to box her in and force Stacy to take it if it didn't feel right to her.

Dara placed her purse and other items on the desk, shrugging into her white lab coat and looping the stethoscope around her neck. She came to the doorway, smiling down at Stacy.

"Doesn't it smell wonderful, Stacy?"

"Y-yes, Dr. McKinley. It sure does." She shyly looked up at Matt and then lifted her chin, looking at Dara. "Does . . . I mean . . . does he always give you flowers?"

"As often as he can," she said gently. "It's always nice to receive something from someone who loves you. My own father? When I was your age? He would pick wildflowers from around the ranch where I lived and he'd bring them in to me and my sister, Callie. We always loved getting them."

"Oh . . ."

Matt felt so many heavy, conflicted emotions around Stacy. She was stunned, unsure, and wanted the lei. Was she feeling as if she didn't deserve it? Or like if she did take it, something bad would happen to her? He knew her feeling of low self-esteem, coming from a dysfunctional home, could be creating that reaction within her.

She frowned and looked to Dara. "Does it mean if Matt gives those to me, he loves me too? I mean, I know he's not my daddy."

Matt's heart broke, hearing the quaver in her soft, unsure voice. Stacy was so fragile. All he found himself wanting to do was protect the child, give her a safe haven, show her that not all men were monsters like her father was. He remained silent, because the question had been directed to Dara, not himself. He saw Dara's face melt with compassion.

"Oh, Stacy," she said. "You *deserve* flowers. You're such a hardworking, responsible young lady. If Matt hadn't thought of it, I'm sure I would have. You should be thanked for all the care and help you gave others yesterday. Flowers are a way to say thank you."

That seemed to make a difference to her, and Matt was grateful that Dara was there to act as a buffer between them. Stacy licked her lips nervously, moving her small hands down her muumuu, as if her palms were damp and sweaty. Matt didn't understand her hesitancy, and he wasn't going to do or say anything to make Stacy feel more agitated or scared than she already was. He saw fear deep in her green eyes. What had he done to make her feel that way? A bad feeling moved through Matt, and he realized that somehow, his innocent gesture to make her feel better was stirring up a lot of unanticipated emotions within her.

Stacy backed off from Matt, moving more toward Dara. She had her finger in her mouth, as if she were a four-year-old faced with a dilemma and not the twelve-year-old she was.

"M-my daddy once gave me flowers," she whispered up to Dara, keeping her voice low, shame in it. "And then . . . he hurt me after I took 'em . . ."

*Son of a bitch!* Matt remained unmoving, hearing the anguish in her whisper. And he got it, big-time. Great, so he was bringing up a truly devastating experience in Stacy's life. Feeling anger and frustration, he slowly rose.

"I have an idea," he told Dara, keeping his voice unruffled, handing her the lei. "Why don't we give this to Alani?" Because there was no way Matt wanted Stacy to see him as anything like her father, who had been charged with child molestation in addition to assaulting his family.

Dara raised her brows, gave him a perfunctory nod. She eased the lei from his hand and said, "That's a great idea, Matt. Why don't we take it up to her right now?"

Matt moved toward the door, giving Stacy the space she needed from him. She looked sadly at him for a brief moment and then quickly looked away. He felt like hell. And there was nothing he could do or say to fix it. Frustration grew in him. "I'll walk with you," he said quietly, keeping his game face on. Turning, he said gently to Stacy, "I know Dr. McKinley is going to need your help today. Thank you for volunteering." He saw her small face lose some of its tension, but he still saw shadows in her large eyes.

"Y-you're welcome," she whispered, chewing on that index finger in her mouth.

Matt turned, cupping Dara's elbow, escorting her down the hall toward the main office section. Only when they made the turn and disappeared around the corner did he pull her to a halt.

"I'm sorry," he muttered, shaking his head. "I really screwed up."

Dara made a soft sound of apology and slid her arm around his shoulders, drawing him to her. "Oh, Matt, don't be! Abused, battered children are always a minefield. You never know what's going to set them off or trigger a bad experience or memory in them." She reached up, kissing the thin, hard line of his mouth, seeing sadness and disappointment in his eyes. He was distraught. "It's okay, really. She'll get over it. You did the right thing, said the right things, so this won't further traumatize her."

"All I wanted to do is make her happy, Dara. Show her that not all men are monsters out to hurt her."

"I understand," Dara whispered, kissing his cheek and releasing him. "It's all right. Really. She'll get over it."

Matt shrugged, rallied, and gave Dara a quick kiss on the lips. "You're good for my soul. I know you have things to do. Go ahead and get started. I'll take the lei out to Alani. We need to start our security inspection of the grounds."

MATT WATCHED FROM the office across from the examination room late in the afternoon as

Dara opened the door, holding a three-month-old baby girl in her arms. The mother was standing nearby, looking drawn. He'd moved into the opposite office to have a place to sit and gather his notes from the walk he'd taken around the charity earlier today with Alani. The exam room had no air-conditioning in it, so sometimes Dara would leave the door half open to get some fresh air into it for herself and her patients. The Madonna-like expression on Dara's face anchored him, filling him with desire, with love and so much more for her. For the moment, the work in his hands was forgotten. She gently placed the baby on the soft blankets across the gurney.

Dara's blond hair was drawn back into a ponytail, as it usually was when she was in doc mode. The baby had huge blue eyes and was kicking her tiny legs; she wore a pink, summery top and a diaper. She waved her arms as Dara leaned over, talking sweetly to her. Something tightened in his chest, a sensation of such powerful love for her that he couldn't breathe for a moment. Matt felt like a thief stealing upon such a priceless, once-in-a-lifetime moment, privileged to glimpse it. Dara's face had transformed, was radiant, her smile tender, eyes misty as she kissed the baby's tiny head, her thin brown curls beneath her lips.

He couldn't tell what Dara said as she turned her attention from the baby to the mother, but the mother looked relieved; he saw her shoulders drop, as if a huge burden had just been lifted away from her. Feeling as if he were interrupting a moment that should be shared between those two, he eased to his feet and quietly closed the door to the office, the look on Dara's face forever branded into his heart and soul. He saw Stacy in the background, being the useful little helper she was to Dara. She seemed almost happy, but he wasn't sure. His pride in Dara, in her being able to work with such wounded children, touched his soul. As he sat down, he pictured Dara with a similar look on her face as she held their son or daughter. His mind shifted and he spread the many notes he'd taken out in front of him. This morning, after rising and before breakfast, he'd sensed several different feelings around Dara.

One was worry, and Matt was fairly sure it was about his leaving once more for Afghanistan after they returned from this vacation. He could almost feel her trying to protect herself emotionally from the reality that he'd be gone for another two months in a land she knew was deadly and dangerous.

Another sensation he'd picked up on was excitement, entwined with strands of anxiety. It was as if she were moving up and down in an elevator, one moment euphoric and hopeful, the next, her hope dashed and a feeling of sadness and loss overwhelming her. Matt had no idea what that was about. He'd always regarded women as an enigma and men as simple in comparison. He supposed women were that way because their hormones were so much more complex than a man's, since they were the ones who carried children and men did not. Still, it bothered him to feel her waffling emotionally like that, and it was something he wanted to address with her tonight.

This was the happiest yet that Matt had felt since meeting Dara at Bagram. Sure, some of it could have been that they were finally alone together, able to explore one another in depth. Matt sensed that their marriage would be like his mother and father's: happy. It didn't mean there wouldn't be challenges, setbacks, or problems to work through. Life was never about being happy all the time. It was always about pain of some sort or another that had to be negotiated and worked through. He was glad his mother had prepared all of them at a young age in that regard, because he saw life as climbing up and down mountains. Right now, Matt considered himself in an "up" cycle. But he knew that soon enough—and he hoped it didn't involve Afghanistan—he'd be sucked into a "down" cycle, where shit happened.

Frowning, he used the mission briefing form that Wyatt Lockwood, Tal's fiancé, had created for Artemis to send in a security report. From there, Wyatt would have the information analyzed. His mother and their board would then be given a briefing. Lastly, decisions would be made, and if an Artemis contractor or team was needed, Tal would approve such an action. If, on the other hand, all that was needed was money to buy the necessary security equipment, the charity would quickly be given that money to keep all of them safer. It would all get sorted out, and Matt was sure that this charity would become safer for those who needed it.

Matt's experience with Stacy bothered the hell out of him. His discussion with Dara last night after making love with her had been about how the young girl needed a positive male role model. In his report, he'd suggested creating a class about the positive father role model. He knew that his mother had created workshops for and given ongoing psychological help to abused and battered women. These abused children needed help to deal with their emotional wounds. Matt knew there were men who were damned good fathers, like his own, like Dara's dad, who would never lift a hand against their wives, much less their children. He decided to push the idea at the yearly international meeting of Delos, which was held at the main headquarters in Alexandria, Virginia. He wanted to get everyone to think about how to bring positive male role models to

Safe House children who had only seen the ugly, dark side of abusive men in their own life. Children like Stacy needed to know that positive, loving men were out there, too. Even though she'd been raised in a hellish environment of pain, punishment, and violence, her perspective could be broadened so that she would begin to realize there were good men in the world, too.

Matt fully admitted he was no psychologist. But he'd stumbled upon something he felt was important. All the employees of the Safe House Foundation were women, and he understood why. It wasn't women who had harmed the mothers or their children. It was understandable that they didn't want to have males on the property. But by not bringing in "safe" men who were healthy role models, Matt felt something was missing and left out of balance. He wasn't sure how it could be corrected, but he wanted to try.

During the security inspection, Alani had told him that some of the children needed new shoes, but Safe House couldn't cover the cost of them. He'd asked for a list of children's names and their shoe sizes, and one of Alani's assistants brought it to him. He'd asked her to fax it to his mother's office in Alexandria with a note to please go to their immense warehouse of clothing donations and find new shoes for the boys and girls here who needed them. Matt knew his mother would get them boxed and sent via UPS to Alani, who could then distribute them to the children. Running a charity was always difficult. Even Delos, the most well-funded charity in the world because of the family's billions, still had shortages. At least this one issue was an easy fix.

Matt became lost in his work, and only a light knock on his door snagged his attention. The door opened and Dara stuck her head inside.

"Hey, it's six p.m. Are you ready to leave? I'm done for the day." She opened the door fully, no longer wearing her white lab coat and stethoscope. Even nicer, she'd released her golden hair from that constricted ponytail and it was now a gold cape around her shoulders, emphasizing the clean lines of her face and those incredible, deep-blue eyes of hers.

"Yeah," he grunted, pushing the chair back from the desk. "I got sucked into this intel," he said apologetically.

She smiled, understanding. "Everyone is gone for the day. We're the last to leave. I'm starving to death, Matt Culver. Why don't you take me out to eat at a nice seafood restaurant? I'd love to put some lobster into melted butter and lemon."

He grinned and gathered up his papers. "I think we can find something nearby."

Matt picked up the sound of bare feet slapping against the tiles in the hall. Someone was running toward them.

Dara turned, looking in that direction down the passageway.

Frowning, he came around the desk.

Stacy ran up to them and came to a halt as Matt stood at the entrance to the office. She was breathing hard, her hair frizzy once more. In her hand was a bright-red hibiscus bloom.

"I-I wanted to give you this," she told Matt solemnly, lifting it toward him in her small hands.

Stunned, Matt stared down at her and then over at Dara. She smiled a little but said nothing, her eyes glistening with unshed tears. He turned, slowly moving into a crouch so he could look directly into the child's eyes and not seem so threatening because he towered over her. Stacy was blushing furiously as she pushed the red bloom into his offered hand. "Thank you," he said, his voice thick and unsteady. Giving her a warm look, he said, "This is beautiful, Stacy. Thank you for giving it to me."

"You can . . . umm . . . put it in a glass of water when you get home if you want. It will stay fresh for tonight. Did you know hibiscuses only bloom for one day and then they close up and fall off the bush after that?"

Matt shook his head. "No, I didn't know that." He smiled a little. "Where did you get this?" He'd seen no hibiscus bushes around the property when he'd walked it this morning with

Alani.

"Oh"—Stacy moved restlessly from one bare foot to another—"well . . . don't tell my mother, but I went behind the barracks and into that nice neighborhood behind us. There's lots of pretty houses there. And the people who live in those homes take really good care of them. I love looking at all the flowers along that street. That's why I knew where to get you a flower."

Matt's heart broke but he kept the smile on his face, the huge red blossom in his open palm. "Well, then I'd say this is a very special gift. Thank you, Stacy. It means a lot to me."

"Or, you could, umm . . ." She pointed up at Dara. "You could put the blossom behind her left ear. It means that she's taken, that she's in love with you, and going to get married."

Touched, Matt nodded. "I'll do that right now." He slowly rose, careful not to startle Stacy by moving too fast and making her feel threatened. Dara smiled and walked up to him, turning so that he could affix the bloom behind her left ear by pulling her blond hair aside. She helped him get it to stay where it belonged.

"What do you think?" Matt asked the child. "Did we do it right?"

Stacy clasped her hands to her chest beneath the muumuu. "Oh, yes! Red looks so good on you, Dr. McKinley!"

Dara laughed and said, "It's my favorite color, Stacy. You must be psychic!" Dara touched the bloom gently and leaned down, kissing the top of Stacy's head. "Thank you. That's so sweet and thoughtful of you."

Stacy colored fiercely and she hung her head, her gaze on her feet.

Matt swallowed hard, a lump forming in his throat. He felt helpless and frustrated that he could not reach out and hug her. But he was sure such a motion on his part would be badly misinterpreted by her. All he could do was rasp, "Thank you, Stacy . . ."

Without warning, she moved swiftly, opening her arms and throwing them around his waist, clinging to him as though if she released Matt, she'd be swept away forever. He hadn't expected this and was momentarily stunned, but his arms automatically moved around her slender, thin shoulders. She pressed her face against his T-shirt across his belly, as if to hide. He held her tenderly, leaning over, grazing her unruly hair. There was so much he wanted to say, but he was so damned afraid of doing the wrong thing. Looking up at Dara for direction, he saw her gulping several times, trying not to cry. Hell, he was on the verge of tears himself.

Stacy was underweight for her age—he guessed she was malnourished, because she was twelve and yet had the height of a girl of maybe ten—and the fragility of her small form saddened him. He'd found out from Alani earlier she'd been molested all her young life by not only her father but her three uncles, as well. And her battered mother had stood aside, allowing it to happen, already beaten down with her husband's fists so much that she couldn't even protect her innocent daughter. That information had sickened him. It served to make his commitment to children like Stacy, to help them heal from their psychic, emotional, and physical wounds, even stronger.

Lifting his hand, Matt followed his heart, praying that as he grazed her hair, Stacy would know that it wasn't a sexual advance on his part, but rather, he was trying to give her love . . . real love. He hoped she would absorb his heart, the care he felt for her. Her little shoulders began to shake and his T-shirt became suddenly damp. *Oh, hell!* It was then that Matt realized just how little he knew about child rearing and how to be a father. He hadn't a clue. And right now, he wished he knew so much more. But Stacy wasn't a normal child, anyway.

Always, as an operator out on a mission, Matt had followed his inner knowing at times when he couldn't pin down a threat. And always, those internal, primal skills had led him to the right path and kept him alive. To hell with it; right or wrong, he was going to get down on one knee and simply hold Stacy and let her cry on his shoulder. Dara believed that tears were healing, and he thought that had never been more true than it was right now. Easing her hands from around his waist, he went down on one knee. Matt opened his arms enough to allow Stacy to come as close or as far away from him as she wanted. The moment he gave her that opportunity, she clung to him, her arms wrapped tightly around his neck, as if she were going to die if she left any space between them. Her sobs got louder, more tears wetting the shoulder of his T-shirt. Enclosing her gently with his arms, Matt rocked her a little, whispering hoarsely that she was going to be all right. That better days were ahead for her. And he lost track of time, fully absorbed in the girl's pain and the anguish tearing out of her contorted mouth, the tears seemingly never-ending.

Dara came over and crouched next to Matt, her hand in the center of Stacy's back, and they knelt in the hall, becoming a protective, loving cradle of arms for the child. Tears came down Dara's cheeks and she didn't try to stop them. Matt's face was hard, set, and he was struggling not to cry himself, but his gold-brown eyes were alive with anguish for Stacy, for her plight, for all the right reasons with this severely wounded child.

Dara's heart went out to Matt, because he didn't know how to handle this and wasn't sure what to do. She could feel him floundering, wanting to fix something that couldn't be fixed. She rubbed her hand tenderly across Stacy's shoulders, whispering loving words near her ear, giving her the affection she so sorely needed. Who had ever held her? From what Dara had seen, in so many broken families like hers, it was the oldest child who became the adult. And the adult, usually the mother, was either so beaten down by the man who abused her or so caught up in simply enabling herself and her children to survive that she became like a child.

Finally, Stacy's tears stopped and she started hiccupping, drawing away a little bit from the front of Matt's damp T-shirt, wiping her reddened eyes with her trembling fingers.

"I-I wish you could both stay here," she whispered brokenly, giving them a pleading look. "Y-you help so many of us," she sniffed, wiping her eyes again.

Matt felt miserable, tongue-tied, unable to say anything of importance. It was Dara, with that compassionate look in her eyes, who wiped the last of Stacy's tears from her small, wan face with a tissue she'd pulled from her pocket. All he could do was allow her to lean against him, his arms loose around her waist.

"Someday," Dara whispered, kissing her damp cheek, "you will come out of this time in your life, Stacy. And there are good people everywhere. Mrs. Alani is helping you and so is your mom. Soon, you'll feel better. You're eating, from what she says. And look how grown-up you were today! You helped me out so much. I couldn't have seen that many babies and children today without your being there." She smoothed Stacy's frizzy hair away from her face. "You are greatly loved. Don't *ever* forget that. No matter how dark or bad it gets, there's light to follow after those storms in your life, Stacy. Will you remember that for us? We love you dearly. We think you're a very beautiful young woman, and you're destined for a wonderful life."

Matt felt tears burn in his eyes and he struggled to keep them at bay. Stacy remained against him, and he could feel she needed that masculine love and support but didn't know how to ask for it or receive it because of the abuse she'd suffered. He was grateful for Dara's sincere words, her extension of love to Stacy, because he could see the girl lapping it up, starved for a little human nurturing when so much had already been stolen from her.

"When we leave, Matt and I will make sure to email Mrs. Alani every so often to see how you're doing. You're such a bright young lady, and we know you can be anything you dream of being. So keep in touch with us through her." Dara looked tenderly into her reddened, tear-filled eyes. Stacy was so broken. So in need of so much. But so was her mother, who was even more fractured. She recognized now more than ever that Delos was a force for good, a shining light of hope for children and adults just like the ones here at Safe House. She leaned over, framing Stacy's damp face with her hands, kissing her like a mother would kiss her beloved child. The fact that Stacy clung to Matt told her that some remaining healthy part of her trusted him even though he was a man. And that was a hopeful sign.

"O-okay, Dr. McKinley . . ." she whispered, trying to smile but failing. "I-I'm glad you like the flower. I-I wanted to thank Matt for what he did for me." She gave Matt a miserable look. "I-I wanted that lei so bad, but I was afraid. I'm sorry . . ."

Tears jammed into his eyes. Matt reached out, caressing her cheek. "It's okay, Stacy. I understood. You just keep getting better. Mrs. Alani and her staff will always be there to help you. And you'll always be able to connect with us in the emails. This isn't the end. It's just the beginning. We will never forget you. We'll be as close as you want us. Okay?"

Giving a jerky nod, she looked away for a moment and then turned, kissing his cheek swiftly. And then she pulled out of his arms, hugged Dara with all her child's strength, and turned, running down the hall, her thin, ragged muumuu flying around her knees.

"Oh, God," he muttered, watching Stacy disappear out the rear door. Giving Dara a sorrowful look as he rose, he said gruffly, "This is a special hell. I don't see how anyone works here. It's too much for me to take, emotionally. All I wanted to do was go find that deadbeat father of hers and her uncles and beat the shit out of them and tell them if they *ever* lifted a hand against Stacy or her family again, it would be the last thing they'd ever do." Matt pushed to his feet, offering his hand down to Dara.

Smoothing out her tan linen trousers after standing, Dara nodded, giving him a sad look. "Men just have a different way of dealing with bastards like her father and uncles."

Snorting, he took her warm hand, walking her down the hall toward the reception area. "Yeah, my reaction isn't PC, is it?"

"No," Dara said, giving him a wry look, "but I don't disagree with you. Men like that are monsters. And most likely, their own fathers sexually abused them and they're just carrying on the bad seed down the family line. Each generation is stained by it until somebody stops it and says no. Stands up to the perpetrator."

"Her mother sure as hell didn't."

"That's because she was so beaten down that she couldn't," Dara said gently. "It's a disease in a family, Matt. Safe House can't fix everything and everyone, but now that Stacy and her mom and her baby brother are here, they have a chance to not only survive this, but heal from it over time. Delos is doing so much good for people across the world." She waited as he unlocked the front door, stepping out to look around before allowing her to walk outside. "I just think your family rocks, Matt. I have so much hope for the Stacys of the world who are lucky enough to connect with one of the Delos charities."

# CHAPTER 9

"I DON'T WANT this vacation to end," Dara admitted, lying on top of Matt, luxuriating in him after they'd made love. She threaded her fingers through his damp hair, drowning in his hooded, lion-like eyes.

"Why? Because we won't be drinking Hawaiian water and we'll lose that great sex we've enjoyed here?" He chuckled, skating his fingertips down her long, sleek back. His heart swelled as she laughed with him.

"That's crossed my mind," Dara giggled, pressing a kiss on his dark-haired chest. She lifted her head, resting her chin on the top of her folded hands, holding his amused gaze. "What if it's true? What if we go back to Virginia and our sex life is dull in comparison? Will we have to visit Hawaii a lot more often, then?" Her lips drew away from her teeth.

Caressing the crown of her head, Matt growled, "If this vacation had done nothing else but give us this incredible new breakthrough with one another, it would be worth every second over here. I don't think we'll go back to the old ways. We like what we discovered way too much. It suits us for where we're at right now." He shrugged. "Nothing stands still, sweetheart. Everything is organic in our life, and it's always going to be changing." He saw a shadow briefly come to her eyes, and she quickly tried to hide it from him, to no avail. "Come here," Matt said gruffly, easing her off him. He fluffed some pillows behind his back, sitting up and leaning against the heavy bamboo headboard. Reaching out, he drew Dara easily across his thighs. Matt was bothered by that fleeting look in her eyes. Settling her comfortably across him, guiding her head to his right shoulder, he slanted a look down at her, imprisoning her with his arms and body. She made that humming sound of pleasure, closing her eyes, surrendering to him in every way.

"I love cuddling with you," she whispered. "I feel so safe, as if I'm suddenly wrapped in a huge cocoon of your care."

A sound of pleasure moved through his chest and Matt kissed her smiling lips, tasting her unique sweetness. "I always want to make you feel safe, my lovely woman." He moved his roughened palm down from the side of her hip, appreciating her long, curved thigh, hearing her sigh of satisfaction as he caressed and continued to please her.

"You are definitely my big, bad guard dog," Dara admitted. "I've always been so independent, a wild cowgirl from the rough country of Montana. But since I met you?" She absorbed the gleam and arousal in his gold eyes, for her alone. "I realize now that sometimes, I want to be held. To feel protected. And it doesn't make me a wimp or whiner or anything."

Matt became serious with her. "When you were little, was there ever an incident in your life that triggered the worry you have nowadays?"

He saw Dara become solemn, her lashes dropping for a moment. "Yes . . . there was an incident . . ."

"Can you share it with me?"

"Sure. I was five years old and I was out with my family in the woods. We gathered firewood in the fall before the snows came. My grandfather Graham would drive the tractor with the flatbed on it, and my father, mother, and grandmother would cut up the trees that had fallen during the year and fill up the flatbed. It was a weeklong event, and we'd go out after breakfast and return just before nightfall. My father and grandfather would then stack the wood in a nearby woodshed near our ranch home.

"I had wandered off into the woods and no one saw me. I was following my nose and pretty soon, I realized I was alone. It scared me, Matt."

"At five? Sure it would," he said. "What did you do?"

"I started crying and calling for them. And no one came. Then I started to run, but I wasn't sure where they were. The trees were thick, the brush heavy, and I got disoriented and lost. I was so scared. I worried about the grizzly bears, because we had a lot of them in the area. I knew they ate little children like me because I had a high, squeaky voice like a baby elk or fawn who was trying to hide and not be discovered by a hungry bear."

"That had to scare the hell out of you, then," Matt said, caressing her cheek, seeing that time branded into her eyes.

"Oh," she said wryly, "it did. I was never so scared. I was so lost. I couldn't hear my parents, and I kept crying out for them."

"They must have found you."

"Yes, near dusk, half a day later." Dara grimaced. "I was dirty, my face, arms, and hands scratched, freezing and shivering from the cold temperature. It was my grandfather who located me. He tracked me through some pretty awful backcountry. Luckily, it had snowed a week before but then melted. He followed my footprints in the mud. It was only many years later that he told me he'd been a sniper in the Marine Corps. I didn't know what that meant, but I do now. Those men and women know how to track, and he'd used that skill to find me." She smiled a little, her voice growing fond. "I had half a day of worry about being eaten alive by a grizzly bear. I was terrified." She gave him a dark look. "Until, that is, that ambush we survived in Afghanistan. It's number one in my book now."

He grunted, considering her story, moving his fingers lightly across her shoulder. "Still, you probably felt abandoned by your parents."

"Oh, I sure did. But I was only five, and I wasn't mature enough to think about doing anything but running and trying to hide. That's when my worry was triggered." She shrugged. "My mom's a worrier, too. And so is my grandmother. The worry gene runs in the women on that side of my family, I guess."

"Yes, and that incident triggered yours, big-time," Matt guessed.

"It did. After that, I couldn't stop worrying about anything that stressed me. My mom and grandmother saw it, recognized it for what it was, and began to work with me on it, to get me to understand worry didn't resolve anything. After I graduated from high school, I had it pretty much in hand. It would only surface in very serious situations."

"But going through medical school? Residency?" he asked, because that was highly stressful.

Shrugging, she said, "I never worried about that. It never triggered it, Matt. The trigger is when I feel like I'm threatened, or feel my life is going to end."

Mouth thinning, Matt began to understand the depth of her anxiety and its originating point. "I didn't see your worry surface the day we got hit by that ambush," Matt said, using his index finger to coax a few gold strands away from the corner of her soft mouth. "You were strong. And you never whined. Even when you sliced your knee open, I didn't even know it had happened until we managed to find a cave to hide in that night. You'll never be a whiner, Dr. McKinley." He tapped the end of her nose gently. "Which brings me to the next topic of conversation that I want to discuss with you tonight."

Her lips curved ruefully and she gave a breathy laugh. "Now you sound like Dr. Phil."

Matt laughed with her and shook his head. "No, I don't have his psychological expertise, I'm afraid."

She curved her palm against his jaw. "What did you want to talk about?"

Looking into her slumberous blue eyes, which were saturated with pleasure, he said, "You worrying yourself to death while I'm back over in Afghanistan for a month and a half. I think you're afraid I'll die over there and you'll lose me." He felt her tense, her eyes suddenly reflecting that concern he'd seen in them before. She tried to hide it from him, but he growled, "Don't dodge me on this, Dara. We *have* to talk about it. We have to get it out so that you don't kill yourself with anxiety while I'm in country." Dara sobered instantly. He felt bad about bringing her down like that, but avoiding the issue wasn't going to help anyone. Especially her.

"I'm not worrying."

"Right. Even your voice tells me you're fibbing, Dara."

Her mouth flexed, brows dipping, and she looked away from him momentarily.

"It's less than two months," he said, making light of it. "I've told you, in the winter, things wind down. We don't do missions. We're all snowed in. And so is the enemy."

"Sure, just like Callie was telling me that Afghan village we were going to was safe, Matt." Dara stared up at him, seeing the calm and strength in his shadowed features. She loved him so much, so deeply, that she couldn't imagine her life without his being a part of it.

"Sweetheart," he sighed, sliding his hand soothingly across her naked shoulder, "we need to figure out how best for you to avoid the worry that keeps you on tenterhooks. I can email you nearly every day. We each get a turn on Skype about every five days so we can talk to our loved ones back home. You'll actually see that I'm alive and kicking." He added a slight, half-cocked smile to go with it, hoping she'd buy his version of life in Afghanistan. Matt knew he had a chance. Callie, her sister, had spent half the year there for five straight years and knew the country's inherent dangers, but Dara did not. Callie knew the rhythm of the black-ops teams and she wouldn't have been fooled at all by what he was saying. He watched Dara's expression, felt her emotions, and it pained him because he knew she'd suffer no matter how logically he reasoned with her.

"What does your family do when you're gone?" she asked.

"My mother worries," he admitted. "Her way of dealing with it is to keep busy. Plus, since my dad is an Air Force general, he can get updates on me and where I'm at when no one else can. There are days when Mom becomes really edgy. She's very psychic, and that doesn't help, either. Some days she senses I'm in a lot of danger. And she's usually right, but I'm not dead. I'm just on an op, that's all. On those days, my dad makes a few discreet requests through certain unnamed back channels, and he finds out more or less what I'm doing and how I am."

"Can I use that back channel?"

He laughed. "I knew you were going to go

for that."

She gave him a dark look. "Well, wouldn't you if it was available?"

"Yes," he cautioned her heavily, "but my CO doesn't like an Air Force general butting his nose into his business, so you can't just use it whenever you feel like it, Dara."

"I hate the nights alone, without you next to me. I get horrible dreams. I wake up screaming sometimes. In fact, I wake myself up because I'm screaming. Not something I like admitting to you, Matt." Dara gave him a pained, apologetic look.

Bringing her against him, holding her solidly, feeling her arm wind around his neck, her brow pressed against his jaw, Matt whispered, "I'm coming home to you, Dara. That's all there is to it. I have so much to look forward to with you. No enemy bullet is taking me out. I promise you." Wincing inwardly, Matt knew he had no way to back up that promise. But if he didn't alleviate her worry, it would eat her up inside while he was gone.

"Look at it this way: you finish your residency on March first. On that very day, I'm leaving Afghanistan and the Army. I'll be home in two or three days after that, depending on the flight schedule out of Bagram. You'll not only be a fully-accredited pediatrician, you'll be putting plans into place for your clinic. I would think that between the two, you are going to be very, very busy. Don't you?" He gave her a wry look, challenging her.

"All that's true," Dara admitted. Tracing an invisible heart on his chest with her fingertip, she said, "I've also been thinking about something else, Matt."

"What?" He picked up her index finger, kissing the tip of it, watching the tension shed from her face.

"I found out from Alani that all the Safe House branches, wherever they are located, have an agreement for a medical practitioner to come in for a visit once a month to see those who need medical attention. It's funded by a stipend. And after it's used up, there's no more money available to pay a doctor. There's got to be a better system put into play to deal with this kind of situation. I've got some ideas, and I want to bend Dilara's ear about them when we get home." Her lips puckered and then she added, "And if she likes my idea, then I want her to hire me as a part-time consultant to be the director of this new medical initiative and get it put into action for all the Safe House charities."

"What about the clinic you want to open for the poor in Washington, D.C.?"

"Oh, I'd do that, too. I'd spend four days a week at the clinic and a day at Delos advising, consulting, and directing the people out in the field once the idea is approved. I'll handle the in-house paperwork."

"Okay," he murmured, "then you're going to be a lot busier than I realized. Don't you feel that all this will keep you so occupied that you'll worry less?"

"No."

Matt bit back a chuckle. Dara was honest, if nothing else. "What can I do to ease your anxiety?"

"Can't you leave the Army early?"

"No, sweetheart. An officer can get away with doing that by turning in his or her commission, but I can't do that without facing a court martial, and I'm not going there."

"But I was talking to your father one day, and he mentioned a hardship discharge."

Matt stopped himself from rolling his eyes. Dara had been creative in uncovering possible routes to get him out of Afghanistan sooner, not later. "Sweet," he murmured, cupping her chin, forcing her to hold his gaze, "a hardship discharge really does mean exactly that. For example, if I were the only son and my father died, leaving my mother destitute, I could request such a discharge and receive it so I could leave the military to go home, get a civilian job, and take care of my mother."

"But I'm not destitute."

"Not by any stretch of anyone's imagination. I'm sorry." Matt meant it, because she was going to be on the razor's edge while he was back in that damned dangerous country. He saw the banked terror in her eyes, and he spread his large, golden tanned hand across her belly. "What about," he rasped, watching her carefully, "the possibility that I've gotten you pregnant while over here? How would that change you, Dara? What would you be focusing on instead?"

Matt knew the answer to all those questions, because in some respects he understood Dara better than she did herself at times. He'd gone through a life-and-death experience with her in Afghanistan.

"I-I've thought about that, too."

All that worry in her eyes dissolved. He intuitively sensed that if she was pregnant, it would short-circuit a lot of her anxiety. She would focus on the baby she carried in her body. "Is there any way you can tell that you might be pregnant?" Because he felt she was, but that was his intuition, his gut call. And he wasn't about to say anything about it. Dara was a doctor. She'd need medical tests to prove it one way or another.

"Yes," she whispered. "When we fly home, I can go to the hospital and have one of my friends at the lab draw blood. She'll be able to tell immediately if the pregnancy hormone is in my blood or not."

"Then why don't we do that? I don't leave for Afghanistan until the day after that. It would be nice to know before I left." He saw her eyes flood with unshed tears, her lower lip quiver, her hand tightening around his neck, holding his gaze. Matt knew how much being a mother would mean to Dara. He knew her secret dream of having as many children as they wanted. She planned to continue her career as a pediatrician and be a mother, too. It would serve her well, and he slid his hand across her belly. "Let's take this one step at a time. I think that if you're pregnant, a lot of your worry will go away. Your focus would be on our child. And I'm going to survive over in Afghanistan just fine and come home to both of you."

MATT WAS OUTSIDE the hospital lab Dara had disappeared into. They still had jet lag from landing yesterday evening at Reagan National Airport in Arlington. The whole Culver family had come out to meet them in baggage claim. It was a feast of happiness, and Matt liked that his mother hugged Dara. They were close and kindred spirits of a kind. As he and his father walked with their luggage in hand to the covered parking lot and their awaiting Suburban, Matt knew his mother would be a strong, caring rudder to Dara while he was overseas.

He slowly paced the hallway outside of the

lab on the second floor of the massive, busy hospital. He'd made them breakfast, and by nine a.m., he and Dara had driven over to the Alexandria hospital. Dara had practically dragged him into the elevator, flustered, worried, and excited. Matt hid his smile because she was anxious and wanted so badly to be pregnant. He wanted it for her, too.

About twenty minutes later, he heard Dara's shriek carry all the way out to where he stood outside the swinging doors. Turning, Matt saw her flying toward the door, waving a piece of paper in her hand, her radiant expression impossible to ignore. He opened his arms and she flew into them.

"I'm *pregnant*!" Dara cried, hugging him fiercely. "Oh, Matt! I'm pregnant!" She sobbed against his neck as his arms closed around her, lifting her off her feet momentarily. Tears of happiness spilled from her eyes as he slowly turned her around in a circle. His laugher reverberated through his chest and through her. She had never felt as close to him as she did in this moment. He gently deposited her feet on the floor, easing away just enough to kiss her long and hard.

Overwhelming joy washed through him from her. Matt framed her face with his hands, tears streaming from Dara's eyes as she sobbed. He understood she was elated, and so was he.

"You're going to be a helluva mother, sweet woman," he managed to say, his own voice strained with tears he was fighting to keep from spilling. Maybe he'd let them fall later. But not here in a busy hospital. Matt wasn't going to cry in front of strangers. He caressed her loose hair, feeling her unfettered response, that luscious mouth of hers stretched into the biggest smile he'd ever seen. Her hands were busy gripping his shoulders, fully embracing him over her joy at carrying their child deep in her body.

"Oh, Matt!" She tried to stop crying and pushed the paper into his hand. "Look! It's real! I'm really pregnant!"

He released her but kept one arm around her waist. Dara was like an overexcited puppy, moving from one foot to another. "I don't know what I'm looking at," he confessed with an apologetic grin. "But I believe you. I really do." He handed the results back to her.

"I'm just so happy, Matt," she said, wiping the tears from her cheeks. "This means so much to me . . . to us . . . I've wanted a family of my own more than anything else."

"Well, you have one now." He eased her forward. "Come on, let's go home. I think you have a bunch of calls to make to your family and friends."

Dara nodded, giving him a watery smile filled with such love that tears drove into his eyes as he led her toward the elevator. Matt sensed that with this shift in her life, she'd have half as much time to worry about his being over in Afghanistan. And he knew his mother would be over the moon about her pregnancy. The Turkish and Greek sides of their global family had been waiting years for the Culver kids to grow up and have children. Matt shook his head, grinning, as he led Dara into the elevator, tucked beneath his arm.

Dilara's three brothers—Matt's uncles—and their wives would rock into a weeklong celebration once they were told, he was sure. They would be ecstatic, because in June, he and Dara were marrying in Kuşadasi, Turkey, where they all lived. Matt could just see the wedding gifts they'd be given—all the aunts, who were stellar at knitting, crocheting, and quilting, would be busily making all kinds of wonderful booties, onesies, baby quilts, and God knew what else.

The elevator doors shushed close. Dara leaned her head against him, wrapping her arms around his waist, hugging him tightly.

"You're going to be a father. Do you realize that?"

He grinned and kissed her temple. "Yeah, and I'm sure as hell going to need a lot of help, training, and guidance in that department." He thought of how awkward and uneasy he'd been with what to say to Stacy. Matt had wanted to show his love to her, but she was so damaged that he wasn't sure how to do it. It brought back starkly to Matt how unprepared he really was for fatherhood. He was hoping his father would be his mentor. God knew he needed one. Matt didn't want to accidentally harm their own child with his ignorance. It would scar his heart forever if that happened.

"Oh," Dara whispered, hugging him tightly and then releasing him as the doors opened, "you'll do wonderfully, Matt. You're a natural father. Look at Robert. He's such a wonderful role model for you to learn from."

"Yeah," he groused, giving her a fond, loving look as he led her toward the main doors of the hospital. "I'm going to need a *lot* of training, Dara." And then he gave her a reassuring look. "I'll get there, so I don't want you to worry about that, okay? I know you have motherhood nailed down."

She slid her arm around his waist, leaning happily against his strong, powerful body as he led them through the doors into the cold morning. Snow had just fallen two nights earlier, and the naked trees were coated with white blankets of it, looking beautiful in the morning sun's light, glistening and sparkling, reflecting how she felt right now. "You'll be *fine*, Matt. I know you will!"

Matt wasn't sure but didn't pursue it. This would be their last day together. He had to leave out of nearby Joint Base Andrews at 1000 tomorrow morning. Today was Dara's day.

"Well, let's just spend the day together. I'm sure your family is going to be really happy to hear from you." Like his Turkish-Greek-American family, the McKinley family had also been pining away for children from Callie and Dara. Matt was sure she would be bathed in the love of her Montana family, and he was sure more happy tears would be spilled during those phone calls.

Wait until his mother found out! She'd probably start sending Turkish food over to Dara's condo tomorrow. Matt was sure that the globe would explode with unabashed joy from his far-flung family. He was also sure, knowing his Turkish aunts and uncles the way he did, that all the aunts would take turns flying over to keep Dara company once they knew he would be in Afghanistan for nearly two months. They would not want Dara to feel lonely or unsupported during this important time in her life. They'd also be sending Dara flowers at her condo, and once an aunt arrived, she would cook Dara Turkish food to eat, to keep her healthy during her pregnancy. And Cousin Angelo and his wife, Maria, would probably send flowers and food from Greece, too. There was a bit of a competition between the Greek and Turkish sides of the family, but it was all in good fun. What they shared was the love of the family's American children: Tal, Alexa, and himself. Matt knew that both sides would surely start immediately planning a baby shower for Dara. They were people of action, and they had the money and heart to literally shower Dara with so much love, attention, and support in his absence that she'd probably forget to worry about him while he was overseas. He grinned; his visiting Turkish aunts, who would care for Dara, were the best possible diversion for his worrywart woman.

Smiling as he settled into the driver's seat and Dara put on her seat belt, he said, "What would you like to do first?"

Dara smiled, her eyes bright with tears. "Let's drive over to your mom and dad's home. I so want to share this with them in person." She reached out, slipping her fingers around his black leather coat sleeve.

"Yeah, that feels right," Matt agreed. And as he drove out of the freshly plowed parking lot, water gleaming here and there along the asphalt of the highway leading toward his parents' house, Matt smiled to himself. This was the single most important time in his life, as it was Dara's.

Matt would make a point of emailing her every day unless he was out on an op. He knew there would be a few, but not as many as there would be in the spring through the summer, when military activity increased markedly throughout Afghanistan. And he knew his visiting aunts would keep his fiancée busy. Dilara would also know the shortcuts to keep Dara occupied so that she wouldn't have time to worry about him. Matt never underestimated the power of women.

But what would really keep her distracted was his Turkish aunts' coming over, one at a time, taking turns, to live in the condo with Dara. His aunts had always promised that if Tal, Alexa, or his wife got pregnant, they would visit if they were alone and without the support of their loved one. The aunt would live with them to be a source of help and support, cook for them, and in general be the big, sloppy, happy Turkish family that they were. The aunts had taught them from childhood onward that the extended family should surround a newly pregnant woman and make sure she and the baby she was carrying stayed happy and peaceful. She became the focus of the family and had plenty of love showered upon her, with the aunts cooking her special food to keep her healthy and the baby growing strong. Dara had no idea this tradition existed, but she would shortly.

Matt smiled again. When—not if—the Turkish aunts took turns flying over to live with Dara, they would keep her looking forward, give her company, and help her with their wise feminine knowledge. They would be there to support and mother Dara with their care and unabashed love.

Matt was sure Maria, their cousin Angelo's wife, would eagerly volunteer to help, too. He wouldn't be surprised if once his Greek side found out that each Turkish aunt was flying in to keep Dara company, Maria became a fixture in Dara's life, too. Maria would enthusiastically cook Greek food; Dara would be in heaven over that. When he got home from Afghanistan, he knew his babysitting aunt would return to Turkey because he could then take over and be there as an ongoing support for Dara and enjoy her pregnancy. His mother would keep making and sending over that special Turkish food to them, however. Matt didn't mind that at all. He knew Dara loved Turkish and Greek food, so it was a win-win for everyone.

His whole life had just been turned upside down in the best of ways. As Matt drove through the wet streets of Alexandria, heading for the Culver home on the outskirts of the city, he shared a smile with Dara. She gripped his hand in her lap, the joy radiating from her face and her tear-filled blue eyes. Yeah, there was nothing better than this moment. Their time in Oahu had been a key turning point in their lives with one another, a very special, heart-centered moment.

Matt gently squeezed Dara's hand, feeling happiness wash through him in tsunami-like waves. He'd never seen her so happy. There was so much to look forward to. So much.

## THE BEGINNING…

Don't miss the novella *Dream of Me*
Only from Lindsay McKenna and
Blue Turtle Publishing.

Available wherever you buy eBooks. Paperbacks
are available through CreateSpace/amazon.com,
and audiobooks through Tantor Media!

Read the sneak peek of *Dream of Me*!

## Excerpt from

### Dream of Me
### by Lindsay McKenna

"GOING ON A hike was *such* a great idea of yours, Gage," Alexa Culver said, her spirits high as she looked back at him as they hiked a trail deep in the Virginia woodlands. Around her, late September leaves were turning red, yellow, and orange. Some drifted down toward them, creating a picture-perfect fall morning. They had just reached the top of a large hill above their recently purchased 1850s farmhouse.

"Anywhere with you is always a great idea." Gage grinned as he picked his way along the steep, rocky trail covered with crunchy, dry leaves. The eighty-degree morning breeze swirled playfully around them as he caught up with Alexa, watching as she absently tucked her auburn hair behind her ears.

Today, Gage was wearing fitted jeans that emphasized his lean, tall body. Alexa always appreciated his lithe energy: like a cougar, he prowled rather than walked. She recognized this was partly from his training as a Marine Corps sniper, but it was also an inborn quality that had served them both well recently.

Even when they'd met last November at the Bagram Army base north of Kabul, Afghanistan's capital, she'd been aware of the powerful, undiluted sexual chemistry between them. But she had never imagined that in a few short days, Gage and his SEAL team would rescue her and eight other women from the Taliban. Since that time, they had grown even closer to each other, and were now back home in the States working for Artemis Security. It was the hidden branch within the largest global charity, Delos.

But those terrifying, life-changing events had been indelibly burned into Alexa's memory. She tried to bury them by working longer, harder hours—in fact, she was in the office seven days a week, and found that when she was focusing on being director of Artemis's Safe House Foundation, she could crowd them out. Whether she could ever completely heal from those two devastating days, during which she had endured verbal abuse, assault, beatings and nonstop sexual humiliation, no one could guess.

Now, Gage slowed his pace, his long fingers wrapped around the red shoulder straps of the large knapsack he carried on his back. "You look as if you belong out here," he said, leaning over to brush her smiling lips with a kiss. His body, as always, hungered for Alexa. He'd missed making love to her, but because she'd been so devastated by her capture by the Taliban, he'd told her he would wait until she was ready to be intimate again.

Gage never kidded himself that he could read a woman's mind, but he did know Alexa well enough to read her body language. Today, she looked particularly attractive in her white shorts and a sleeveless cotton tee the color of her auburn hair. She was free of makeup, and he saw the light sprinkling of girlish freckles peeking out across her cheeks.

He loved her. Gage knew her so well that he could read her moods from her eyes. He had learned that when the brown flecks in her eyes were prominent, she was emotionally upset about something. But if the green and gold were front and center, she was happy and at peace.

"Look at this," he said, leaning down and capturing a red leaf at their feet. Holding it up, he brought it up near her ponytail lying on her right shoulder. "The colors almost match," he said, placing the recently dropped leaf next to her hair. Gage drew in her scent, which made his growing erection harden even more. Alexa gazed down at it, a playful look on her face; both were aware that they'd had no sex together for five days.

Now, she stepped forward and pressed her

breasts against his chest, and, unable to resist, Gage pulled her to him and captured her mouth, now soft and willing beneath his. Reluctantly easing away from her, drowning in those green-flecked eyes that showed how much she loved him, Gage breathed in the scent of almond oil in her hair, a fragrance that always aroused him.

Alexa's mother, Dilara, who was Turkish with a bit of Greek, put a few drops on her own hair every morning to make it shine, and her daughter tended to follow her mother's example—from her high-fashion clothing to her perfect makeup to her skillfully arranged coiffure.

"Wow," Alexa laughed. "That's quite a match." Her eyes crinkled with humor as she examined the leaf. "Hey, are you calling me a dried up old leaf, Hunter?"

He chuckled. "Not hardly, Ms. Culver." His heart swelled. It was rare, since her capture and rescue, that the Alexa he'd met and fallen in love with had resurfaced. And the wicked smile on those beautifully shaped lips, combined with the dancing glint in her eyes, boded well.

Gage silently congratulated himself on having dragged Alexa kicking and screaming away from the office for this noontime hike up into the hills. She had been getting ready at nine a.m. on Saturday to drive into work, but her face reflected the strain she was under. Gage had avoided telling Alexa what to do since her ordeal with the

Taliban, whenever possible urging her to take control of her activities. But this time, he was damn glad he'd coaxed her into taking this five-mile hike into the Virginia hills above their farmhouse. Already, the strain and smudges around her eyes were gone. The young woman standing before him right now was the Alexa he'd met at Bagram, and he couldn't feel more grateful to have her back.

"It's beautiful up here," Alexa breathed, gesturing around the hilltop crowned with colorful trees. The sky was a deep marine blue with a few fluffy clouds drifting overhead. Breathing in deeply, she leaned against him, her hand on his chest, looking skyward. "I love the smell of autumn leaves, Gage." Turning, she gazed at his ruggedly handsome face, his light blue eyes warm with love.

"Do you wish you were flying your Stearman biplane instead of being chained here to the earth?" he teased, lifting his hand to graze her rosy cheek with his thumb. His touch always aroused her, and he watched her pupils grow larger, her lips part. He fought his desire to take her right there. They had been together for five days, and it hadn't been the right time or place to resume their steamy connection.

"I don't know," Alexa murmured. "It's a perfect day to fly. But right now"—she smiled as she moved her hips suggestively against the thick bulge beneath his jeans—"I like being earth-bound with you." Alexa saw how Gage's expression changed from loving to lusty, and it made her inner thighs dampen even more. She grazed his recently shaven cheek, feeling completely loved and cared for as he tightened his arm around her shoulder. Slowly moving so their hips touched, she pinned herself against him. "I can't really pilot the Stearman and make love with you at the same time."

# The Books of Delos

Title: ***Last Chance*** (Prologue)
Publish Date: July 15, 2015
Learn more at:
delos.lindsaymckenna.com/last-chance

Title: ***Nowhere to Hide***
Publish Date: October 13, 2015
Learn more at:
delos.lindsaymckenna.com/nowhere-to-hide

Title: ***Tangled Pursuit***
Publish Date: November 11, 2015
Learn more at:
delos.lindsaymckenna.com/tangled-pursuit

Title: ***Forged in Fire***
Publish Date: December 3, 2015
Learn more at:
delos.lindsaymckenna.com/forged-in-fire

Title: ***Broken Dreams***
Publish Date: January 2, 2016
Learn more at:
delos.lindsaymckenna.com/broken-dreams

Title: ***Blind Sided***
Publish Date: June 5, 2016
Learn more at:
delos.lindsaymckenna.com/blind-sided

Title: ***Secret Dream***
Publish Date: July 25, 2016
Learn more at:
delos.lindsaymckenna.com/secret-dream

Title: ***Hold On***
Publish Date: August 3, 2016
Learn more at:
delos.lindsaymckenna.com/hold-on

Title: ***Hold Me***
Publish Date: August 11, 2016
Learn more at
delos.lindsaymckenna.com/hold-me

Title: ***Unbound Pursuit***
Publish Date: September 29, 2016
Learn more at:
delos.lindsaymckenna.com/unbound-pursuit

Title: ***Secrets***
Publish Date: November 21, 2016
Learn more at:
delos.lindsaymckenna.com/secrets

Title: ***Snowflake's Gift***
Publish Date: February 4, 2017
Learn more at:
delos.lindsaymckenna.com/snowflakes-gift

# Everything Delos!

**Newsletter**

Please sign up for my free monthly newsletter on the front page of my official Lindsay McKenna website at lindsaymckenna.com. The newsletter will have exclusive information about my books, publishing schedule, giveaways, exclusive cover peeks, and more.

**Delos Series Website**

Be sure to drop by my website dedicated to the Delos Series at delos.lindsaymckenna.com. There will be new articles on characters, my publishing schedule, and information about each book written by Lindsay.

# ETHICS AND THE GOSPEL

*Ethics*
AND THE GOSPEL

T. W. MANSON

CHARLES SCRIBNER'S SONS
NEW YORK

# CONTENTS

# INTRODUCTION

The six chapters of this book were originally given as the
Ayer Lectures in 1952, and subsequently as an Extra-
Mural evening course in Manchester University. They
were repeated later in 1953, in substantially the same form,
as the Ayer Lectures at Colgate-Rochester Divinity School
in the United States of America. In the case of the first four
lectures Professor Manson had prepared a fairly full manuscript; in the case of the last two he had assembled little
more than a synopsis. Five of the lectures were taken down
at Manchester as they were delivered. The first three follow
the manuscript fairly closely, but there is some expansion
and the style is more popular and, indeed, racy in places.
The typescript of the fifth and sixth is of course a great
expansion of the scanty notes. The fourth lecture was
apparently not taken down verbatim (the typescript merely
follows the manuscript); that is why it is shorter than
the others, for there is no record of the way in which
Professor Manson expanded his manuscript in giving the
lecture.

Professor Manson had begun the revision of the first
lecture for publication and the first few pages of the second.
His revision chiefly took the form of adding a number of
references, re-writing colloquial passages and removing
allusions to passing events. The process of preparing these

lectures for publication has therefore consisted in continuing the revision along the same lines. Professor Manson did not work by a series of provisional manuscripts; what he prepared he did slowly and with great care. There is, therefore, scarcely any doubt what he wished to say.

The Biblical passages in the text of the lectures are given exactly as Professor Manson spoke them; some are probably from the new English version of the New Testament due to be published in 1961 (drafts of which he was in the habit of using in lectures), some may be his own translations, and some are from the existing English versions.

The work of checking Biblical references was begun under the direction of Professor Matthew Black of St Andrews, who is Professor Manson's literary executor, by the Revd Alan Quigley, now of Dunedin, New Zealand. It was completed in Manchester by Mr J. W. Rogerson, a student of the Faculty of Theology and of St Anselm Hall, who also undertook most of the checking and searching out of other references.

RONALD PRESTON

*St Anselm Hall*
*University of Manchester*

## *one*

# THE OLD TESTAMENT
# BACKGROUND

IT is possible to begin discussions about ethics along various lines. One of them is the philosophical. Here we begin by recognizing that there is a certain area of human experience which can be called the moral or the ethical field, and that when people start to talk of it they naturally tend to use a number of technical terms like 'good' and 'bad', 'ought' and 'ought not', 'conscience', 'duty' and so on. Then we can set to work by making a careful examination of the technical terms and trying to ascertain exactly what they mean; and go on from that to study different codes of morality and to discuss such questions as whether there is such a thing as an absolute ethical code. Or if we do not care to do that, we can ask ourselves whether there is any general formula which will express what we mean when we talk about things being good and bad. We can, for example, define 'good' as the greatest happiness of the greatest number.

I am not going to attempt anything like this. I propose to begin in a strictly empirical way, and to put before you a survey of the teaching about morality which the Bible offers to anyone who wishes to go into the matter and to know more about it. Let us begin at the beginning, with the Old Testament background. We will take as the starting point of our study a very simple fact, with which most of us are by now quite familiar. Whenever there is a project of some kind of social change, for example the provision of better houses for the masses, almost certainly two voices will be heard in the discussion. One says that the only way to make the slum-dweller better is to remove him from his present environment and put him into better surroundings. It is urged that if you do that and give him a fair chance in a better house with proper amenities and pleasant surroundings, he will adapt himself to his new environment and become a respectable citizen. The other voice, less hopeful, says that if you put the slum-dweller into a better environment before very long he will be storing an extra coal supply in the bath and cutting up the banisters for firewood; and in a few months he will have brought his new house down to the level of the property which he has just left. One party or group says: 'If you want people to live better, you must improve their living conditions'; the other says: 'If you want to improve conditions, you must have better people.' I mention this not in order to adjudicate between these two points of view: it is in fact impossible to do so. You can go and take a look at the average housing estate and you will find parts of it in perfectly good order, while others reflect slum conditions. I mention the fact because it seems to reflect another fact, that our ethical ideas go back to two ways of tackling the problem of living, the Greek and the Hebrew.

For the understanding of the Greek approach it is important to remember that in the great classical expositions of the subject given by Plato and Aristotle, ethics and politics are not two separate sciences but two inseparable parts of a single discipline. That is a point made long ago by John

Burnet.[1] Plato's *Republic* takes it for granted that the basic
problems of personal behaviour and those of communal
organization are essentially the same problems. The only
real difference is that personal behaviour is on a small scale,
while communal behaviour is on a large scale. Aristotle's
*Ethics* and *Politics* are published as separate books but, as
Burnet showed, they are really parts I and II of the same
philosophical enquiry and complementary to one another.
In this way of tackling the problem the chief questions to
ask are (1) what is the essential nature of the good life for
man? and (2) under what social and political conditions
can this good life be realized? It is as simple and practical
as that. First define what you mean by the good life, and
secondly discover how it is attainable. It is understood that
you can, by clear thinking, define the goal, and by appropriate action, get the conditions right. The conditions, of
course, include a great variety of things, of which the most
important is an elaborate educational system. If the conditions are satisfied, people will achieve the good life; or if
they cannot achieve all of it, they will at least achieve as
much as lies within their several capacities. Plato's *Republic*
has no idea that all men are free and equal: in fact no Greek
ideal state is based on the idea that men are equal. Every
Greek state, real or ideal, depends for its economic existence

---

[1] *The Ethics of Aristotle.* Introd., pp. xxiv–xxxi, esp. p. xxvii. 'The
*Ethics* asks the question "How is the Good for Man realized?" and the
answer it gives is that legislation is the means of producing character, and
that upon character depends the possibility of that activity which consti-
tutes Happiness or the Good for Man. The *Politics* takes up the inquiry at
this point and discusses everything connected with legislation and the
constitution of the state. The whole forms one πραγματεία [*pragmateia*] or
μέθοδος [*methodos*] and there is no word anywhere of ἠθική [*ethikē*] as a
separate branch of study.'

in the first place on slavery, and Plato's ideal republic is one of the most sharply defined class societies that was ever invented. The rigid class system runs through it from top to bottom, and it is recognized that within that large society only a very small minority will ever attain the good life in its completeness and perfection. The classes that rank below the philosopher-kings will have a relatively good life; they will do the tasks that lie within their capacity and enjoy such pleasures as are available to them. The defenders of the community will have a satisfying military career; the workers will do their appointed jobs; and in that elaborate system of grading each class will do the task for which it is best fitted and receive a satisfying recompense. At the bottom of the social scale the worker, freeman or slave, can expect but little; at the top the philosopher-king may approach a really full and satisfying life—by Platonic standards; while in between there can be very varying degrees of competence and achievement. It seems to me, looking back on it, that the Greek way is a thoroughly scientific and completely unsentimental way of dealing with the question of individual morality and social organization. No sympathy is wasted on the underdogs; their job is to hew wood and draw water that the system may work efficiently. There is no attempt to assert the principles of liberty, equality, and fraternity. There is no declaration of the infinite value of the individual human soul.

When we turn from the great philosophers of Greece to the great prophets of Israel, we are at once struck by the difference of temper, attitude and approach to the problems of human life. The difference goes very wide and very deep and it is important that we should try to define it as clearly and accurately as we can.

First let us consider the relation between man and society, between the individual and the national or racial or social group to which he belongs. For this purpose we may take, on the one side, the attitude of the Athenian citizen to Athens and compare it with the attitude of the Israelite to Israel. What was it that made the Athenian prize his Athenian citizenship above all earthly goods? I cannot help thinking that, more than anything else, it was the fact that the brilliant culture and civilization of Athens belonged to him. As a citizen he shared in the ownership of the masterpieces of Greek art and architecture, master-pieces which even in ruin still capture the imagination and make us wish we could see them as they once were. The Athenian citizen knew and loved them: they were his, he helped protect them as a soldier in the citizen army; and as a member of the citizen body he had a voice and vote in the maintenance and control of the political system in which they had been produced. He was consciously proud of his membership of a cultured and civilized society and he was complacently contemptuous of the 'Barbarians', who had no such background to their rough and unmannerly life. He was keenly interested in the intricate mechanics of the running of a city-state, and jealously restricted the right to share in the job. More than that, of course, the city-state was a relatively small and manageable concern. It is very difficult for us to appreciate that a city-state, governing an area which in England would come under one of the smaller county councils, could have the power of life and death; power to declare war and make peace; power to do all the things which in our case are done by the Queen's ministers and the Houses of Parliament. And all this power lay in the hands of a relatively small group in which everybody knew everybody else and in which rights and privileges were very jealously guarded.

The Israelite's attitude to Israel is different. The outstanding feature in it is the intense awareness of corporate solidarity. The members of a clan or tribe in Israel feel themselves as parts of a single living whole. The kind of thing that is involved is expressed in the Book of Hosea (2.21–23): 'And in that day, says the Lord, I will answer the heavens, and they shall answer the earth; and the earth shall answer the grain, the wine, and the oil; and they shall answer Jezreel. And I will sow him for myself in the land. And I will have pity on Not pitied; and I will say to Not my people, "You are my people"; and he shall say "Thou art my God".' This refers back to the first chapter of the book, where the prophet has children: first a boy named Jezreel (1.4); then a daughter who, by God's command, is called Lo-ruhamah, meaning 'Not pitied' (1.6); the third child is a boy who has to be called Lo-'ammi, 'Not my people' because God has disowned Israel as his people (1.9). I am not at all sure that 'Not pitied' is the right translation for the girl's name; I think that what is really involved in both cases is the presence or absence of kin-feeling between God and Israel. It really means 'They are no relation of mine, no people of mine'. It is the reversal of recognition, and it goes back to the normal formula for claiming relationship in the semitic world. If you wanted to claim relationship with someone else you said, 'I am bone of your bone and flesh of your flesh'.[1] If your claim was admitted, the answer was 'Yes, you are bone of our bone and flesh of our flesh'. What is claimed and recognized is that you and the others are all part of one living

[1] Cf. Genesis 2.23; 29.14; Judges 9.2f; II Samuel 5.1.

organism. It is very difficult for us to understand this because we are accustomed to thinking of ourselves as individuals, and very much individuals. It is extremely hard to
think ourselves to the point of view where everyone within
the tribe or clan is part of 'one flesh'; where if one member
of the tribe is wounded or killed the tribe says not 'So-and-
so's blood has been spilt' but '*Our* blood has been spilt'.
That intensity of feeling for corporate solidarity has to be
kept in mind continually. It comes out in a very striking
way in Romans 11.14 where Paul speaks of stirring up 'his
flesh' to jealousy, and it is quite clear that 'his flesh' means
his fellow-countrymen, the Jewish people. It underlies his
whole teaching about the Body of Christ.

The difference between the Greek and Hebrew ways of
thinking may be expressed in this way. One Athenian
regards another Athenian as 'fellow-citizen': they are citi-
zens together of the same city. In Hebrew I do not think
there is any term corresponding to fellow-citizen.[1] If one
Hebrew wanted to express relationship to another Hebrew
he had two terms at his disposal, first *rē'a* meaning 'neighbour', and second '*āh* meaning 'brother', and which of
them he used depended on circumstances. The normal
thing in Hebrew usage was to say 'neighbour' if the idea
was uppermost of being members of the same nation by
physical descent, 'brother' if the emphasis was on the sharing of a common religious faith and loyalty. 'Brother' is the
term of relationship when you are thinking of the group in
its religious capacity; 'neighbour' when you are thinking
of it in its political and economic capacity.

[1] *Sunpolitēs* is not used in the Septuagint, and *politēs* is not common.
In the seven places where it can be compared with a Hebrew original, in
one it represents the Hebrew *ben-'amim*, in another '*amith* (fellow, associate, relation), and in the remaining five *rē'a* (neighbour).

That brings us to a further point, the relation between God and Israel. The Greek ethic is concerned with the relation of the individual and the community to certain discussible and definable ideas and ideals: the Hebrew with the relation of the individual and the community to the will of a personal God. In Hebrew ethics the governing factor is the relation of human persons to a Divine Person; and that means that the good is not so much the object of philosophical enquiry as the content of divine revelation. *'He has shown* thee, O man, what is good; and what doth *the Lord require* of thee but to do justly and to love mercy and to walk humbly with thy God?' (Micah 6.8). The emphasis is on God and the things revealed by him; it is a matter of acceptance and obedience. The relation between God and the single living corporate body called Israel is a covenant relation. The terms of the covenant are the commands given and the promises made by God. If Israel will do God's will, then he will be their God and they will be his people. This covenant, with its provisions of commands and promises, is the charter of Israel's existence as the Chosen People of God. The promises are the never-failing source of the national hope and confidence: the commandments are the ever-present challenge to the conscience of the nation as a whole and of every member in particular. *And the important thing is that the commands, no less than the promises, are the gift of God to his people.*

We can now take a further step. Granted that both the commands and promises are a gift from God to Israel, we may add that they are a gift in which God reveals himself; he gives a glimpse of his own nature to his people. This is expressed by a formula that keeps on recurring in the Jewish Law: 'Ye shall be holy, for I Yahweh your God am holy.' That is the ultimate ground of Hebrew ethics: 'You must be holy because Yahweh your God is holy.'[1] We must constantly bear in mind that for the ancient Hebrew what we call the moral imperative came as a revelation of God and was, by that very fact, a call to the imitation of God. 'You are to be holy as I am holy.' This principle runs right through the Bible, till in the Gospel we find Jesus saying 'Be ye perfect, as your heavenly Father is perfect' (Matthew 5.48), 'Be ye merciful, as your Father is merciful' (Luke 6.36), and so on. The last ground of moral obligation is the command of God; and the supreme ideal is the imitation of a God who is at once king and father, who exhibits in the field of nature and history, and above all in his dealings with Israel, the qualities of holiness and righteousness, mercy and faithfulness, love and covenant-loyalty, which are to be the pattern for the behaviour of his subjects and children. It is extremely significant in this con-nexion that the promulgation of the specific laws which go to make up the Old Testament code of conduct is closely and constantly bound up with the record of what God has done for Israel. Regularly when God lays some specific obligation on them, it is prefaced by what he on his part has done for them; and so God's action becomes the stan-dard and pattern on which they are to model themselves. The Ten Commandments begin not with a command-ment, but with a statement: 'I am Yahweh thy God who brought thee out of the land of Egypt, out of the house of bondage' (Exodus 20.2). The code of Deuteronomy is preceded by a detailed history running to four chapters and telling of the marvellous way in which God has led Israel

[1] Cf. Leviticus 11.44 f., 19.2, 20.7, 26; Numbers 15.40 f.; Psalm 16.3, 34.10 (in Hebrew); Daniel 8.24.

from the beginning up to that day. The first three chapters of Deuteronomy give a resumé of the events from the time when the Hebrews left the neighbourhood of Horeb-Sinai until they were on the point of beginning the invasion of the Promised Land. It is made clear that throughout this period the guiding and controlling hand has been God's. It is this fact that justifies the call in Deuteronomy 4 for unswerving loyalty to God and willing obedience to his Law. Only after all this do we come to the actual promulgation of laws and Moses says 'Hear, O Israel, the statutes and ordinances which I speak in your hearing this day, and you shall learn them and be careful to do them' (5.1), and we come to the Deuteronomic form of the Ten Commandments. In the next chapter we reach what has become a central principle of Judaism, the binding together of command and promise: 'Hear, O Israel, and observe to do it; that it may be well with thee, and that ye may increase mightily, as the Lord, the God of thy fathers, hath promised unto thee, in a land flowing with milk and honey' (6.3). But these present duties and future hopes are not set out until it is first stated what God has done for his people in the past. Again, if we take the Pentateuch as a whole, we find that the entire body of the legislation, with its 613 specific commandments (248 positive and 365 prohibitive), is set in a framework of narrative which rehearses the mighty acts of God from the beginning of the Creation down to the eve of Israel's entry into the Promised Land.

This setting of God's requirements in the framework of God's gifts is a phenomenon that constantly recurs in the Bible. It appears in the New Testament and most clearly in the Epistles, where the account of the mighty acts of deliverance wrought by God in Christ is put first and is the prelude to the demands of Christian conduct. See, for example, Romans, Galatians, Ephesians, I Peter. The first eight chapters of Romans deal with the work of salvation which God has accomplished in Christ. In chapters 9 to 11 we have the application of what has been expounded in 1–8 to the special and difficult problem created by the Jewish rejection of their Messiah. Then, when the nature and purpose of God's saving work have been fully and clearly set out, we come (12.1–15.3) to what it expected in the conduct of those who have received God's great gift. The same thing occurs in Galatians, where Faul spends four chapters explaining the inner meaning of the work of Christ and then goes on in the fifth chapter to say something about the nature of Christian freedom. Then, at the end of chapter 5 and the beginning of chapter 6 we have some plain instructions about ways of Christian living, but not before the fact and the quality of God's gift have been established. The same thing also occurs in Ephesians, exposition of divine goodness (1–3); exhortation to Christian living (4–6), and in I Peter, where the work of the Saviour is described in 1.1–2.10, and the duties of the saved in 2.11–5.11.

The importance of all this lies in the fact that it brings us face to face with the essential relation between the kingship of God and the ethical teaching of the Old Testament. In order to have a clearer appreciation of this we must look for a moment at some of the characteristic qualities of Semitic kingship. For this purpose it is useful to consider not only the works of scholarship dealing with the subject, but also the reports of men and women in modern times who have lived and worked among Semitic peoples, particularly among the Bedouin tribes of Arabia. Among the works of scholarship one thinks, for example, of Robertson Smith's *The Religion of the Semites* (with S. A. Cook's additional notes), and Pedersen's *Israel*. One can learn an immense amount from these works of scholarship; but in a different way a vast amount of illumination can be gained from Doughty's *Arabia Deserta*, or Lawrence's *Seven Pillars of Wisdom*, or the works of Miss Freya Stark and other modern writers. In some respects the most helpful works of all are those which deal specifically with the exploits of such men as Feisal and Ibn Saud. Here we can see directly what Semitic peoples look for in a king, what are the qualities in the ruler which alone will command the loyalty and obedience of the people. They can be brought under three main heads.

The first is personal courage and military skill. One of the recurrent themes of Lawrence's *Seven Pillars of Wisdom* is the immense difficulty of organizing the Arab tribesmen into military formations, and of keeping them together as a fighting force for any length of time. Almost the only thing that will do this is the personal prestige and force of character of some individual who stands unmistakably head and shoulders above his fellows in military skill and personal courage. The tribesmen will follow a leader who really leads, who can endure all the hardships that they endure, and more; who will face all the dangers that they face, and more; who knows what he means to do and is not to be cajoled or driven from his chosen path. It is of the essence of the matter that the commander is not a remote military potentate issuing orders from a GHQ away behind the lines. He is in the battle-line in person. In the thick of the fray he is the rallying-point for his men, and if he falters or fails his army will just melt away. In all this there is little difference between the Arabs in the twentieth century A.D. and the Hebrews in the eleventh or the second century B.C. A Saul or a David or a group of Maccabean brothers could rally the people and by winning victories win a throne. But equally any failure or defeat quickly brought the cry, 'To your tents, O Israel!' (I Kings 12.16).

The second special responsibility of kingship among Semitic peoples is the administration of justice. This takes place in public, and that means under the unwinking gaze of a vigilant and highly critical crowd. The king must be able to do two things superlatively well. He must master the great and growing mass of laws, customs and traditions and be able to find and apply the appropriate one in any given case. And he must have all this at his finger-tips ready for use at short notice. So far as I can discover Semitic legal procedure had little room for the reserved judgment. The good judge sees the real issues in the case and gives the right decision on the spot. Not only must he have the knowledge of the law and the ability to apply it; he must also have that peculiar genius that can leap to a fair decision where there is no guidance to be got from the existing law. He must know and apply law; and, if need be, he must make it. In that connexion we may recall the case of the two mothers claiming the one child and Solomon's decision on the matter (I Kings 3.16–27). That is the kind of judgment that never fails to impress Semitic people. The king must be able to say authoritatively what is 'done' or 'not done' in Israel; and he must be able to create new and acceptable rules and precedents to guide future generations. Swift nemesis waits on any failure to carry out that function. One recalls the account, in II Samuel 15.1–4, of the propaganda campaign preceding Absalom's revolt. Absalom is able to say to the litigants, 'See, your claims are good and right; but there is no man deputed by the king to hear you.' It may be questioned whether Absalom could have won over as many people as he did if his father had not been getting a little past full efficiency in his judicial functions. It is no accident that the same root *shāphat* covers both the executive and the judicial activities; and that the men whom the Old Testament calls *shōphĕtĭm*, judges, were also national heroes and rulers of the people.[1]

The third royal activity is connected with worship. In modern travellers' accounts we can read of Arabian kings like Ibn Saud conducting prayers and giving religious addresses. We can find some parallels to this in the history of the Hebrew monarchy, for example Solomon's prayer at the dedication of the Temple, which he had built and furnished (I Kings 8.22–53). And, of course, there is the very striking case of the Hasmonean dynasty, who combined the offices of Highpriest and king.

The ruler may thus be said to stand for the people in face of their enemies, to drive away dangers from outside, and in face of wrong doers within to purify the community from injustice and oppression. He also represents his people before God. At every turn he is intimately bound up with them; and his right to continue in office is closely related to the efficiency with which he discharges his royal tasks. The acid test of the monarchy is the adequacy of the king to meet the needs of his people for security: to give them freedom from fear, freedom from injustice, and freedom to

[1] Cf. the constitution of the great Tyrian colony of Carthage in N. Africa, founded about the end of the ninth century B.C. Here the chief magistrates (judicial and executive) were the two *shōphĕtĭm* (Latin *suffetes*). The word is the same as that used for the 'Judges' in Israel.

worship. This is summed up in the New Testament in the *Benedictus*, where the crowning mercy for Israel under the Messianic King is 'that we, being delivered from the power of our enemies, and free from fear should serve him (God) in holiness and righteousness, remaining in his presence all our life long' (Luke 1.74 ff.).

The ruler who conscientiously and efficiently discharges these duties is in a very real sense God's agent. He can be thought of as God's gift to his people, specially raised up by God to realize God's good purposes for Israel, and to lead them in ways that God will approve (cf. *Psalms of Solomon* 17). Within the limits set by human frailty and fallibility and the shortness of human life the good king does what God does on the grand scale. But no king, however good and efficient he may be as a king, can ever be more than God's agent. God remains the principal; and, in the Old Testament, the measure of a man's adequacy as king is the depth of his loyalty to God and the faithfulness with which he follows God's guidance. The divine verdict on a good king runs like this: 'My servant David, who kept my commandments, and who followed me with all his heart, to do that only which was right in mine eyes' (I Kings 14.8) or this: 'Josiah . . . did that which was right in the sight of the Lord, and walked in the way of David his father, and turned not aside to the right hand or to the left' (II Kings 22.2). By the same token the bad king is thus described: 'Manasseh . . . did that which was evil in the sight of the Lord, after the abominations of the heathen, whom the Lord cast out before the children of Israel . . . And Manasseh seduced them (Israel) to do more evil than did the nations whom the Lord destroyed before the children of Israel' (II Kings 21.2, 9).

We have gone quite a long way without saying anything about what is commonly regarded as the mainspring of Hebrew religion and ethics, the ideals of the Hebrew prophets. I am not going to say much about prophetic ideals because I think that we are apt to misunderstand the prophets if we think of them as setting ethical ideals before their contemporaries. We shall be much nearer the truth if we think of them as the messengers of God to Israel, and in particular to the rulers of Israel. When we look at the great prophets of the period from the rise of Saul to the downfall of the last king of Judah, we cannot but be struck by the extent to which their concern is with the concrete practical issues that confront successive rulers. Time and again the prophet comes on the scene to announce the divine decision about the course of events in the immediate future, a decision that calls for immediate action by the ruler. Or again the prophet comes to pass judgment in the name of God on some act of the king, whether in his public policy or his private life. As two examples out of very many we may take David's census of the people (II Samuel 24) and his treatment of Uriah the Hittite (II Samuel 11–12).

It has been suggested by Wheeler Robinson,[1] and the suggestion has much to commend it, that the Hebrew prophet normally speaks as one who has been allowed to attend the private Council of God. That is to say, when he uses the formula, 'Thus saith the Lord' or 'It is an oracle of the Lord' he is in effect promulgating a divine decree. The most striking example of this is the famous case of Micaiah ben Imlah in I Kings 22. Some of these decrees are concerned with the divine control of history, some with the

[1] Wheeler Robinson, *Redemption and Revelation*, pp. 138 ff.; *Inspiration and Revelation in the Old Testament*, pp. 167 ff.

divine standards of righteousness. In the latter case, what happens is that the prophet formulates in God's name a demand for certain kinds of behaviour or condemns others as intolerable to the living God. So far as the prophetic concern with conduct goes, we might almost say that the prophet is appointed by God to publish the statute law of Israel, to declare the will of the supreme Lawgiver to his subjects. In contrast to this the task of the king is to administer and enforce the statutes of God, and in so doing to produce a certain amount of what we should call 'case law'. The final codification in the *Torah*, with its 613 'Thou shalts' and 'Thou shalt nots', is in large measure the result of many generations of prophetic teaching and of governmental and judicial activity. And, be it noted, the final product is not in the form of a discussion of the nature of the good or of the categorical imperative: it is rather a catalogue of concrete things that must be done or not done, because that is the will of God.

## two

# JUDAISM AND
# THE LAW OF MOSES

ONE very important conclusion from the preceding discussion is that when we speak of the Kingdom of God we are not to think of it primarily as a political organization which can be brought into existence by despotic decree or democratic legislation. For the Hebrew mind it is above all a personal relation between a king and his subjects. The relation is marked on the one side by the complete regal competence of the king, and on the other by the complete trust and loyalty of his subjects. This being so on the human level when the ancient Hebrew used the concept of kingship to describe the rela-tion between God and his people, he thought in terms of complete sufficiency on God's part and complete loyalty on man's. One aspect of God's sufficiency consists in his being the final authority on matters of right and wrong; and com-plete loyalty on man's part calls for total obedience to such direction as God gives. That direction is embodied in what the Hebrews call the *Torah*, a term which is regularly trans-lated in the Greek Bible by the word *Nomos* and in the English versions by the word 'Law'. 'Law' is in many ways a misleading translation because the fundamental idea of the Hebrew word *Torah*, and of the root from which it is derived, is not the idea that in our minds is associated primarily with law. We think of it in the first instance as

something that has been put on the statute book by enact-
ment of some competent authority, and the chief thing
about it is that it imposes an obligation on the subject to
obey an obligation backed by sanctions; so that he incurs
penalties if he does not do what is commanded and refrain
from what is forbidden. The idea that underlies the word
*Torah* is not primarily the formulation of a series of categorical commands and prohibitions with appropriate sanctions, though such an idea is part of its meaning. It is
rather a body of instruction regarding man's place in God's
world and his duties to God and his neighbour. The *Torah*
is the divine guidance as to the right way in which man
should behave as a subject of the heavenly king.

This great corpus of rules of conduct and concrete examples is traditionally ascribed as a whole to Moses. We
should rather regard it as the product of long development
over many centuries, with Moses having had a very large
part in setting the development in motion. This living,
growing body of rules, traditions, and examples becomes,
in the period after the Exile, the Rule of Life for Israel, the
formulation in plain terms of what might be called the
Israelite ideal. It becomes a fixed belief that the truly wise
man is the man who studies and comes to know intimately
this code of conduct, this completely reliable guide to the
art of living. That can be illustrated over and over again
from the Old Testament. Take for example these verses
from Psalm 19 (7–11):

*The law of the Lord is perfect, restoring the soul; the testimony
of the Lord is sure, making wise the simple. The precepts of the
Lord are right, rejoicing the heart; the commandment of the Lord is
pure, enlightening the eyes. The fear of the Lord is clean, enduring
for ever: the judgements of the Lord are true, and righteous*

*altogether. More to be desired are they than gold, yea, than much
fine gold: sweeter also than honey and the honeycomb. Moreover
by them is thy servant warned: in keeping of them there is great
reward.*

It is easy to see what is involved here; the study and practice of the *Torah* is for the devout Jew something more than
a religious exercise, something more than a way of behaving
well; it is a liberal education. By studying it you may not
only achieve virtue; you may also acquire the true wisdom.
The whole activity of the people whom the New Testament calls 'scribes' and Judaism 'Rabbis' is based on this
principle. By constantly turning this law of God over in
your mind and studying every detail of it you can become
a completely educated person. So the content of this code
comes to be looked upon as the very essence of wisdom.
There is nothing more worthy of man's attention and
study.

Similar sentiments are expressed by the author of that
amazing encomium of the *Torah*, Psalm 119. Verses 97 to
104 are a typical section:

*Oh how I love thy law! it is my meditation all the day. Thy
commandments make me wiser than mine enemies; for they are ever
with me. I have more understanding than all my teachers; for thy
testimonies are my meditation. I understand more than the aged,
because I have kept thy precepts. I have refrained my feet from
every evil way, that I might observe thy word. I have not turned
aside from thy judgements; for thou hast taught me. How sweet
are thy words unto my taste! yea, sweeter than honey to my mouth!
Through thy precepts I get understanding: therefore I hate every
false way. Thy word is a lamp unto my feet, and a light unto my
path!*

Just by concentrated attention to the *Torah* this man

claims that he is wiser than his enemies, and more understanding than his teachers and his seniors. He is no more
dependent on human guidance, for he has found the secret
of all wisdom and knowledge. Job 28 and Proverbs 8 and
9 tell a like story. No praise is too high for the *Torah*, and
in the end we find it identified with the wisdom of God
himself!

From the books of Proverbs, Ecclesiasticus[1] and the
Wisdom of Solomon we get the idea of wisdom as existing
before the creation of the world; and on the rabbinic side
this is matched by the idea that the Law existed before the
creation. The second century Rabbi Aqiba says 'The
instrument by which the world was created was the Law.'[2]
We may compare what is said in Proverbs 8.22–31. In the
pre-Christian era the word 'wisdom' has a variety of
senses. On the one hand it is the self-revelation of God, and
on the other it is the highest reach of man's knowledge. But

[1] Ecclesiasticus 15.1: 'He who fears the Lord', that is seeks wisdom,
'and he who takes hold of the Law will find her (wisdom)'.
Ecclesiasticus 34.8: 'The Law will be fulfilled where there is no false-
hood and wisdom will be the perfection of a trustworthy mouth.'
Ecclesiasticus 21.11: 'He who keeps the Law masters its meaning and
purpose, and wisdom is the crown of godly fear.'
Ecclesiasticus 19.20: 'All wisdom is fear of the Lord; and in all wisdom
there is the doing of the Law', that is to say three things, religion, wisdom
and obedience to the Law are aspects of the same achievement.
Ecclesiasticus 24.7–12. Here we have wisdom personified, speaking for
herself. Wisdom says 'With all these', that is all peoples and nations,
'I sought for a resting place and where I should lodge and in whose
inheritance I should find my lodging. Then the creator of all things gave
me a command, and he who created me set my bound and he said,
"Dwell thou in Jacob and take up thine inheritance in Israel". So I took
root among an honourable people in the portion of the Lord and of his
inheritance.'
[2] *Pirkē Aboth* 3.15 (see H. Danby, *The Mishnah*, p. 452).

31

that reach can only be achieved by accepting what is given by God, and it is at the same time the best possible achievement of man's effort.

We have now got to the point where we have a community, a nation whose governor is God. Its members have from God this clear idea as to where they will find their wisdom and their best life, and they are convinced that in following that revelation they can achieve true wisdom and a good life. Let us look a little further into the matter. We probably all realize that there is more to ethical conduct than just finding out what is the wisest thing to do, and then doing it successfully. We realize that underneath everything that is worth calling conduct in any serious sense of the word there lie springs of conduct—ideals, hopes, fears and so on—and that it is these that give character and quality to conduct. If the beggar calls at the back door it may or may not be that the right thing to do is to hand him half a crown or a packet of sandwiches. But if we only give them in order to get rid of him, that is a very different thing from giving because of sympathy for his hard lot. Nor must we suppose that that interest in the psychological background of behaviour is a completely new thing. The Jewish ethic is just as much aware of the motives of conduct as we are. It will clear up our ideas of ethics in Gospel times if we try to find out what were the springs of conduct for the devout and observant Jews.

The first clue is given by the daily religious obligations of every Jew, which is to recite morning and evening the passage known as the *Shĕmaʿ*. The *Shĕmaʿ* occupies in Judaism the place that is occupied in Christianity by the Apostles' Creed and the Lord's Prayer combined. If you can conceive an obligation on every devout Christian to say both

these morning and evening, that would be about equiva-
lent to the Jewish obligation to recite the *Shĕmaʿ*. It consists
of three passages of Scripture in this order: Deuteronomy
6.4–9, 11.13–21; Numbers 15.37–41. It is called *Shĕmaʿ*
because of the first word of Hebrew 'hear' ('Hear, O
Israel, the Lord our God is one Lord'). When the Jew per-
formed this daily ritual in his private prayers he 'took upon
himself the yoke of the kingdom'.[1] The 'yoke of the kingdom' at once called up a picture of two pairs of oxen doing
work for some Jewish farmer. When the devout Jew recited
this daily prayer he felt that he was harnessing himself to
God's plough, God's wagon, God's chariot, putting himself at God's disposal to do whatever God demanded him
to do. He did not go exploring on his own account: rather
he submitted his will to the will of the heavenly King and
went where he was commanded to go and did what he was
commanded to do. The technical name for the whole
system of obedience that is embodied in the Law is the
Hebrew word *hālăkhāh* which literally means 'walking'.
For the devout Jew the *hālăkhāh* is a royal road to walk in,
the King's highway, and it is laid down and marked out
and sign-posted. When the Jew in his public prayers in the
synagogue took part in the recitation of the *Shĕmaʿ* that was
regarded as the proclamation of the kingdom of God.
When you had the whole unit saying in unison the *Shĕmaʿ*,
each one speaking for himself, the kingdom of God was
proclaimed as a present fact. To proclaim the *Shĕmaʿ* was to
promulgate it as a royal decree.

Suppose there is a convert from paganism to Judaism,
what happens then? There is a fixed ritual for the reception
of proselytes, a ritual of initiation into a community whose

[1] See C. G. Montefiore and H. Loewe, *A Rabbinic Anthology*, p. 3.

life is to be lived in obedience to the will of God. At every stage it is impressed on the convert that this is the kind of life that he has to embrace. When he receives the prose/lyte's baptism he has selected commandments read to him, including not only what we should call the important ones dealing with the weighty matters of the Law, but also those that we might consider trivial or relatively unimportant, so that the stress is on the necessity of obedience to the revealed will of God in its wholeness and completeness. Both for the born Jew and the convert to Judaism it is a taking on one/self of the yoke of the Kingdom of God, and a proclama/tion of the kingdom in the life and worship of the com/munity. How is that worked out in detail? We may begin the answer in the light of a saying of the famous pre/Christian Jewish teacher, Simeon the Righteous, who declared that the world is based upon three things, that is to say a true and lasting civilization rests upon three foun/dations, the Law, worship, and 'the imparting of kind/nesses'.[1]

We have already said something about the Law. As it is presented here as a foundation of society it means the whole codified body of commandments giving the revealed will of God, a comprehensive system of rules covering the whole life of the Jew from the cradle to the grave, regulating his work and his worship, his family life and his relations with his neighbours. The development of it as a code extended over many centuries; and the form in which it was taken into the Old Testament canon was the form reached at the time that Palestine was part of the Persian Empire in the fifth century B.C. and the beginning of the fourth. What had been put together up to that time was attributed to Moses,

[1] *Pirkē Aboth* 1.2 (see H. Danby, *The Mishnah*, p. 446).

34

though in fact it was the result of contributions made by judges and kings, prophets and priests during a period of at least eight hundred years. It had two main characteristics. The first is an undivided loyalty to God. The Ten Commandments begin with an unqualified demand for this. It is important to remember the difference between Hebrew monotheism and the monotheism which we derive from Greek philosophical thought. The Greek comes to monotheism through the search for a single explanation for the variety of existence; what the Greek philosophers had been searching for from the beginning is a primary reality or first cause. The Hebrew comes to monotheism by a different road. He comes through the elimination of conflicting claims on loyalty and devotion. Hebrew monotheism is a worship that cannot and must not be shared. The second feature of Jewish Law is its full respect for human personality. There is, incidentally, a striking contrast in this respect between Hebrew law and Roman law. Hebrew law is much less concerned with the rights of property and much more concerned with the rights of personality. Hebrew and Jewish law, both the 'statute law' of the Pentateuch and the 'case law' of the scribal and rabbinical decisions, is primarily concerned with the rights of persons. This is brought out by Finkelstein in his book, *The Pharisees* (p. 66), in which he compares the Sadducees and the Pharisees. There were a number of legal issues on which they took different views, and a detailed examination of these goes to show that the rabbinical or Pharisaic view of the law and the application of it is almost always concerned to assert the rights and dignity of human beings without regard to their social status. They may be free or slave, it does not matter, but they have certain rights and dignities which must be preserved and safeguarded, and the interpretation of the Law is the way of seeking to do that.

Simeon's next foundation of civilization is worship. That means primarily the worship of the Temple, but in process of time it is expanded to cover the worship of the synagogue and the private worship of the individual. It is a highly significant fact that many of the rules concerning Jewish worship are embodied in the Law. That is contrary to the modern tendency in the West, which is to think that nothing of a religious nature is a matter of law. Acts of worship and acts of justice and mercy are alike part of the whole duty of man in Israel. By New Testament times the worship had developed far beyond ʹ.hat was prescribed in the Pentateuch. The rules there governed the Temple ritual; but many Jews seldom, if ever, took part in that ritual. Many never even saw the Temple; perhaps once in a lifetime they might get there for one of the major feasts, but as so many lived elsewhere the rules of the Pentateuch simply did not apply. A Jew living in Rome was under an obligation to present himself in Jerusalem three times a year. That was part of his religious duty. If he had tried to do it he would very likely have had to cease living in Rome altogether. Under such conditions a great many Jews could have kept the letter of the Law only by living in Palestine for six months of the year and going back home in the winter. Clearly this was not feasible, and Jews who were in this position obviously did not derive much good from the daily services in the Temple. They tried to find their normal form of worship in their private devotions and in the services of the synagogue. These things were part of the good Israelite's duty, his duty to God. His prayers and praises, his study of God's word, all were thought of as an offering to God. We are too prone in these days to think of acts of worship in psychological terms. Our main interest is apt to be in their effects on the worshipper. Many people assume that if they are not consciously uplifted by going to church there is no reason why they should continue to go. The Jewish way of looking at the matter was much more concerned with whether or not these acts of worship would be acceptable to God. The punctual performance of religious duties, with due reverence and a turning of the mind and heart towards God, was an obligation and a privilege whether the worshipper felt like it beforehand or not, and whether he felt better for it afterwards or not. The question whether he wanted to go to the synagogue at a set time had nothing to do with the case. His business was to be there. The question whether he felt better afterwards was also irrelevant. It is quite easy, as we all know, for dutiful worship of this kind to degenerate into the mechanical performance of rites that have ceased to have any real meaning to the performer. I do not think that is a serious danger today. We are more exposed in these days to the peril, from which the Jew was set free, of ceasing to worship because we are never in the mood, or because our half-hearted attempts produce no immediate and exciting emotional result.

The last of the three items in Simeon's list is the imparting of kindnesses. This is a phrase almost impossible to translate, yet it is of vital importance for our understanding of Jewish ethics. To say 'the imparting of kindnesses' hardly begins to bring out the wealth of meaning involved. *Hesed* is commonly translated by words like 'mercy' or 'loving kindness'. That brings us nearer to the root meaning, but it is not quite satisfactory because mercy is apt to be somewhat arbitrary. A good deal may depend on the mood at the moment of the person involved. I am much less likely to be merciful if I have a raging headache, when it is difficult to take a detached, much less a merciful, view. But the 'imparting of kindnesses' is not a matter of whims or liberality of decision, it is a settled way of maintaining personal relations; and it is always connected with the maintenance of relations between people who are in a covenant relation with one another. When we use the word 'covenant' the simplest way of understanding what is involved is by considering the relationship between husband and wife, parents and children, friend and friend, or members of the same society who have their association governed by common interests and common obligations. One can act according to the strict letter of the law in such relationships. In that case there is no 'imparting of kindnesses'; there is only justice. 'Imparting of kindnesses' comes in when we start doing more than is required by the strict letter of the law. Strict justice may require that I give three-quarters of my salary or wages to my wife for housekeeping; that is an obligation. But then there is the extra packet of cigarettes or the occasional brooch; that is where 'the imparting of kindnesses' comes in. When some member of a covenant group has not played the game, 'imparting of kindnesses' really means saying, 'So-and-so has behaved in such a way as to forfeit all his rights, but we will not let him lose them. His rights are going to be preserved in spite of the fact that he has forfeited them.' In human society this loyalty to the covenant relation and all that it involves expresses itself in acts of kindness and helpfulness which are the outward and visible expression of an inward and spiritual unity. The 'imparting of kindnesses' is the active kindness, comfort, and support, given by members of the covenant-people to one another, and springing from a deep sense that they are members one of another. It is something that cannot be legislated for, because its very nature is to be the spontaneous and gracious response of brotherly love to a brother's need. In practice, of course, it can be both a very exalting thing and a very degrading thing. We can practise it until it merely means 'you scratch my back and I'll scratch yours'. We can also lift it up to a level of spontaneous feeling of unity.

There are, then, these three foundations of any true and lasting civilization: the standard of conduct, the worship, and a brotherly feeling for one another. If any one foundation is missing the whole structure will suffer. There is an increasing number of people today who think that the defect of our civilization is the lack of the second of the three. We have rules and regulations in plenty. We have a number of striking instances of corporate solidarity. It is the lack of worship that poisons the other two. Let us take a further look into the way of achieving the good life, as it appeared to the Jews, and consider what should be the motives of action in the three areas of life which Simeon stresses. What is required in the attitude and spirit of the doer in order that his fulfilment of the Law, or his act of worship, or his brotherly kindness may be genuine? The Jewish answer to that is again in two technical terms.

*Kawwānāh* has to do with the inward attitude of the doer towards his actions. A rabbi said, 'It does not matter whether you achieve much or little: it does not matter whether you have a big job or a little job, the thing that matters is whether your heart is directed to heaven, whether your mind is directed to God.'[1] The nature of the occupation does not count. It does not matter whether the man in question is a rabbi or a farm labourer: it is all one. What does matter supremely is whether or not in doing the work his intention is to serve and obey God. *Kawwānāh* characteristically belongs to 'religion', in the technical sense, and to ethics as well. In religion, it is the concentration of the mind and heart in acts of worship so that they are a real offering of the self and not just a mechanical performance of the rite. In ethics, it is the intention to do the good act or abstain from the evil deed in conscious and willing obedience to the will of God. Rabbi Me'ir said 'Everything depends on the *Kawwānāh* of the heart.'[2] 'He who prays must direct his heart towards God'[3] (remembering 'heart' in Old Testament and rabbinic usage is regularly used when we should say 'mind'). Another rabbi, Raba, said, 'For *doing* a commandment *Kawwānāh* is *not* required; for committing a sin *Kawwānāh is* required'.[4] That is, the good intention and the good deed have each a value. Man has credit with God for doing the good act. He has credit for intending the good act even if circumstances prevent him from carrying out his intention; but best of all if he has the good intention and carries it out. On the other hand, the intention to do wrong is the thing that makes the wrong act really bad; the act may be done in error or unintentionally without serious stigma. Rabbi Nehemiah said, 'If a man purpose to commit a sin, God does not reckon it to him till he has done it, but if he purpose to fulfil a command, then although he has had no opportunity to do it, God writes it down to him

[1] Montefiore and Loewe, *A Rabbinic Anthology*, p. 272.
[2] *Op. cit.*, p. 272.
[3] *Op. cit.*, p. 274.
[4] *Op. cit.*, p. 275.

at once as if he had done it.'[1] It all comes to this, 'to the rabbis the love of God becomes both the supreme command of the Law and the supreme motive'.[2] This direction of the heart towards God simply means that the final governing motive of all ethical action must be a desire to please God, and that means that the spring of action becomes in the last resort the love of God, so that the command and the motive run into one another.

The other important technical term is what is called *Lishmāh*.[3] Taken literally it means 'for its name'. We can best translate it by saying 'for its own sake'. You do the thing that is right simply because it is right 'for its own sake' and have no ulterior motive whatever. Here again are a few rabbinic examples. Rabbi Banna'ah used to say, 'If one studies the Law for its own sake it becomes to him an elixir of life; but if one studies the Law not for its own sake, it becomes to him a deadly poison.'[4] 'He who busies himself with the Law for its own sake causes peace in the upper and the lower family (i.e. among the angelic hosts and among the sages); he is as if he had built the upper and the lower palace; he protects the whole world; he brings near the redemption.'[5] 'For God's sake, out of love, and *lishmāh*, are really all equal to one another.'[6] 'Do the words of the Law for the doing's sake, and speak of them for their own sake. Make them not a crown with which to exalt thyself, or a hoe with which to weed.'[7] In other words, do not use the study of the Law either to foster your own pride, or to increase your own profits. 'God said to Moses, "Go

---

[1] *Op. cit.*, p. 275.  [2] *Op. cit.*, p. 276.
[3] See G. F. Moore, *Judaism*, vol. II, pp. 96 ff.
[4] *A Rabbinic Anthology*, p. 277.
[5] *Op. cit.*, p. 277.  [6] *Op. cit.*, p. 278.  [7] *Op. cit.*, p. 278.

and tell the Israelites, 'My children, as I am pure, so be you pure; as I am holy, so be you holy, as it is said "Holy shall ye be, for I, the Lord your God, am holy".'[1] 'All man's good deeds must be done in conscious relation to God, and with the thought of love of him continually in his mind. To him alone is the glory, and he must ever be praised.'[2] And finally the statement often repeated and very important, 'All is in the hand of heaven except the fear of heaven.'[3] That is to say, everything is in the power of God except to compel man's reverence. God can do everything except compel someone to worship him. The two concepts, *Kawwānāh* and *lishmāh*, both lie behind that saying.

I do not think that there can be any doubt that, for the rabbis, to do something for the sake of God is more fundamental than to do it for its own sake. This appears from the frequency with which the doing of the will of God is stressed as the motive of conduct. The idea that a good deed should be done for its own sake is present; but it takes second place to the idea of obedience to God. Thus it is not allowed to ask why commandments dealing with what look like minor matters are given the same unqualified status as those dealing with highly important duties. It is pointed out that the same reward is attached to the 'major' commandment to honour father and mother as is attached to a 'minor' commandment. This is to show that it is not permissible to discriminate in this way. Again, you must not ask why a garment of mixed stuffs is forbidden. It is enough that this is the will of your Father in heaven. Your business is to be swift and strong and courageous in obeying it, just because it is his will, and because to conform your will to God's is the only way to a secure and satisfying life.

[1] *Op. cit.*, p. 280.      [2] *Op. cit.*, p. 281.      [3] *Op. cit.*, p. 291.

# three

## JESUS AND
## THE LAW OF MOSES

WE have considered some of the principal ingredi-
ents in Jewish ethics in New Testament times,
and it is clear that we are unjust if we represent
Judaism as being indifferent to the motives for action. The
contrary is the case: while the Jewish Law lays great stress
on the punctual and meticulous performance of the duties
published in the Law, it also lays stress on the necessity of
doing the command for the right reasons. We saw that the
two principal motives to which special value is attached are
the doing of God's commandments just because they are
his commandments and with a view to pleasing him, and
doing a good deed for its own sake without any regard to
what profit it is going to bring you. The one they called
*kawwānāh* and the other *lishmāh*. The two are not incon-
sistent with one another. It is quite possible to do something with the idea of pleasing God and at the same time
to do it for its own sake.

Up till now we have been looking at the ethic of the Old
Testament as developed in the experience of the Hebrew
people through the impact of divine revelation on the facts
of life and history. It is important to remember that the
ethical system set out in the Old Testament, and developed
in the *Mishnāh* and *Talmûd*, is not an ethical system produced by philosophers thinking in the abstract. It is worked

out in the direct experience of life, by the impact of revelation on the hard facts of life and history; and they were hard
facts. Life in Palestine for the Chosen People was an affair
of almost constant turmoil and recurrent crises. There were
only two brief periods in the whole history of the Hebrew
occupation of Palestine when it could be said that the
people enjoyed relative peace, prosperity and security. These
periods, both short ones, covered the greater part of the
reigns of David and Solomon and the decades when the
Maccabean dynasty was in charge in the second and first
centuries B.C. The rest of the time life in their not very
fruitful land was under constant threat from neighbouring
great powers. Century after century the great Empires swept
backwards and forwards in a struggle for mastery of the
Fertile Crescent, and out of that constant crisis the Hebrew
people produced two things: a creed and a code; Jewish
monotheism and the Jewish Law. We have tried to look at
the creed and the code as they were seen by the contemporaries of Jesus, the firstcentury Jews. Now we must
take the next step and try to see them as they were seen by
him.

Is it necessary or desirable to do this? Would it not be
simpler to leave aside the Old Testament and Jewish background and start straight away on the New Testament?
That is something that the Christian Church from the
second century onwards has constantly refused to do, and
for very good reasons. Early in the second century of the
Christian era there was a very devout and saintly heretic
called Marcion who did his best to persuade the Church
to cut completely loose from this Jewish tradition. It was
his view that true Christianity had no roots in the Jewish
past. It was a completely new beginning. Christ had no

Jewish parentage: he appeared without warning, miracu-
lously, mature and full-grown in the synagogue at Caper-
naum on the Sabbath of which Luke tells us in chapter 4
of his Gospel, to reveal a God who had nothing in common with the God of the Old Testament. Marcion did not
deny that the Old Testament was true or that the God of
the Old Testament was a real God. What he did deny was
that the God of the Old Testament had anything to do
with the God and Father of Jesus Christ. They were two
quite different people. But the Church of the second century would have nothing to do with this theory. It held, as
the Church has held ever since, that the entire heritage into
which we have entered is precious. Jesus comes not to
destroy the Law and the Prophets but to fulfil them. He
fulfils them first by understanding them in their deepest
meaning, and second by going beyond them in action.

We must now try to follow Jesus' understanding of the
Jewish Law as it existed in his day. For that purpose we
can hardly find a better focusing point for our study than the
Sermon on the Mount, for it covers a great deal of the
ground in which we are interested. Before discussing its
details I must refer to the background of the Sermon as it is
understood as a result of what may be called the commonly
accepted critical studies of the Gospel of Matthew. We
have there a book made up by adding to the framework
supplied by Mark materials drawn from two other sources,
the source Q (from which Luke also borrowed) and the
source which for convenience is called M, covering the
material that is peculiar to Matthew. That is the usual
critical view. I should add a further element: the religious
and literary gift of St Matthew himself, whoever he was.
That literary and religious gift is often overlooked. It is

what St Paul calls a *charisma*, and I use the word advisedly in connexion with Matthew's editorial activities. We must not think of the evangelists as literary hacks producing gospels by stringing other people's work together; they were genuine composers, with gifts as authentic as those of the poet or the musician or the artist, and a good deal more important.

We must also realize that the five great discourses in Matthew, of which the Sermon on the Mount is the first, are not shorthand records of actual addresses delivered by the Prophet of Nazareth on specified dates at specified places. They are systematic presentations of the mind of Christ on various matters of great moment to his Church. The modern critical position is stated clearly enough by Dibelius in his book, *The Sermon on the Mount* (p. 105), in four propositions:

(1) The Sermon is made up by combining single sayings, which Jesus uttered on various occasions to different people.

(2) These sayings, combined by St Matthew or his source, no longer proclaim a heavenly kingdom, but describe a Christian life on earth.

(3) This involved some adaptation of particular sayings.

(4) The Sermon on the Mount is not the only programme of Christian conduct in the New Testament; but it overshadows all others as the great proclamation of the new righteousness.

I have a few comments to make on each of these four propositions.

(1) The statement that the Sermon is made up by combining 'single sayings'. That is true up to a point. But there is ample evidence in the Sermon itself that some of the

material that is given in it was more than 'single sayings', and that sayings were already combined into short pieces of teaching. For example we have in chapter 5 a number of passages which have a common form: 'You have heard that it was said to them of old time . . . but I say unto you . . .' It is quite clear that we have there a systematic treatment of a number of commandments in the Jewish Law, and I do not think it is in the least likely that this systematic treatment began life as a collection of oddments. It is much more likely that it comes from Jesus himself, and that he dealt with these half-dozen or so commandments at once and not merely in a series of separate sayings. The same holds for chapter 6, where we have a collection of three sayings about various kinds of religious observances.

(2) I think that Dibelius' second point is true. We have a good deal of evidence outside the Sermon on the Mount that parables and sayings, which originally were warnings to the man in the street to flee from the wrath to come, have been adapted by the early Church and have become pieces of good advice for those within the Christian community. One of the simplest and most striking is the piece of advice about coming to an agreement with your adversary in a lawsuit while still on the way to court, in case he takes you and hands you over to the judge, and the judge to the jailor, and you find yourself in prison until the last penny is paid! (Matthew 5.25 f.; Luke 12.57 ff.). It is probable that the original moral of that story was that men and women are living on the edge of judgment, that any moment now they may be called upon to render an account, that it is God with whom they will have to reckon, and that if they have not made their peace with God by repentance here and now they will be liable to find themselves in serious

trouble. The parable says in effect, 'If you are engaged in a lawsuit you have got enough sense to know it is better to settle it outside the court if you can. You have all got a law-suit with the Almighty and the day is coming when out-of-court settlement will no longer be open to you. Be warned!' But as we have it in the Gospels it has become a piece of good advice to Christian people in their everyday relationships. There are a number of other cases where a similar process can be discerned.

It is important to note that the contrast between the heavenly kingdom and life on earth can easily be pushed too far. In the first century men and women lived in a 'three-storey universe'; heaven above, earth on the ground floor, and the abode of shadows underneath. That of course is out of date scientifically. The important point about it for our purposes is that it was taken for granted by those who believed in it that the universe was one single establishment; it was not a three-storey establishment. Therefore an effective kingdom of God was not one which was only effective on the top storey and had no application anywhere else. It had to be effective on all three floors; and the belief that this is indeed the case runs through the New Testament. The Lord's Prayer says: 'Thy will be done on earth as in heaven.' Jesus also said: 'If I by the finger of God cast out demons, then the kingdom of God has come upon you' (Luke 11.20). It is not possible to make a complete distinction between a heavenly kingdom and life on earth. What we may observe is a certain shifting of emphasis, and I think that Dibelius is right in pointing out that the main emphasis has shifted from the future consummation to the present realization. But I should hold that both elements are part of the authentic teaching of Jesus.

(3) It is true that the teaching involves some adaptation of particular sayings, but the amount can easily be exaggerated.

(4) On the point that there are 'other programmes of conduct in the New Testament than the Sermon on the Mount', that is also true, but it has to be understood in the light of considerations that I shall bring forward later.[1]

We have seen that the sources for the Sermon on the Mount from which the Evangelist has drawn his material are the document Q and his own private treasury, which has been called M. A great deal of the material used in the Sermon on the Mount was published in written form, and I should think in Aramaic, round about AD 50, and probably on the early side of 50. The other material, which is peculiar to Matthew, we cannot say very much about: it may or may not have been in documentary form before Matthew got it. All we can say is that it provides a group of teachings that have a strong family likeness.[2]

[1] See Chapter 4.

[2] Abbot B. C. Butler, *The Originality of Matthew*, gives priority to Matthew and regards the document Q as an unnecessary hypothesis. I do not think that this case will stand up to close criticism. We have to look at the material in Matthew's Sermon and compare it with the corresponding sections in Luke. Critical orthodoxy says that the pieces that we find in Luke are part of the raw or partly cooked material out of which St Matthew made the Sermon. Butler says that the Sermon is the source of the scattered fragments in Luke. That seems to me very fanciful. What we are asked to believe is that St Luke, who was himself a very considerable literary artist, found this noble discourse and could think of nothing better to do with it than hack it to pieces. Having done so he planted the battered torso in his own Gospel as the 'Sermon on the Plain', scattered some of the bits and pieces in other more or less unsuitable contexts, and discarded the rest. The motives suggested by Butler for the committing of these atrocities by St Luke (pp. 37–48) seem to me to be quite inadequate; and I find it more rational to suppose that St Matthew created the Sermon than that St Luke deliberately destroyed it.

If the Sermon on the Mount is genuine composition (and I say 'composition' and not 'compilation' or 'fabrication'; 'compilation' was the idea of the older literary criticism; 'fabrication' is what more recent and more radical criticism amounts to, even if it is not said outright; I say 'composition' and I use the word as I should use it of a classical symphony), then careful analysis of the argument is the first step towards understanding it. It is bad procedure to *begin* by trying to break it up into authentic sayings of Jesus, adapted sayings of Jesus, editorial glosses, and the like. That kind of work can only be done at the end of the enquiry. The first task is to understand what the Sermon as a whole and as it stands is trying to say. The task has often been attempted. The most fruitful analysis up to date is that of Windisch.[1]

We begin with a short narrative setting of the scene (5.1 f.). These two verses make a number of important points. They represent the Sermon not as broadcast propaganda, but as formal instruction given to a group of disciples assembled at a suitable quiet place to receive it, the hill-country of Galilee, which was less thickly populated than the plains. At the very outset we are warned against indulging in one of the most insidious and mischievous forms of wishful-thinking, that which says 'If only the principles of the Sermon on the Mount were accepted and applied by politicians, statesmen and industrialists how happy the world would be!' The Sermon is addressed to disciples, not to mankind in general. It does not deal directly with the affairs of the world at large. And in any case it is hardly to be expected that it should find a ready

[1] H. Windisch, *Der Sinn der Bergpredigt*; ET: *The Meaning of the Sermon on the Mount* (Westminster Press, Philadelphia).

market among men of the world, many of whom find even the ten commandments intolerably irksome. The Sermon is not saying: 'This is how men in general should live if they really want to build the kingdom of God on earth.' It is saying: 'This is how you who are in the kingdom of God must live if your citizenship is to be a reality.'

That brings us to the Introduction. The Sermon is addressed to disciples and it begins with Hearty Congratu/ lations, commonly known as Beatitudes (5.3–12). Note that beatitudes and woes are not the same things as blessings and curses. Jesus never cursed the scribes and Pharisees: he uttered woes about them. It is one thing to utter woes and another to utter curses. What he said about scribes and Pharisees was that they were more to be pitied than laughed at. It is one thing to say that X is in danger of damnation and another to say 'X be damned'. Neither are beatitudes identical with blessings. They are congratulations to people on their present position, 'Yours is the kingdom of Heaven'; and on their future prospects, 'You will inherit the earth', 'You will be comforted and satisfied'. These blessings really mean how fortunate are those concerned, how lucky the poor in spirit, for the kingdom of Heaven is theirs; how lucky the meek for they shall inherit the earth. The fact is that these people are actually enjoying or about to enjoy great privileges. However there are no privileges without responsibilities, and so in 5.13–16 we have a statement of these responsibilities. The disciples have to be the salt of the earth and the light of the world. Where much is received, much is required. That is the order in which things happen in the Sermon. First the congratulations, the status, the promise; and only after that the charge, the responsibilities, the tasks. The gift of new life can only be appropriated and enjoyed by living the new life. It is the nature and quality of this new life that is now to be described in detail.

The description is divided into three main sections. I suggest that this threefold division is based upon an ancient and familiar maxim preserved in what was, and is, pro-bably the most popular part of the rabbinic literature, the *Pirkē Aboth*, the Sayings of the Fathers.[1] There we are told the teaching of Simeon the Righteous, to which I have already referred, that the world rests upon three pillars: the Law, the worship and the 'imparting of kindnesses'.[2] The *Torah* is the law of the kingdom of God, that is to say God's revealed will as the standard and pattern of human con-duct; the worship is the divinely ordained means of access to God's presence, the way of fellowship with him, and the 'imparting of kindnesses' is the practical expression of brotherhood and corporate solidarity within Israel, a mutual loyalty within the covenant, shown in thought, word and deed.

The Sermon takes these fundamentals of Judaism and restates them as fundamentals of the New Israel living under the New Covenant. So we have the New Law (5.17–48), the New Standard of Worship (6.1–34), and the New Standard of Corporate Solidarity (7.1–12). The account of the New Law has a clearly marked beginning and end. It begins in verse 17 with the statement 'Do not imagine that I have come to destroy the law or the prophets: I have not come to destroy but to fulfil. For I tell you that until heaven and earth pass away, one jot or one tittle shall in no wise pass away from the law, till all be fulfilled.

[1] See H. Danby, *The Mishnah*, pp. 446–460.
[2] *Pirkē Aboth* 1.2 (Danby, p. 446).

Whoever therefore shall relax one of the least of the commandments, and teach other men to do so, shall be called least in the kingdom of heaven: but whoever does and teaches them he shall be called great in the kingdom of heaven. But I tell you that unless your righteousness exceeds the righteousness of the scribes and Pharisees you shall by no means enter the kingdom of Heaven.' There it begins, and it goes steadily on to verse 48 where the matter is summed up in a single statement: 'You therefore must be perfect, as your heavenly Father is perfect.' That means that the ultimate standard is God the Father himself. But when we turn to the actual content of the Law as set out, we find that knowledge of the Father is through the Son: there is real concrete instruction given in the form '*I* tell you'. This 'I tell you' is something that is presented to the followers of Jesus both in word and deed. It is very difficult to find anything in the way of positive instruction in the Sermon on the Mount that cannot be paralleled in the actual conduct of the Preacher of the Sermon. Whatever else may be true of the Sermon on the Mount, it is not a sermon that says 'Do as I say and not as I do'. This is borne out by the introduction of the New Law, particularly in 5.17 f., and especially in the words 'I have not come to destroy but to fulfil'. It is to be noted that these words are said not of prophecy alone, but of the Law and the Prophets. 'Do not suppose that I come to fulfil *either* the Law *or* the Prophets. I come to fulfil both now.' That means, in the broadest sense, that what has to be fulfilled is the terms of the covenant, including both the commandments and promises of God. The commandments are in the Law and, roughly speaking, the promises in the Prophets. These two things together make up the terms of the covenant between

God and his people. You fulfil a prophecy by making it come true: you fulfil a command by obeying it. To fulfil the Law and the Prophets is thus to make the New Covenant a reality, a reality into which men may enter forthwith. When they do, they become subject to its New Law; and the New Law is the holy will of God made visible in the obedience of Christ.

Turning to the contents of the New Law we observe that the framework is in the form 'You have heard that it was said to them of old time . . . but I say to you'. That formula occurs five times, introducing pronouncements on such things as murder, adultery, perjury, punishment, and communal loyalty. The tendency in the past has been to make the difference between Jesus and those who went before him something like this: that the old Law simply insisted on the outward good, whereas Jesus insists on the inward motive. This will not do. We have already seen that the Jewish ethic *did* insist on inward motive as well as on outward good. The difference lies elsewhere, and we will come to it in due course.

I turn now to the second important section, dealing with the new Worship (6.1–34). Here again we have a recurrent formal structure. There is the general introduction: 'Beware that you do not your righteousness before men, to be seen of them; else you have no reward with your Father which is in heaven. When you are doing charity do not sound a trumpet before you, as the hypocrites do in the synagogues and in the streets, that they may have glory of men. Verily I say unto you, they have received their reward. And when you are praying do not be like the hypocrites: for they love to stand and pray in the synagogues and in the corners of the streets, that they may be seen of men. Verily I say unto you, they have received their reward.' In verse 16 we come to the third section which has to do with fasting. 'When you fast do not be like the hypocrites, of a sad countenance: for they disfigure their faces, that they may be seen of men to fast. Verily I say unto you, they have received their reward. But when you fast, anoint your head, and wash your face; that you be not seen of men to fast, but of your Father which is in secret: and your Father, which seeth in secret, shall reward you.'

In these three instances we have the fixed form in which the teaching is presented. It is interesting to pause for a moment on the three things that make up the content of worship as understood in the Sermon. Prayer and fasting are not entirely surprising, but why almsgiving as a particularly religious exercise? It is significant that after the destruction of the Temple in A.D. 70 and the consequent cessation of the sacrificial ritual, it was laid down by the rabbis, who set to work to pick up the pieces of Judaism, that almsgiving would be in God's eyes an acceptable substitute for sacrifice. It is therefore perhaps not surprising that the section on the new Worship has a lot to say about almsgiving. Matthew 6.2–4 prescribes secret almsgiving as parallel to secret prayer and fasting. Another passage further on (6.19–21) deals with treasure in heaven; and we learn from other sources how treasure in heaven is acquired (Mark 10.21). Then there is the further saying about the good and evil eye (6.22 f.). In this context it is more than likely that the good eye signifies generosity and the evil eye meanness. Finally there is the statement in verse 24 that the kind of service that the new worship calls for cannot be divided between two masters, 'You cannot serve God and Mammon'. As a corollary to this, freedom from care and anxiety is inculcated in 6.25–34. Almsgiving, prayer and fasting alike point this way. The simple trust in God which is involved in true prayer, the generosity of true almsgiving, the self-denial of true fasting, all involve a certain sitting loose to possessions and a consequent release from anxiety.

In chapter 7 we have a statement of the need for right relations with our neighbours, the demand for a new spirit of corporate solidarity. It opens, interestingly enough, with a prohibition of censoriousness. One of the standing dangers of moral achievement under any ethical system is that we begin 'to trust in ourselves that we are righteous and despise others' (Luke 18.9). That is one of the things that cannot be tolerated in the New Israel. And it is very significant that the first duty towards one's neighbour is the duty of not looking down one's nose at him. At the same time there must be some discrimination, 'Do not give the holy thing to the dogs and do not cast pearls before swine.' What is in mind is that there must be, in the nature of things, some reserve; there is a duty to maintain and safeguard good and holy things, as well as a duty to be kind to others. Christians are required to follow the 'friend of publicans and sinners' (Luke 7.34), but they have also to keep constantly in mind that the level of the association was fixed by him and not by them: they met on his ground and not on theirs. This section ends with a general statement of the covenant rule for relations with our neighbours. That is expressed in the Golden Rule; things that you would like people to do to you, you should similarly do to them, for this is 'the Law and the Prophets', or as we might put it, this is the essence of the covenant.

In 7.13–29 we have the summing up of the whole matter. First in verses 13–14 it is emphasized that there is a choice to be made and a decision taken; in verses 15–20 there are warnings against people who would divert attention from the real issues; in verses 21–23 there is a clear statement of the necessity for real decision as distinct from mere verbal profession; this is followed in verses 24–27 by the parable of two believers. In verse 28 the evangelist ends with his regular formula 'And it came to pass that when Jesus had finished these sayings, the multitudes were astonished at his teaching: for he taught them as one having authority, and not as their scribes'.

When we look at the Sermon as a whole, we have to ask whether it gives a fair picture of Jesus's attitude to, and his understanding of, the Jewish spiritual heritage. I think that in the main it does. There is a great deal in it that can be paralleled from Jewish sources. That was brought out in a rather polemical way by a well-known Jewish rabbi, Gerald Friedlander, in his *Jewish Sources of the Sermon on the Mount*. His main thesis was that any good in the Sermon on the Mount can be paralleled from Jewish sources, and that nothing that cannot be paralleled from Jewish sources is any good. That is a distorted and polemical way of saying that the Sermon on the Mount takes the best and deepest things in the Jewish creed and code of conduct and adds to them the still deeper insights of Jesus himself. If we ask what these deeper insights are, the answer must be they are the things embodied in his Messianic Ministry. And it is to that we must now turn.

# *four*

## THE FOUNDATION OF CHRISTIAN ETHICS: FOLLOWING CHRIST

I HAVE suggested that Jesus summed up the New Law in the commandment: 'Be ye perfect as your heavenly Father is perfect.' This does not mean setting up some completely new and unheard of ethical standard to replace the existing standard of the Old Testament and of Judaism. On the contrary the very form of the new commandment immediately reminds us of the old commandment of the Law: 'Ye shall be holy, for I the Lord your God am holy' (Leviticus 19.2). The Jewish rabbis had fastened on that commandment and construed it in their own way as calling upon God's people to be separated from all the abominations of the surrounding heathenism. The required holiness was to be modelled on the white-hot purity of God in whose presence evil cannot survive. Jesus does not deny that ideal. He adds to it. He asks not merely that his followers should keep clear of the contagion of evil; but also that they should show in their lives some positive quality akin to the positive creative goodness of God.

'Be ye perfect as God is perfect.' That is a very tall order. It is worth our while to pause for a moment on this motion of 'perfection'. A good way of approaching it is by considering what is meant by the doctrine of the 'sinlessness' of Jesus. Obviously this cannot be historically demonstrated: we know only a small fraction of the total thoughts, words, and deeds of Jesus. Anything we say must be based on these samples. If we predicate that Jesus was perfect as his Father in heaven is perfect, it must be in virtue of some discernible quality in the samples of his conduct that we possess.

Here it becomes relevant to consider 'perfection' as we use the term in relation to a work of art. For every artist there comes a moment when he has to say, 'This is as good as I can make it. Any change after this will be for the worse.' Not only can he not better it. Neither can we. The art in question may 'progress' in all kinds of ways; but not even Beethoven attempts to revise Bach or Mozart. But a Brahms can write variations on a theme of Haydn. Is there not about the words and deeds that make up the ministry of Jesus a moral quality analogous to the artistic quality that makes a great masterpiece of music or poetry or painting? And is not the challenge of 'Be ye perfect . . .' a challenge to produce words and deeds of a quality similar to that which we discern in those of the Master, and to follow him (Matthew 19.21)?

Is there any brief and compendious way in which we can describe what is involved in following Christ? One thing can be said right away. To follow Christ is not to go in pursuit of an ideal but to share in the results of an achievement. Christ does not ask anyone to go where he has not already been himself, or to do anything that he has not already done himself. The stiffest question he asks a disciple is, 'Can you drink the cup that I drink, and share in the baptism that I undergo?' (Mark 10.35–45; Matthew 20. 20–28). With him we are never on uncharted ways for he is always ahead of us. He sends no man to warfare at his own charges. Or in the words of Richard Baxter[1]

[1] Lines from his *Poetical Fragments* (1681) which appear in many hymn books in stanzas beginning 'Lord, it belongs not to my care'.

Christ leads me through no darker rooms
Than he went through before;
And he that to God's kingdom comes
Must enter by this door.

Now we can go a step further in the search for what is
involved in following Christ. The starting point is the
story told in St Mark (12.28–34):

One of the scribes, who had been listening to the
debate between Jesus and the Sadducees, and had ob-
served how well he answered them, came forward and
put the question, 'Which is the first commandment of
all?' Jesus replied, 'The first commandment is, "Hear O
Israel, the Lord our God, the Lord is one: and thou shalt
love the Lord thy God with all thy heart and all thy soul
and all thy understanding and all thy strength." And
here is the second, "Thou shalt love thy neighbour as
thyself." There is no other commandment greater than
these.' 'Well spoken, Master,' said the scribe; 'What you
say is quite true. For he is one, and there is no other
beside him; and to love him with one's whole heart and
understanding and strength, and to love one's neighbour
as oneself is a far bigger thing than all the burnt offerings
and sacrifices.' This reply showed Jesus that the man
was thinking seriously, and he said to him, 'You are not
far from the kingdom of God.' After that nobody ven-
tured to put any more questions to him.

It has often been suggested that here we have the quintessence of Christian ethics. The two great commandments
sum up the whole duty of a Christian man; and the great
originality of Jesus lies in the fact that out of the vast corpus

of Jewish Law and tradition he chose just these two precepts and gave them an absolute priority over all the others. There is a measure of truth in this view; but it has to be qualified in several points. Let us look at the incident a little more closely. What is reported is a talk between two Jews in Jerusalem in the early thirties of the first century. One is a professional scholar, an expert in the interpretation of the Law and the tradition. The other is the Galilean teacher Jesus of Nazareth. They are discussing the Jewish way of life, and the particular point in debate is whether it is possible to find in the Law any single, simple, and all-embracing rule of behaviour. Jesus says 'Yes: among all the commandments, that found in Deuteronomy 6.4, "Hear O Israel . . ." comes first' (it was part of the *Shĕma'*, and therefore part of the daily obligation of every devout Jew to repeat in his prayers); 'and—for good measure—the second is "Thou shalt love thy neighbour as thyself" (Leviticus 19.18). No other commandment takes precedence of these. All others give place to them.' The parallel passage in St Matthew (22.40) has the statement that the whole of the Law and the Prophets depends on these two commandments.

All this, however, adds up to the somewhat unexpected result that the two great commandments are presented by Jesus and accepted by the scribe as the quintessence, not of Christian ethics, but of the Jewish Law. It can further be urged that closer examination of the second great commandment shows that it lacks something. I am to love my neighbour as I love myself. How do I love myself? Most of us, if we are candid, must answer 'selfishly'. To love my neighbour as myself may therefore be no more than a kind of sublimated selfishness. Be that as it may, there is no escape from the fact that these two commandments are the quintessence of *Jewish* ethics.

What then is the differentia of Christian ethics? The answer to this question was clearly expressed a century ago by the famous English preacher F. W. Robertson of Brighton. It is in the sixteenth sermon of the series preached at Brighton.[1] The secret is the text in the Fourth Gospel (13.34): 'I am giving you a new commandment; it is that you love one another. As I have loved you, you are to love one another.' 'As I have loved you'; that is the character, istic and hall-mark of the gospel ethic. The injunction is repeated later on in these Farewell Discourses in St John's Gospel: 'This is my commandment, that you love one another as I have loved you' (15.12). We may note the occasion of these sayings. They belong to the night before the Crucifixion. The first promulgation of the *new* commandment comes in the discourse after the footwashing and can be linked up with an earlier statement concerning it, 'I have set you an example, that you should do as I have done to you' (John 13.15).

Why was Peter unwilling that Jesus should wash his feet? He wanted Jesus to love him, but he also wanted Jesus to keep his dignity. This utter self-giving shocked him: it seemed to him abject and almost grovelling. 'Lord thou shalt never wash my feet' means, 'You don't know what is due to yourself; I do, and I am not going to let you demean yourself in this way.' But Jesus insists on demeaning himself in this way and doing for his friends what was slave's work.

[1] F. W. Robertson (1816–53). His sermons have been published in various editions since they were first issued posthumously in 1855, 1857 and 1863.

The second promulgation of the new commandment comes later the same evening. Its immediate context is the thought of the swiftly approaching Passion and the laying down of the Messiah's life for his friends. 'Love as I have loved you' calls for a love which has forgotten the meaning of self-regard, of what we call 'looking after number one'. It is totally unselfish. It is love of the quality that marks the Ministry of Jesus all through and reaches its crowning manifestation on the Cross. As St Paul puts it, 'He loved me and gave himself for me' (Galatians 2.20). This total self-giving is the characteristic feature of the ethic of Jesus. We may note four key points about it:

(1) It is not merely an ideal: it is act and deed. It is the way Jesus carries out his life-work.

(2) It goes beyond the highest requirement of the existing Hebrew-Jewish code by requiring a more complete love of neighbour than is involved in loving him as much as, or in the same way that, I love myself.

(3) In doing this it does not abrogate the old standards; for *love* is still the essential thing in the teaching of Jesus as it is in Leviticus and Deuteronomy. It does not abrogate: it fulfils. Jesus shows what is really involved in love of neighbour; and shows it in thought, word, and deed.

(4) As we have already seen it is not the case (as many think) that Jesus stressed the inward springs of action, the motives by which we are led, as against Judaism which was concerned merely with outward acts. Not only is such a view unjust to Judaism, which had a lot to say about *kawwānāh* and *lishmāh*, but it also fails to bring out the true significance of the teaching of Jesus. Hatred and lustful desire are not just unhealthy psychological conditions in the person who has them: they are wrongs done to the

person towards whom these thoughts are directed. What Jesus is saying is that if you are to love your neighbour with the kind of love that God requires you must not only treat him rightly and speak to him rightly; you must think about him rightly. To love as Christ loves means to put so high a valuation on your neighbour that it will be as impossible for you to harbour evil thoughts about him as to do him a physical injury.

It may be asked what harm hate in the heart or lust in the eye do to anyone but the person who harbours them. But it does not require much sensitiveness to the nuances of human behaviour to know that hate can be felt outside the hater without a word spoken or a hand raised; and there can be a horrible awareness of the predatory eye. In fact the modern emphasis on the inner springs and motives of action is appropriate to the formulation of the ethical ideal as one of self-realization rather than that taught and lived by Jesus. It is this ethic of self-realization which leads to the explicit or implied corollary that wrong-doing is most harmful to the wrong-doer. So we get in many quarters a general attitude that forgets the wrongs done to the victims of crime (always more than the wrongs of the individual actually robbed, raped, or murdered) in concern for the psychological health of the criminal and enthusiasm for reforming him. The Prodigal does not say 'I am the victim of a psychological upset'; he says, 'I have sinned *against heaven* (i.e. God) and in thy sight' (Luke 15.21). More concern about the wrong done would balance matters, and that means at least two things, that the wrong-doer must admit that he has done wrong, and that he must make reparation.

The new commandment given and lived by Jesus therefore goes beyond Jewish ethics, but does not abrogate it.

'I am not come to destroy the Law and the Prophets but to fulfil' (Matthew 5.17). We can see how profoundly true that is when we put three sayings together. *The Law* says: 'Ye shall be holy, for I the Lord your God am holy.' *The Sermon on the Mount* says: 'Be ye perfect as your heavenly Father is perfect.' *The Farewell Discourse* says: 'Love as I have loved you.' The ethical demands of the Law and the Prophets are not cancelled; they have become flesh and have dwelt among us in the person and work of our Lord Jesus Christ.

What then? Are we left with a new and still more exacting code than that of the Jewish law? Are we left with a supremely noble and heroic example which we are to try, however vainly, to follow? This is no good news! It also leaves two major problems on our hands. The first is that of seeing how the new standard is to be applied to the life of our own day. The second is that of finding the power to put into action what we see to be the right and good thing. These are in fact our urgent and practical problems, but the Christian way of approaching them frees them from the feeling of being an intolerable burden as they might at first appear to be.

We must recall the fact that the ethic of the Bible, from beginning to end is the ethic of the kingdom of God. In the Christian era that means that Christ is reigning in the world as God's vicegerent. He is *reigning*. In terms of Semitic kingship, that is of kingship as understood in the Bible, it means that we can look to him for reliable direction on our moral problems, as Semitic peoples looked to their kings. The nature of Christ's kingship, however, is such that it has very different corollaries for the problems of Christian behaviour.

(1) We cannot fall back on mere legalism. The Sermon on the Mount, if made into a new cast-iron Law, will only produce a new Pharisaism, more intolerant and more intolerable than the old.

(2) We cannot be content with mere mechanical imitation of Christ. Progress in painting does not come by copying the old masters, though copying is an essential part of the artist's training. Jesus called the Twelve to be with him and learn his ways, and then to go out and do things for him. Each situation that calls for our action is unique and demands a unique response.

(3) We must bring to the task of Christian living a creative initiative, based on the Law and the Prophets, instructed by the words and deeds of Jesus, and able with him as guide to deal constructively and imaginatively with the problems of our time.

An illustration from the world of music will give an indication of what I mean. Sir Donald Tovey writes: 'Classical counterpoint is harmony stated in terms of a combination of melodies: classical harmony, when correctly translated from whatever instrumental conditions may have disguised it, is the result of good classical counterpoint where the minor melodic lines are not meant to attract attention. Modern counterpoint tends actually to avoid classical harmony. It prefers that simultaneous melodies should collide rather than combine; nor does it try to explain away the collisions. It wishes the simultaneous melodies to be heard; and if they harmonize classically the combination will not assert itself as such. Hence modern counterpoint is no longer a technical matter at all; its new hypothesis has annihilated it as a discipline. But this very fact has thrown new responsibilities on the composer's imagination. A technical discipline becomes a set of habits which, like civilization itself, saves the artist from treating each everyday matter as a new and separate fundamental problem. The rule-of-thumb contrapuntist need not trouble to imagine the sound of his combination; his rules and habits assure him that it cannot sound wrong. The composer who has discarded those rules and habits must use his imagination for every passage that he writes without their guidance. It is by no means true that mere haphazard will suit his purpose. Nor, on the other hand, is it true that any great classical master used rules as a substitute for his imagination. One of the first essentials of creative art is the habit of imagining the most familiar things as vividly as the most surprising. The most revolutionary art and the most conservative will, if they are both to live, have this in common, that the artist's imagination shall have penetrated every part of his work. To an experienced musician every score, primitive, classical, or futurist, will almost at a glance reveal the general question whether the composer can or cannot use his imagination.'[1]

Something like this has to happen in the ethical sphere. We are living in the kingdom of God under the rule of Christ. Christ is adequate to all the demands that we can make on him. As with the good king in the Hebrew idea of kingship, we can rely on his judgment. This means that we are not tied hand and foot to a written code. Equally we are not left to our own devices. We have before us the records of the kingdom in the Old Testament, the New Testament, and Church History. From those records we can learn about the ways of the kingdom. But we have also

---

[1] *Essays in Musical Analysis*, vol. iii, pp. 220 f. Quoted by kind permission of the Oxford University Press.

a living king; and we have the assurance of his direct aid through his spirit as we seek to understand and apply the will of God in our own affairs. The springs of revelation are not dried up. The living Christ is there to lead the way for all who are prepared to follow him.

More than that, the strength to follow is there too. The living Christ still has two hands, one to point the way, and the other held out to help us along. So the Christian ideal lies before us, not as a remote and austere mountain peak, an ethical Everest which we must scale by our own skill and endurance; but as a road on which we may walk with Christ as guide and friend. And we are assured, as we set out on the journey, that he is with us always, 'even unto the end of the world' (Matthew 28.20).

# *five*

## THE EARLIEST
## CHRISTIAN COMMUNITY

U P till now we have been surveying the ethical ideals of the Old Testament and of early Judaism, and we have tried to understand the way in which Jesus fulfilled these ideals in the words and deeds of his ministry. That ministry had a sequel. There came into existence a new social organism, the Christian community, the Church, the New Israel, the Body of Christ. In the next chapter we shall see how this community held as one of its most treasured possessions the *corpus* of teaching which laid down the law of Christ and which showed ways in which its principles could be applied to human affairs in all their variety and complexity. But first we must consider the Church itself as the *milieu*, the environment, of Christian ethics; the order of society in which the law of Christ is the law.

It is important that we should avoid the anachronistic reading back into the first century of later ideas and actualities. It is through doing this that many people have come to deny the authenticity of the sayings about the Church attributed to Jesus in St Matthew 16.18 and 18.17. You start off with the idea that Church means an ecclesiastical organization with Archbishops, Bishops, Moderators, Sung Eucharists, Prayer Meetings and the like: then you realize that these things were probably not in existence in

the early decades of the Church and that Jesus cannot have
had them in mind; then you conclude that he cannot have
used the word 'church'. But this is simply because you have
already put your own meaning on the word 'church' and
have not stopped to ask what he meant by it, supposing he
used it. As a matter of fact the word 'church' was in existence long before the time of churches—at least the word we
translate by 'church'. The Hebrews had a word for it; the
Greeks had a word for it; the Greek-speaking Jews had a
word for it. The word put into the mouth of Jesus in
Matthew is the word *ecclēsia*. It is quite a common word in
the Septuagint (or Greek version of the Old Testament).
It is regularly used to translate perfectly the Old Testament
word *Kāhāl*. Now the *Kāhāl* was something that had been
in existence for centuries before the beginning of the
Christian era. The idea of the *Kāhāl* was already familiar
to the Christians of Galilee, Judæa, Jerusalem and Damascus in the second quarter of the first century. But *ecclēsia* in
Greek and *Kāhāl* in Hebrew did not mean the kind of
church structure that we find in the third quarter of the
second century where there is a well-organized community
of bishops, presbyters, deacons and readers, organized
primarily for what we should call religious exercises in the
strict sense of the word.[1] It meets at regular intervals, under
proper direction, to hold religious services, of which the
most important is the eucharist. This is at the latter end of
the second century; but it is not there in the first half of the
first century.

We can go further than this. If it is wrong to think of the

---

[1] Cf. *The Apostolic Tradition* of Hippolytus (various editions) which
contains details of rites and practices presumably in use at Rome in the
early third century.

Christian community of the thirties and forties of the first century as much the same kind of institution as we find 150 to 200 years later, it is nearly as wrong to suppose that the Christian community immediately after the resurrection should be thought of as a synagogue of the Jewish pattern, or even as an eccentric kind of synagogue. The forms of worship in the Church borrowed a good deal from those of the synagogue. But, so far as I can see, all the evidence from the New Testament suggests that the members of the primitive Church in the thirties and forties thought of themselves neither as a synagogue, nor as a church in our way of thinking, that is primarily as a group for holding religious services. Historically the *Kāhāl* or the *ecclēsia* is not primarily a prayer meeting or religious gathering. It is the people of God, functioning as a people in the full exercise of all their communal activities and not just in their organized religious observances in some sacred edifice. I am very much inclined to think that we should look for the nearest analogy to the structure of government of the primitive Palestinian Christian community in those other communities of which we have begun to learn a great deal more in recent times. We have had for a long time a certain amount of information, limited in quantity but interesting in quality, regarding the community of the Essenes. We know about them from Josephus[1] and other authorities. We also know from Philo[2] about another community in Egypt called the Therapeutae. The discovery of a great horde of Jewish documents in the old synagogue near Cairo[3] at the end of last century brought to light another sect or group, that known under various names but most

---

[1] See *The Jewish War*, II. viii. 6.
[2] *de vita contemplativa* 2 (12).     [3] See P. Kahle, *The Cairo Geniza*.

frequently as the Covenanters of Damascus. The recent discoveries of the Dead Sea Scrolls have shed more light on that particular group, or if not on that group, on some other group very closely allied to it; but they look as if they were the same. The characteristic of all these groups, with the possible exception of the Therapeutae, is that they are not content simply to organize religious beliefs and worship; they are concerned with the whole range of the life of the society. In some ways they resemble monastic communities in that the members share a common life, which includes a great deal of religious observance, but also includes other things which we should not regard as directly religious work, meals, friendship, intercourse with one another, all governed by the rules of the community.

When we look at the early Church as it is described in Acts, we are apt to be a little blinded by the fact that it is so full of public addresses. Periodically St Peter gets up and preaches sermons to the general public: these sermons occur so regularly[1] that we tend to think of the life of the early Church as having consisted in meetings for public worship at which somebody preached a sermon. If we look a little more closely we get a different impression.

Let us begin with the question in the first chapter of Acts, where at verse 6 we are presented with a picture of the disciples talking with the Risen Lord after the resurrection and putting a question to him: 'Lord, are you restoring the kingdom to Israel at this present time?' He answered, 'It is not for you to know the times or the seasons, which the Father has set under his own authority. But this is what will happen: you will receive power when the Holy Spirit has come upon you, and you will be my

[1] Acts 1.15–22; 2.14–36; 3.12–26; 4.8–12.

72

witnesses both in Jerusalem, and in the whole of Judaea and Samaria and to the farthest limits of the country (or the earth).' That is the first intimation of what the original followers of Jesus were looking for after the resurrection, and of what they were instructed to expect. They were looking for the restoration of the kingdom of Israel, that is the restoration of national autonomy. At this point I refer you to Vernon Bartlett, the church historian, for an exposition of the bearing of this conversation on our ideas of the Catholic Church. He points out rightly that this question, by its national conception of the kingdom to be restored, was a purely Jewish view of the form of the kingdom. It was on a national and not on a universal basis: that is to say, it was not a Catholic Church at all.[1] What they are to expect is not the restoration of national autonomy, still less the establishment of an Israelite world empire. What they are to expect is the visitation of the Holy Spirit, which will bring to them power, and in that power they will be witnesses in Jerusalem, Judaea, Samaria and to the farthest frontier of the country, or the earth as the case may be (the word *gē* can mean either). It is interesting to notice that only Judaea and Samaria are mentioned: there is nothing about Galilee. It has been suggested by Lohmeyer that Galilee did not need to be mentioned because it was already well filled with Christians. It was already Christian territory.[2]

As the chapter continues we learn that after the departure of the Risen Lord the disciples returned to Jerusalem and went into the upper room. Then it says: 'All these were assiduous with one accord in prayer, along with the women

[1] V. Bartlett, *Church Life and Church Order*, pp. 26 ff.
[2] *Galiläa und Jerusalem*, p. 52.

and Mary the mother of Jesus and with his brethren. And at that time Peter stood up in the midst of the brethren and said (and the number of persons gathered together was about 120).' That is significant, for according to the *Mishnah* 120 is the minimum number of Jews to form a community and to have a Sanhedrin of their own.[1] Then we learn how they took steps to fill the vacancy caused by the death of Judas Iscariot. Now what is the purpose of that step? The first thing to be realized is that it is unique in the history of the Church: it is never done again. In Acts 12.2 we read that Herod Agrippa put James the son of Zebedee to death; but no attempt was made to fill that vacancy. Evidently, the place of James was not regarded as vacant, unlike the place of Judas. You cannot lose a place by death, you can only lose it by misconduct; Judas had lost his place not by the fact that he was dead, but by the fact that he was a traitor.

This way of looking at things can best be understood if we keep in mind that the early Church was thinking in terms of a speedy return of Christ to wind up the present order and to bring in a completely new order. One of the things that would happen at his coming was that the martyrs, the righteous dead, would be raised to receive their reward. The obvious reward of a man like James the son of Zebedee would be to receive what in fact was promised to the Twelve in the Gospels, where Jesus says 'I covenant to you as my Father has covenanted to me a kingdom, and you shall sit at table with me in my kingdom, and you will sit on thrones judging the twelve tribes of Israel' (Luke 22.29–30; cf. Matthew 19.28). That promise could not be nullified by the violent action of a secular ruler; it could

[1] See H. Danby, *The Mishnah*, p. 383.

74

only be violated by man's own misconduct. We must realize that it is the filling up of a vacant place on the ruling body of the New Israel that is in question. This post, to which Matthias was appointed in the place of Judas, is described by three different names: episcopate (Acts 1.20; AV 'bishopric'); superintendence (Acts 1.25; AV 'minis-try'); apostolate (Acts 1.25). Episcopate makes us think of all the ideas which we now associate with bishops, but we must take the word in its plain meaning and not as an ecclesiastical technical term. The post is next called a diaconate, so we will have to make Matthias a deacon as well as a bishop. The deacon is minister or servant. And in the third place the post is called an apostolate, which means that Matthias would be similar to the apostles. Apostolate here, I think, means something like delegated authority. When we look at these three terms in their first-century context they add up to a combination of superin-tendence, authority and service. We are presented with a picture of a community in which the elders or rulers exer-cise their authority by being its servants, which is precisely what Jesus himself laid down as the correct way of organ-izing his community. 'He who would be chief among you shall be servant of all' (Mark 10.44).

In Acts 2 we have a description of what happened on the day of Pentecost: the coming of the gift of the Holy Spirit to the new community. The phenomena which fell upon the disciples caused a certain amount of unfavourable comment from the general public; some of them thought that the disciples were drunk. Peter felt it necessary to put them right on this matter, and he did so in a speech which divides into three distinct parts. The first runs from verses 14 to 21, the second from verses 22 to 28, and the third from verses 29 to 36. The speech is marked by the occurrence of direct vocatives. He begins in verse 14 by saying 'Men of Judaea and fellow Jews'. In verse 22 he starts again, 'Fellow Israelites', and in verse 29 he says what is usually translated 'Men and brethren'. I do not really know how to translate *andres adelphoi*; the first word means just 'men' in general and the second means 'sharers of the same faith and worship'.

The first part of the speech appeals to Scripture. The things that have happened and the extraordinary manifestations that have taken place are an indication that an important prophecy in the Old Testament is being fulfilled, the prophecy from the Book of Joel (2.28–32). This means that the Day of the Lord is at hand; consequently the question of salvation or its opposite has become extremely urgent.

The second part of the speech goes on to deal with recent history and to link what has happened not only with the Old Testament but also with the public career of Jesus. It says in effect 'You may have thought that with the crucifixion you were finished with Jesus for good and all, but you are not. God has raised him from the dead and we are here as witnesses of that, to testify to you concerning a Messiah who has indeed been killed but has been raised from the dead and is the effective force in all history from now on.'

The third part of the speech links these events once more with the old messianic hope and appeals to one of the Psalms (16.10), which is taken to be a Psalm of David in which he prophesied that he would not be left to lie in the underworld but would have a better fate than that. 'But,' says Peter, 'the fact is that David is in his grave, has been for centuries and still is.' What he was prophesying about was not himself, but his descendant Jesus, and (verse 30) the crucial point is that David, who was in fact a prophet and knew that God had sworn by an oath that he would set someone physically descended from him upon his throne, spoke about the resurrection of the Messiah that 'he would neither be left in the abode of the dead nor would his flesh see corruption. And it was this Jesus that God raised up, and we are all witnesses of it. So he, having been raised to the right hand of God and having received the promise of the Holy Spirit from the Father, has poured out this, which you see and hear.' Verse 30 is the important verse; it expresses the expectation of the Messiah, a descendant of David who would be the ruler of God's people and seated on the throne of David.

There is a practical application of that argument in verses 37–42. As a result of what was said the hearers were impressed—deeply impressed—and they asked Peter and the others what they were to do. Peter said, 'Repent and be baptized in the name of Jesus Christ for the remission of your sins; and you will receive the gift of the Holy Spirit, for the promise is to you and your children and to all those who are far off, as many as the Lord our God shall call.' 'And with many other words he testified and exhorted them saying, "Save yourselves from this crooked generation".' 'Save yourselves from this crooked generation' is a reference to Deuteronomy (32.5). Peter exhorts God's people to separate themselves from their rebellious compatriots. A large number took this advice and were baptized, and about three thousand people were added to the church on that day. Acts 2.42 goes on to tell us that they were assiduous in attending on the teaching of the apostles and on the fellowship and the breaking of bread and the prayers.

This is the first picture in any kind of detail of what made up the life of the primitive Christian community and it is just as well to take a look at it as it stands. There is, first of all, the *teaching* of the apostles. Actually it is called the *didachē* of the apostles. Again our immediate reaction is to translate it into terms familiar to us and to think of a Bible Class of three thousand or the Annual Conference of the Society. But this will not do. We can see what this expression meant at the time because we have a little book called *The Didachē of the Twelve Apostles* which was discovered about eighty years ago. It was written in the second century and is a book of regulations for a Christian community. It starts off by describing two ways: the Way of Life and the Way of Death, and it lays down a lot of very sound principles regarding conduct, good and bad. Then it goes on to give detailed instruction about how the life of the community is to be carried on. In other words, the *Didachē* is a book of primitive Church law, the rules and regulations or constitution and bye-laws of the Christian community. It seems, then, that the apostles were regarded as custodians of the Law, the Christian *Torah* (and we have already seen that the Hebrew word *Torah*, which we commonly translate Law, really means instruction). The Community was under the guidance of the apostles.

The second word is the *Fellowship* (*Koinōnia*). It is not certain what it means. Fellowship is a very elastic term: it could mean any one of four things. It could mean fellowship with the apostles or association with them; it could mean fellowship in material possessions by sharing their things with one another (which we know from other statements that in fact they did); or it could mean fellowship with the community in general and particularly the fellow-ship of the common meal, the Christian common meal, the 'breaking of bread' as it is sometimes called; or fourthly it could mean charitable gifts, sharing their good things with other people less fortunate. My own view of the matter is that it probably means the practising of mutual helpfulness and kindness. I am very much inclined to take *koinōnia* in the sense of mutual kindness. In that case what is there called *koinōnia* is in Simeon the Righteous called 'the imparting of kindnesses', the practice of mutual help-fulness as the expression of corporate solidarity.

The third thing referred to in verse 42 is the *breaking of bread*. There are two important possibilities here. 'Breaking of bread' could mean either an ordinary meal, or a ritual observance involving the breaking and sharing of bread and the eating of bread. Jeremias has pointed out that in Jewish usage 'the breaking of bread' is not a normal ex-pression for taking a normal meal,[1] so that we should probably prefer to think of 'breaking of bread' as a ritual meal. The rest of the evidence seems to bear this out. We know that our Lord himself attached great importance to certain ritual acts connected with the sharing of food. We have an example in the accounts of the feeding of the multitude, where we are told how he took bread, blessed it and broke it. That was in fact the normal procedure for saying grace according to Jewish custom, but it is more than likely that Jesus had put more into the common meal than ordinary Jewish practice did. That is to say that while he said grace, as heads of Jewish households would say grace, when he said it and shared out the food the meal

[1] J. Jeremias, *The Eucharistic Words of Jesus*, p. 83.

took on a special significance: it became a messianic meal. One of the ways in which the Jews pictured the golden age to come was as a great banquet, and it seems that under-lying this meal of Jesus and the multitude was the idea that even if it was not a banquet in the proper sense, even if they could only share a crust of bread, it was a real messianic banquet in the sense that all the essentials of the messianic banquet were there. And that idea is carried over into the early Church.

The fourth element is the *prayers*. We will say more about this presently. When we go on from verse 42 to verses 44–46 we have a further description of the life of the believers, and again we are told four things about them. The first is that they were altogether: that is, I take it, that they formed a united group. I do not think it would be going too far to think that that group was united under the leadership of the Twelve. The second thing is that they 'had all things in common'. They sold real and personal property and divided it amongst all as anyone had need. That is, they pooled their resources. It is not necessary to go into the question whether this procedure was sound economics or not; doubtless it was not, but when people are expecting that the present age is going to be wound-up any day they will not take very long-term views of economic questions. The third thing in verse 46 is that they were 'assiduous in one accord in the Temple' and that, I think, belongs with number four, the breaking of bread. If we letter the four elements in verse 42 thus:

(*a*) Teaching
(*b*) Fellowship
(*c*) Breaking of bread
(*d*) Prayers

and call the four elements in verses 44–46, 1, 2, 3, 4, then 1 corresponds to (*a*), 2 to (*b*), 3 to (*d*). Number 4 in verse 46 is the breaking of bread in private houses where they shared their food in 'gladness and singleness (or generosity) of heart, praising God and having favour with all the people'; this corresponds to (*c*).

Let us look further at this account. The prayers, that is the worship, gives us the second item noted by Simeon the Righteous.[1] So here we have the three pillars, the three foundations, on which the world rests—the Law (instruction), the worship and the imparting of kindnesses. The Law becomes the instruction of the apostles; the imparting of kindnesses becomes the united fellowship and the pooling of resources; the worship becomes the prayers. The worship Simeon had in mind was the worship of the Temple, and it was to the Temple that the primitive Christians went for worship. They did not go to the synagogue, they went to the Temple. The breaking of bread does not fit entirely into this picture, for the very good reason that here we have something particularly Christian, deriving from an action of Jesus right through his Ministry, and done in a particularly marked way at the Last Supper. If we want to bring it under one of these heads we should have to bring it under 'worship', but it has also got something to do with the imparting of kindnesses.

We can now go further, and see these items appearing in the narrative of the history of the primitive Church. In Acts 3.1 we have prayers and worship. Peter and John are on their way into the Temple at the hour of prayer, namely the ninth hour, or 3 p.m. The prayers are connected with the offering of the evening sacrifice. If we jump to Acts

[1] See above, p. 34.

81

4.32, we have 'And there was one mind and one soul among the multitude of believers', which is the same thing as is described by 'They were all together'. There was genuine unity of mind and spirit in the community, and that mind and spirit I take it came from the fact that they enjoyed a single guiding authority, that of the Twelve. 'And not one of them said that any of his possessions was his own, but all things were common to them'—that is, they sold private property and pooled their resources. 'And with great power the apostles witnessed to the resurrection of the Lord Jesus and great grace was upon them. For there was not a single person among them in want, for all who were possessors of lands or houses sold them and brought the proceeds of the things they had sold and laid them at the feet of the apostles and it was distributed to each according as anyone had need. And Joseph, who was surnamed Barnabas by the apostles (a name which means 'son of consolation') a Levite, a Cypriot by race (or family), to whom a field belonged (or a piece of land), sold it, brought the price and laid it at the feet of the apostles.' That is the Fellowship (*koinōnia*), the pooling of resources. Then in chapter 5 we have a further development of this theme, in the story of Ananias and Sapphira who sold some property but did not hand in the whole of the price, with disastrous consequences to themselves. Peter this time appears not only as giving instruction but also as a kind of judge passing sentence. In verse 12 we have a description of 'signs and wonders' wrought by the apostles, and it goes on to say that they were all in the porch or colonnade of Solomon. I assume this means that the cloister of the Temple was the regular meeting place of the community. That is natural enough. No private house would be big enough to hold an assembly of 3,000 people. If they were to meet anywhere they had probably got to meet in the open. And there again we have the unity, the 'altogether-ness', of the community.

In Acts 5.33–42 we have the account of how the Jewish authorities were displeased by the way in which the Christian community was growing and the steps they took to arrest its leaders. This produced a debate in the Sanhedrin as to what should be done with these people, and in the course of the debate the famous rabbinical teacher Gamaliel addressed the assembly. That is the Gamaliel who is claimed as the teacher of St Paul.[1] Gama-liel does not compare the Christian movement in Palestine to a curious Jewish sect, or an eccentric synagogue, or a hierarchical group. He compares it to the revolutionary movements of Theudas and Judas of Galilee. The picture that Gamaliel is represented as having before his mind's eye is the picture of a revolutionary community, not a queer sect of a religious character. It is as much political as reli-gious and, from Gamaliel's point of view, even more political than religious; and he says 'Let it alone.' Now if it were a matter of wrong theology or bad ethics I do not think that Gamaliel would have said 'Let it alone.' If he

[1] There has been a great deal of fuss about Gamaliel's speech; it is said that it could not have been made by him because one of the incidents which he speaks about did not occur at the relevant time. Theudas (to whom he refers in verse 36) made his insurrection in A.D. 44, and the speech of Gamaliel cannot be put as late as that. We are still quite near to the crucifixion, probably still in the early 30's. But that is not the point at the moment. Whether Gamaliel actually made this speech or whether somebody put it into his mouth, the point is that this is the kind of speech that either Gamaliel did in fact make or that would have been suitable for Gamaliel to make at this time. For our immediate purpose it does not matter which.

had thought of it as something which undermined the faith or the morals of Judah, something heretical in doc/trine or immoral in practice by Jewish standards, he could not have tolerated it. But if it was thought of as a political movement, then he could say 'Let it alone, if God is behind it, it will prosper, if not it will perish'. I do not say that to regard it as a political movement is anything like the whole truth about the primitive Church, but it is a strong indication as to what it looked like to outsiders at that time.

If we turn to Acts 6.1–6, we have the appointment of deacons, and again we have got to clear our minds of modern notions. In my communion deacons are the people who take care of the collections, spend them to the best advantage and see that the buildings are kept in good repair. The first thing to notice about this passage is that the brethren are not in fact called deacons. 'Now in those days there came a complaint from the Christians of Jewish Greek origin against the native Hebrew Christians that their widows were overlooked in the daily ministration.' Something had gone wrong with the distribution, with the 'pooling of resources'. 'The Twelve called together the main body of the disciples and said to them, "It is not satisfactory that we should neglect the word of God in order to look after the rations" (serve tables, in other words), "therefore, brethren, seek out from your number seven men of good reputation, full of the Holy Spirit and wisdom, whom we will set over this task. As for us, we intend to apply ourselves strictly to prayer and the ministry of the word." And that proposition found favour with the entire gathering and they chose Stephen, a man full of faith and of the Holy Spirit, and Philip, and Prochorus, and

Nicanor, and Timon, and Parmenas, and Nicolas a proselyte of Antioch, and they presented them before the apostles and they prayed and laid their hands upon them.' They are not called deacons at all. They are the seven. The only place where they are mentioned again is in Acts 21.8, where they are called 'the Seven'. The title seems to be parallel to 'the Twelve'. This is quite clearly an organization for dealing with the *Koinōnia*, the sharing of the common goods. I think it is possible that the ritual meal may also be involved though that is less certain.

When we put all this evidence together and ask ourselves what picture of the primitive Church it presents, I think we get something rather different from any religious organization with which we are acquainted. It does not tally with anything that we know, from Roman Catholic to Baptist or Quaker. This is something which is like nothing but itself. In particular we must realize that the first community that sprang up in Palestine as a result of the Ministry of Jesus was a community whose interests were as wide as the normal affairs of human life, and was not in the narrow sense religious at all. It was, in fact, an attempt to constitute the ideal Israel. Indeed one of the claims it made was that it *was* the New Israel. We have seen that Israel was something wider than just a worshipping community: it was a community which included worship along with a whole range of other activities. My own guess would be that the only thing that differentiated the Christian community from the surrounding Judaism so far as scope of interests were concerned was the fact that the Christian community was expecting the existing order to windup fairly soon and was therefore not likely to make any longterm programme on the economic side. The

Church in the first and second centuries was not just a worshipping society; like Judaism it was a community in a very much wider sense, it included worship, and many other things besides.

## six

# THE ORIGINAL TEACHING OF JESUS
# AND THE ETHICS OF THE
# EARLY CHURCH

WE have been studying the messianic community, the early Church, as a new kind of social organism. We have now to consider that this Church preserved a body of Jesus' teaching, and that from what was preserved it is possible for us to get adequate illumination for living in our own time. A good starting point is Mark 10.32–45. This sets out clearly the main issue that confronted Jesus and his followers in the course of his Ministry. 'They were on the way going up to Jerusalem, and Jesus was leading the way; and they were dumb-founded and those who followed were afraid. And taking again the Twelve he began to tell them the things that were going to happen, saying, "We are on our way to Jerusalem, and the Son of man will be betrayed to the chief priests and the scribes, and they will condemn him to death and hand him over to the gentiles, and they will mock him and spit on him and scourge him and kill him; and after three days he shall rise again".' That is a picture of the destiny of suffering and sacrifice that has been reserved for the Son of man.

Appended to it there is the story (beginning at verse 35) of the request of James and John. 'Master do for us what-ever we ask.' And he said, 'What do you want me to do

for you?' And they replied, 'Grant us to sit in your glory.'
That is, 'Allow us to sit in state with you, one on the left
and one on the right.' Jesus replied, 'You do not know
what you are asking. Are you able to drink the cup that
I drink? or to be baptized with the baptism that I am
baptized with?' And they said, 'We are able.' And Jesus
said unto them, 'The cup that I drink ye shall drink; and
with the baptism that I am baptized withal shall you be
baptized; but to sit on my right hand or on my left hand is
not mine to give: but it is for them for whom it has been
prepared.' Now the Ten heard this, and they began to be
annoyed with James and John (not because James and
John wanted the chief places, but because they had jumped
the queue!). Jesus called to them and said to them, 'You
know that those who rule over the Gentiles lord it over
them; and their great ones wield authority upon them. But
it is not that way amongst you. On the contrary, whoever
wishes to become great among you shall be your servant:
and whoever would be first among you shall be servant of
all. For the Son of man did not come to receive service but
to give it, and to give his life a ransom for many.' We could
not have a clearer statement of the contrasted hopes and
ideals of Jesus and his contemporaries. Here side by side
are two conceptions of the messianic task; one looks to the
triumph and rule of the Messiah who sits on his throne and
gives his orders; in the other there is a picture of the
messianic Ministry in which the function of the Messiah
is to be supremely the servant of all.

The messianic ideal cherished by Jesus is put by him in
the form of a statement about the Son of man; the Ministry
of which Jesus speaks is the Ministry of the Son of man; the
sacrifice is the sacrifice of the Son of man. 'Son of man' is

in one way an ambiguous term.[1] It means 'People of the saints of the Most High' (see Daniel 7), the people within Israel who are completely devoted to the worship and ser-vice of God, for whom the will of God is their supreme rule, who know no higher loyalty. But 'Son of man' can also be used as a name for the Messiah, in so far as the Messiah is himself the representative and embodiment of this 'People of the saints of the Most High'. The meaning can oscillate between the sacred community as a whole and its head, so that when it is said by Jesus that the Son of man must suffer that can mean—and probably does mean—either or both of two things. It can mean that the 'People of the saints of the Most High' must suffer, and it can mean that the Messiah must suffer. When it says that the Son of man must serve, it means that the 'People of the saints of the Most High' must serve and that the Messiah himself must serve. Jesus says to the sons of Zebedee, 'Can you drink the cup that I drink?' 'O yes, we can,' they reply. 'All right,' says Jesus, 'You will.' But when it comes to the point they did not; they all forsook him and fled, which is probably what most of us would have done in similar circumstances.

The Messiah says 'I do serve and I will suffer.' His acceptance of this challenge is found in two passages in Luke 22. The first is verses 24–27, which is Luke's version of the passage we have just considered in Mark. 'So now considerable contention developed among them as to who was the greatest. And he said to them, "The kings of the nations lord it over them and their men of authority are called benefactors. But you are not like that. The great man

[1] See T. W. Manson, *The Teaching of Jesus*, pp. 211–234, and *The Bulletin of John Rylands Library*, XXXII (1950), pp. 171–193.

among you let him become as the junior, and the leader as the servant. For who is greater, the diner or the waiter? You say the diner, but I say the waiter. I am among you as one giving service".' This passage does not only say that it is better to give service than to receive it; it makes the positive statement 'I am among you as a servant'.

Jesus' acceptance of the Messianic vocation of suffering occurs in the same chapter (verses 35–37). 'And he said to them, "When I sent you out without purse, wallet, or sandals, were you ever short of anything?" They said, "No." He said to them "It is different now; whoever has a purse had better take it and notes in a wallet too; and if anyone is short of a sword he had better sell his cloak and buy one. Why? Well, I can tell you that this text is about to have its fulfilment in me." ' Then Jesus quotes from Isaiah 53.12: 'he was reckoned among the lawless ones'; and he adds: 'For my career is coming to its close.' 'And they said, "Master, here are two swords"; and he said to them, "Well, well".' All this is very elusive, but the words allude to the tragedy of Jesus' ministry. The first part of the passage refers to a time of Jesus' popularity and acceptance, the second part is a very strong way of expressing the fact that they are now surrounded by enemies so ruthless that the possession of two swords will not help the situation. The messianic task can only be fulfilled in one way, and that the way indicated in the fifty-third chapter of Isaiah. This means that the Messiah must accept a destiny of suffering and death, as well as a task of service, which brings us back again to the passage in Mark about rules and the true test of greatness. When Jesus says 'Whoever would be great among you shall be your servant', he is not saying that those who are ambitious will be punished by being compelled to do menial tasks, and *vice versa*. Precise correspondences of that sort do not exist in the messianic kingdom. In it greatness *is* service, and service *is* greatness; no decoration is given for a life of service, the life of service is the decoration.

The phrase in Mark 10.43, 'But it is not so among you', has a history going back to the Old Testament, where we find it translated 'It is not so done in Israel' (II Samuel 13.12) to describe conduct that is incompatible with being the People of God. So the Christian ethic has its first acceptance within the Christian community. It is 'done' or 'not done' among 'you'. From there it may spread to the outside world, but if it does not begin there it is not likely to begin anywhere. But if the Christian ethic begins within the Christian fellowship it cannot stay there: the service and sacrifice of Christ are 'for many' (Mark 10.45; 14.24). Jeremias has shown that 'many' in these verses has an inclusive meaning; it is a way of saying that the Son of man who 'gave his life a ransom for many' is really giving his life for the common good.[1] There is an interesting parallel to this statement in the words of institution at the Last Supper: 'He said to them, "This is my covenant blood, which is shed for many"' (Mark 14.22). Again it means for the general good. It follows that as the Messiah sacrificed himself for the common good, so the community or people of the saints of the Most High must be expendable also for the common good.

It was not very easy for the early Church to accept this in its full meaning and with all its practical implications. It was no easier for it than it is for us. Even when it had got away from the idea of a messianic triumph and the shaping

[1] See J. Jeremias, *The Eucharistic Words of Jesus*, pp. 148 ff.

of an Israelite world empire, there was still the standing temptation for the Christian community to become a 'saved Remnant' rather than a 'saving Remnant',[1] to think of themselves as elected for privilege rather than for service, and so to make the words and deeds of Jesus the standard and pattern of their internal discipline rather than the inspiration of an apostolic mission.

When we read the Acts of the Apostles it would seem as if the apostolic or missionary task was forced upon the primitive Church. What really started its missionary work was the persecution that followed the martyrdom of Stephen (Acts 8.1). Another factor that set the missionary work going was the outburst of missionary zeal that took place in Antioch (Acts 13). This outburst does not appear to have been initiated by any influence from Jerusalem: the entire credit is given to the Holy Spirit poured out on the community at Antioch. It is probably only when Paul went up to Jerusalem and started talking about foreign missions to the leaders of the Jerusalem Church that they decided to make some arrangements for carrying them on.

On the other hand the narrowness of outlook at the beginning of the primitive Church, chiefly concerned with shaping itself as an elect body separated from the surrounding wickedness, has its good side. If the primitive Church tended to keep Jesus to itself, at least it did take him seriously. One of the ways in which it did so was by turning his teaching inwards upon itself. If we think in terms of strict historical documentation these early Christians were guilty of tampering with the evidence. But they did not regard themselves as bound to store up archives for the

[1] Cf. T. W. Manson, *The Teaching of Jesus*, p. 179.

investigation of historians nineteen centuries later. They saw themselves as the messianic community, and the words of Jesus their Master as full of instruction for them. They were prepared to take his sayings and apply them to their own case, and if in the process sayings which had originally been intended to serve other purposes were diverted, that did not appear to them to be a serious matter. This process has lately been made the subject of close and detailed study by C. H. Dodd[1] and J. Jeremias,[2] and in what follows I am making a good deal of use of what they have to say.

We can see the process at work most clearly in the case of the parabolic teaching of Jesus. Every authentic parable had originally its own actual situation in the life of Jesus. There was a day, a set of circumstances, and a definite group of people; and it was on that day, in those circumstances and to those people that the parable was first uttered. But not every parable has succeeded in keeping its original context. By the time they have been included in the Gospel, many have been given a new situation in the life of the early Church. Once we have got over the shock of realizing that the parables have been treated in this way to meet new situations, the fact is encouraging rather than otherwise, because it really means that the men of the early Church did not normally invent sayings of Jesus to express their own convictions, but rather that they selected from the mass what they thought was relevant. Admittedly the chosen words of Jesus may have been misunderstood or made to speak to a new situation in ways not originally intended by Jesus. The early Church remembered better than it under⁄stood. This means that the better we understand the mind

---

[1] *Parables of the Kingdom*, chapter 4.
[2] *The Parables of Jesus*, pp. 20–38.

of the early Church, the more likely it is that we shall be able to reverse the process that went on in the first decades, to strip off mistaken interpretations and applications and see the utterances in their original intention. We may not be able to reconstruct the actual situation, but we should be able readily to conceive the kind of situation in which it would be very much to the point.

This process of adaptation of the sayings of Jesus has two important characteristics. One is that the audience to which the saying or parable is addressed is changed. It is possible to go through the sayings of Jesus classifying them accord, ing to their audience—disciples, opponents or the general public. One fact that emerges when one goes into this in detail is that some of the sayings that appear in more than one Gospel are addressed to opponents in one and to disciples in another. There is evidence of a tendency to transfer sayings originally spoken to opponents to dis, ciples; but there is no evidence of traffic in the other direction, of sayings originally spoken to disciples being re, addressed to people outside. Now why does this change take place? What is it that makes the tradition turn polemical utterance designed for outsiders into exhortations addressed to members of the community? I suggest that it is tied up with the fact that the primitive Palestinian community thought of itself as a kind of Israel within Israel; that it thought of itself as receiving a new Law from Jesus, and of Jesus as a new Moses (cf. Deuteronomy 18.15 ff.). Given a community of this kind, which thought of itself as Israel within Israel receiving Law from its messianic prophet, the oracles of that messianic prophet would all be precious, and the more precious where they could be understood as legislation for the community. That some of

these oracles had been spoken in the first instance to those
outside did not matter very much. Those outside had
rejected the new Law in much the same way that the
nations of the world had rejected the Law of Moses. The
Christian community accepted and claimed the new revelation as Israel had accepted and claimed the old. Thus we
are witnesses of a process by which the day-to-day answers
of Jesus, his ways of dealing with the particular concrete
situations that arose during his Ministry, are turned into the
laws and customs of the Church. It is significant for the
general question of the reliability of the Gospels as historical documents that it is the absorption and adaptation
of existing material and not the creation of new material,
with which we are presented.

The second element in the process of adaptation is the
turning of teaching which was eschatological in its intention and very often threatening in its meaning into exhortations and ethical advice for the community. The solemn
warning to the outsider becomes wise counsel to the church
member or the church leader. That is illustrated in a very
striking way by a short parable in Matthew 5.25.[1] There,
in the context of the Sermon on the Mount and in a general
passage dealing with the necessity of having a conciliatory
and friendly attitude to one's neighbour, Christian disciples
are told to come to terms with the adversary quickly while
they are still with him on the way to the court, in case the
adversary delivers them to the judge and the judge to the
prison-keeper and they are thrown into prison, where they
will be kept until the last farthing is paid. Here the parable
shows the Christian community the necessity of being
reconciled to its neighbours and being on decent terms with

[1] Previously referred to above, p. 47.

them. But when we turn to the parallel passage in Luke (12.54 ff.) it is a very different story. Now it is addressed to the crowd, the general public. 'He said to the crowd, "When you see a cloud rising in the west you say, 'We shall have rain'; and when you observe the east wind blowing you say, 'There will be a heat-wave'. And so it is. Hypocrites, you know how to interpret the phenomena of the earth and sky; why can you not interpret this present situation? You can judge the seasons; why do you not judge what is right by yourselves? For as you are on your way with your adversary to the court take the opportunity to be quit of him." ' Here the hearers are asked to consider the gravity of the times and the need to 'get right with God' while there is still time. What has happened is that the urgent and very necessary warning to outsiders in Luke has been adapted in Matthew to meet the needs of a Church whose members are not in need of any such warning because they *have* come to terms with God. The parable is now used as an exhortation to Christians to be conciliatory and to come to an agreement with their neighbours.

Another example can be taken from Luke (16.1–13), where we have the story of the 'Dishonest Steward' who was accused by his master of embezzlement and falsifying the accounts. The master orders an immediate audit, and the steward realizes he is likely to lose his job, so he sets to work with people owing money to his master and hopes to establish them as friends who will take care of him when he is out of work. This parable has always caused a lot of uneasiness to Christians because of verse 8, 'And the master commended the unrighteous steward because he had done wisely'. It looks as if Jesus is commending shabby tricks. But the fact that Jesus applauded his cunning does not mean he approved of the man. The steward was a scoundrel, but a pretty smart scoundrel all the same. Let the children of light be equally alert! There follows (from verse 9) a number of commands in the mouth of Jesus himself. 'I say to you, Make yourselves friends by means of the mammon of unrighteousness; when it runs out they may receive you into everlasting dwellings. Men reliable in the smallest matters will be reliable in big things. He who is dishonest in small matters will be dishonest in big.' Then there is another detached reflection: 'If you have not turned out faithful or reliable in the unrighteous world; if you have not been reliable with other people's goods, who would give you your own?' 'No servant can serve two masters, for either he will hate the one and love the other; or else he will stick to one and despise the other. You cannot serve God and mammon.' All these give the impression of being detached sayings that have been linked to this parable because of something to do with reliability, or with the question of serving one master or several. The original force of the parable has nothing to do with the morals of the steward. This dishonest steward—dishonest to begin with and dishonest to the end—finds himself in a fix, and being in a fix he takes steps to get himself out of it. Granted that the steps he took were as dishonest as the steps that had brought him into the fix, but he did take energetic action to get out once he was in. The primary intention of the parable is to say to people in the world at large, 'You also are in a fix and the evil day for you is not very far away. If you had any sense you would take steps, and urgent steps, to get yourselves out of the fix while there is still time.' In other words, the dishonest steward and the man on the way to the law court are in origin similar cases, but when the early Church adopted them they also adapted them for a community which had already made its peace with God, and therefore had to apply them in some way to fit its own situation.

The parable of the labourers in the vineyard (Matthew 20.1–16) is another example of what appears to be change of audience. Here again is a parable which has worried a lot of good people, who feel a certain sympathy with the men who worked all day and at the end got no more than those who had laboured only for the last hour. But this is to miss the point. The essential meaning of the parable is in verse 15, 'Or is your eye evil, because I am good?' Everybody got the basic minimum wage, one *denarius* per day, which was just enough to keep a working man and his family, and no more. The people who worked the full day got the full day's pay; to give the people who had worked less than the full day something less than the day's pay would be to inflict hardship on them, because the one *denarius* was the minimum wage. The force of the parable is to emphasize the goodness, the kindness, of the employer who gives the one group of workers what they are entitled to, and to the others what they are not entitled to but what, in fact, they need.

The parallel to these workers is the case of the two brothers in the parable of the 'Prodigal Son' (Luke 15. 11–32). There the party is open to both brothers, they are both entitled to come in and have a plate of veal and stuffing and everything else that is provided. The trouble is that the elder brother is not content: he either wants more himself or the prodigal to have less; this kind of equality of treatment irks him. It is probable that the parable ends with a rebuke to the scribes and the pharisees who wanted God to discriminate. They wanted the undeserving to get less. They did not want 'parties for prodigals'. What the prodigal should get is a good plain suit of clothes, a good plain diet and plenty of work: discipline would be good for him. But God does not measure or discriminate in that way. When the parable came to be used in the early Church it was a community where some worked harder for it than others, and the parable became a warning to such folk that they must not expect special consideration because they had been particularly loyal; even the Twelve should not expect a lot of extras. In any case one is not dealing here with things that can be weighed and measured: one is dealing with the love of God, which cannot be divided up into parcels of different sizes for different people.

A further example of a change of audience is found earlier in the same chapter, the parable of the man who has a hundred sheep and loses one, and goes to seek the lost one and does not rest until he has got it back (Luke 15.3–7). In Luke this is addressed to the pharisees and scribes and is a rebuke to them for criticizing the way in which Jesus deals with publicans and sinners and is so friendly with them. In Matthew, however, it appears in a different context (18.12–14). Here it is in an address to the disciples concerned with the internal organization and discipline of the Christian community, and it has become a warning to those within the Church not to be harsh and censorious to their brothers. An original rebuke against a harsh attitude towards people *outside* the Christian community has now become an exhortation to preserve a spirit of kindness and brotherly love *within* it.

It is possible to go on multiplying examples. Take, for instance, the parable of the 'Great Feast' (Matthew 22.1–10;

Luke 14.16–24). In its original setting in the ministry of Jesus the parable was a reproach to his contemporaries for their unwillingness to accept what was being offered to them; a reproach for their refusal to enter the kingdom of God when the doors were standing wide open. As it now stands in the Gospels we can see it has been turned into encouragement to missionary effort on the part of the Christian community. The emphasis is now on the idea of going out to bring people in. It is interesting to see that in Matthew the instructions to the servants are to make only one expedition 'into the streets and lanes of the city'. In Luke there are two expeditions, one 'into the streets and lanes' and the other 'into the highways and hedges', in the country. It is quite possible that that extra expedition has in mind the expansion of the Christian community beyond Judaea to the Gentiles.

Again there is the picture of the thief in the night (Matthew 24.43 ff.; Luke 12.39 ff.). If the householder had known what time the thief would come he would have been watching. This was originally intended as an appeal to those outside the group of followers of Jesus to realize the urgency of the times and to take steps to deal with the situation. Jesus says, in effect, to his contemporaries, 'You are living on the edge of a volcano and it is urgent that you should do something about it before it erupts on you.' By the time the Church took it over it had become a warning to church members and leaders to be watchful and alert because at any moment the second coming may take place. The parable of the ten virgins (Matthew 25.1–13) is a warning to outsiders by Jesus that a crisis is at hand, but as applied in the life of the Church it is an exhortation to church members to be prepared and equipped. The original setting of the parable of the doorkeeper (Mark 13. 33–37; Luke 12.35–38) was a warning to the leaders of the Jewish community that the crisis of the coming king, dom is at hand, and that they are neglecting their duty if they do not see it coming and help their fellow countrymen to appreciate the urgency of the matter. But in the Christian community it becomes an exhortation to church members and church leaders not to become lax because the second coming is delayed. The same may be said about the par, able of the pounds (Matthew 25.14–30; Luke 19.12–27).

It is important to realize what has happened. While Jesus was going about his own ministry he often reproached his hearers because they had the wrong attitude to God and to their fellow men, and tried to bring them to a different attitude. That situation had passed and a new one had taken its place, a situation in which Jesus had already suffered and died and risen. The Christian community was now trying to learn from his sayings and doings, and they took them and found ways of applying what had been said, for example to scribes and pharisees, to their own case. It is arguable that they misunderstood a great deal of what they adapted. No doubt they did. I have already said that there is very little doubt that they remembered far better than they understood. The point is that they *did* remember, and they *did* try to understand. Because they did these two things they preserved for us the chance of understanding more fully and of having a clearer picture of these words and deeds of Jesus which are a standing inspiration and challenge, and as often as not a standing rebuke, to us all. They could not have done it if they had not taken these words and deeds of Jesus with complete seriousness and accepted them as applicable to themselves. This is a striking contrast to the attitude which sees how well a rebuke applies to someone else, or how pointed advice is for someone else, but does not accept it for onself. We can give the early Church full marks for diverting the rebukes that were given to outsiders and asking itself 'where does that touch me?'

We have come to the end of our study, and the points that I would like to stress are few but important. The first is that the ethic we are dealing with is the ethic of a king- dom: the ethic of a society with a leader and ruler; and the primary quality of the ethic is that it comes from the ruler himself, who is the interpreter and exemplifier of it. This holds if we think in terms of the kingdom of God, in which God himself gives the rules of life and exemplifies them; 'you are to be holy as God is holy; perfect as he is perfect; merciful as he is merciful.' It still holds if we think of it in the terms of a messianic kingdom. It is the Messiah whose life and death exemplifies and interprets the ideal which is summed up in the commandment 'Love as I have loved you'. In the last resort the Christian ethic inevitably comes back to Christ himself. It is from him that it derives its content, its form and its authority. Its force is most likely to be felt by those who belong to the community which he founded and maintains, the community which belongs to him. And the power to carry it into effect is most likely to be found in living association with that community and with its head.

If the Christian ethic is anything at all it is a living, growing thing. 'Love as I have loved you' is not to be construed solely in the past; if there is anything in the Christian religion 'I have loved you' is true of the past, the present, and the future. 'I *have* loved', in the perfect tense, means that it is a past thing which continues into the present until the end of time. Further, just as the power and inspiration of the Christian ethic is represented in a living person and a living body, so the achievement of Christian ethics is always something new and original. Christian ethics is certainly not a slavish obedience to rules and regulations. It is active living, and therefore it has the power to go to the heart of every ethical situation as it arises. It has the power to see what response is called for in terms of feeling, word and act, and the power to make that response, and make it creatively and effectively. In short, Christian ethics is a work of art.

# INDEX OF BIBLICAL REFERENCES

# GENERAL INDEX